TREAD SOFTLY, ALICE

Alice Ware, aged 18, is pretty, charming and impetuous. At home in Yorkshire, she is determined to seize any fresh opportunities and experiences that come her way. The arrival of a new neighbour, the elegant and scandalous Mrs Emma Cheevey, leads to visits from her two highly eligible soldier sons. Alice is instantly drawn to Matthew, the younger brother – and then Captain Steven Cheevey arrives home from South Africa. Alice's choice is made, her future secure ... until a reckless decision throws the lives of three people into turmoil.

TREAD SOFTLY, ALICE

TREAD SOFTLY, ALICE

by

Jessica Blair

Magna Large Print Books
Long Preston, North Yorkshire,
BD23 4ND, England.

British Library Cataloguing in Publication Data.

Blair, Jessica
    Tread softly, Alice.

    A catalogue record of this book is
    available from the British Library

    ISBN   978-0-7505-4292-0

First published in Great Britain in 2016 by Piatkus

Cover illustration © Lee Avison by arrangement with
Arcangel Images

The moral right of the author has been asserted.

Published in Large Print 2016 by arrangement with
Little, Brown Book Group

Magna Large Print is an imprint of Library Magna Books Ltd.

Printed and bound in Great Britain by
T.J. (International) Ltd., Cornwall, PL28 8RW

For my great-grandchildren

Jacob Spence, born 16 November 2014
Olivia Hudson, born 7 December 2014

Remembering
Joan

and for
Anne, Geraldine, Judith and Duncan

As always
for Jill

1

Eighteen-year-old Alice Ware breathed in the sea air as the ferry *Victoria,* heading for Dover, cut through the choppy waters of the Channel. She hugged herself as if to lock in place the exhilaration she felt and keep it alive for ever.

But she knew this sense of liberation would not last. Even though the shackles of certain conventions governing the lives of women in particular were slackening, many still governed her conduct and prospects. However, Alice was determined to make the best of her new life as an adult, after being raised by loving and understanding parents, receiving a convent education in England and spending a final year in the home of French friends. Now, in July 1900, as the new century got under way, she was determined to grasp whatever opportunities came along.

She unfastened the ribbon tied under her chin, swept the narrow-brimmed hat from her head and let the wind blow her fair hair free. Her blue eyes sparkled at the thought of the surprise her mother would feel on seeing her again. A year ago Alice had left Wooton Hall, her family home in the North Riding of Yorkshire, very much a schoolgirl still and one her mother was reluctant to let go. Now she was returning from France a confident young lady, one she was sure her mother would welcome and admire.

Unconcerned by the rolling of the ship, Alice took a stroll around the deck, pausing to look back along the foaming wake towards the diminishing coastline.

Her mind drifted back to the happy stay she had enjoyed with the Berger family, in particular their daughter Alexis. Friendship had blossomed immediately between the two girls when they'd met in their final year at the convent to which Alexis had been sent to strengthen her English. At the end of that time Monsieur and Madame Berger had invited Alice to live with them for a year, an invitation she was keen to accept and of which her parents enthusiastically approved, recognising that a good command of another language would be an asset to Alice whatever life might hold for her in future.

With that year over, Monsieur Berger and Alexis had taken Alice to Calais to see her safely on to the *Victoria,* knowing that her father would be at Dover to meet her.

Recalling their parting, Alice gave a little sigh of regret but immediately comforted herself with the thought of what lay ahead. She was going home! Shortly afterwards her eye was caught by the familiar sight of the white cliffs welcoming her back.

Sir Raymond Ware was impatient to greet his daughter after her long absence. She was eighteen now, and with a mind of her own, no doubt. His eyes roamed over the passengers crowding the rail of the cross-Channel ferry closing in on a Dover dockside.

'Where is Alice, Raymond?' asked his wife

Cecilia. 'I can't see her.' His wife's grip tightened on his arm.

'There! Just in front of the ship's steward,' Sir Raymond exclaimed, waving his hand to attract Alice's attention.

'Ah, yes I see her!' His wife's face was alight with joy. 'She's waving.'

Sir Raymond started to give directions to the porter standing beside him.

'I've seen her, sir,' said the man. 'She has one of the ship's crew close by. He'll escort your daughter ashore and then I'll take over.'

Sir Raymond nodded as he dug into the pocket of his overcoat. 'I may not have another opportunity when my daughter comes ashore...' he thrust some coins into the porter's hand '...share that with whoever is helping Miss Ware.'

'Thank you, sir. I will.' The man knew from the weight of the coins that the tip had been a generous one.

Once the vessel had docked and passengers were allowed ashore, Lady Cecilia, her eyes damp, was soon embracing her daughter. Then Alice's slender frame was engulfed in her father's arms until he stepped back a couple of paces to view her better. 'You've grown up,' he said. Her mother nodded in agreement. 'We've lost our little girl,' he observed, a tinge of regret in his voice.

Alice dismissed this, laughing. 'No, you haven't, Father, I'll always be here for you both.'

'Until some handsome young man whisks you away,' he observed.

She ignored the implications and asked, 'How is Nicholas?'

'Your brother is well,' replied her mother. 'He loves working on the estate.'

'Though he has some extraordinary ideas about its development,' her father put in. 'We have to keep a tight rein on him.'

'Where are we going now?' Alice asked.

'Train to London, spend tonight at the Clarendon, then another train tomorrow from King's Cross to York where Sam will meet us with our carriage.'

'That sounds exciting,' Alice observed.

'It will be,' agreed her mother, linking arms with her. 'Oh, it's wonderful to have you home.'

'It's wonderful to be home. Or almost.'

The railway porter had gathered together their overnight luggage. 'Follow me, sir, ladies,' he said. 'You are in first-class carriage A, with compartment B for your exclusive use. That same designation has been reserved for you on the eleven a.m. train out of King's Cross tomorrow. As requested the rest of your daughter's luggage has been taken care of, sir. It should be delivered to your home in four days' time.'

'Thank you,' said Sir Raymond. 'That sounds most efficient.'

'We aim to please, sir,' replied the porter. He saw them comfortably seated and bade them a good journey.

Once they had settled themselves and the excitement of being together again had eased, Alice's father asked, 'You enjoyed your year with the Berger family then?'

'Yes, Father. They made my time most pleasant and rewarding.' She gave a little smile and rattled off a few French phrases, knowing he would not understand a word of them.

He held up his hand to stop her. 'Very commendable, I'm sure, but if you want to keep your French up don't use it on me.'

'Oh, Father,' Alice said, her expression regretful, 'and I was so looking forward to teaching you.' She was teasing, of course, but he took her up on the offer.

'Never! English is good enough for me, so long as there is a touch of Yorkshire to it. And don't forget, your great-grandfather fought at Waterloo.'

Seeing her mother wink at her, Alice suppressed a smile as she said, 'I would never do that, Father.' When he grunted for reply she asked, 'What news of home?'

He quickly warmed to this subject, regaling her proudly with information about her mother's local charitable work.

'I've been helping ease the lot of two small village communities that have suffered since Deepdale Manor and its estate were left deserted. Only the minimum of work on the estate was organised by the solicitor handling probate,' Cecilia told her.

'And there's no sign yet of whoever has inherited it?' asked Alice.

'We haven't heard anything,' her mother replied.

'Couldn't you buy Deepdale, Father?'

He chuckled. 'Wooton is enough for me to handle and keep viable. It's a fine inheritance for you and Nicholas as it is. Besides, Deepdale will need some capital spending on it after being

15

neglected so long since the last owner died. I see no need to alter our circumstances. Everything is nicely settled at Wooton.'

Alice felt a deep sense of satisfaction on hearing the resolve in her father's voice as he made this statement. She loved Wooton Hall and would hate to see any major changes made there. She only hoped her brother Nicholas felt the same. Although he worked alongside his father with enthusiasm, she knew he had ideas of his own that might be brought in once he formally took over. Only time would tell.

Their stay at the Clarendon was comfortable and relaxing so that the next day they were refreshed before the eight-hour journey to York.

There, porters took charge of their luggage and led them to the Station Hotel where Sir Raymond had booked rooms for the night so that they would not be overtired for the twenty-five mile onward journey to Wooton Hall. He knew Cecilia wanted Alice to enjoy the final part of her homecoming.

The following morning as they finished a hearty breakfast they were informed that their carriage had arrived.

Half an hour later as they left the hotel, thankful that the day was warm and the sky clear, their coachman Sam Clark greeted Alice with, 'Welcome home, Miss, it is good to have you back.' The greeting came with a touch of his cap and a broad pleasant smile, just as she would have expected from the long-serving groom who was a favourite with her. After seeing them comfortably seated, Sam climbed to his seat, took up the reins and set the coach in motion towards the hall.

Emma Cheevey left the dining room of Heatherfold Hall after luncheon and strolled into her study, where she knew Betsy, her personal maid, would have placed the mail that always arrived at lunchtime. She crossed the room to her Regency escritoire, pausing for a moment to look out of the window at the rolling hills of the Scottish Borders, a view she always admired.

She sat down at the escritoire, placed so that light from the window fell across it from the left, and picked up the five envelopes that were awaiting her attention, hoping there might be some communication from her husband Colonel Robert Cheevey or their son Captain Steven Cheevey, both of whom were serving in South Africa in the hostilities that had developed from England's dispute with the Boers there. Her disappointment deepened when she saw there wasn't even a letter from her second son, Lieutenant Matthew Cheevey, who was still in England but expecting to be posted to South Africa before long.

Seeing one envelope addressed in what had become a familiar hand to her during the last six months, Emma slit it open immediately and withdrew a sheet of paper.

Dear Mrs Cheevey,

I believe I am nearing a solution to the problem that has troubled us for the last six months. I would like to deliver my latest findings in person next Friday the 20th July and hope this will be convenient.

My best wishes and regards,
John Smyth

She smiled to note the way he had signed the letter – a little crack in the formality that had previously existed in his manner towards her, though she had, early in the relationship, sensed that he wished for an easier association between them. Emma had to admit to herself that she felt flattered by the admiration of this good-looking bachelor whose politeness to her was always accompanied by a certain warmth that she believed he did not display towards all his clients. She would look forward to his visit, she decided.

'Mr Smyth has arrived, Ma'am.'

'Thank you, Betsy.'

After the door had closed behind her maid, Emma stood up, smoothed her dress and examined her face in the mirror. She patted a mischievous wisp of hair into place then went downstairs.

'Good day, Mr Smyth.' Emma sailed into the drawing room, holding out her hand in greeting.

He took it and made a small bow. Since Miss Penelope Owens, owner of the Deepdale Estate in North Yorkshire, had died two years ago at the age of ninety, he had devoted his time to discovering who was now its rightful owner. His enquiries had led him down a number of byroads and he had met various potential claimants, though none as charming as this vivacious woman to whom his quest had led him six months ago. Then, the link to Deepdale on her mother's side of the family had seemed tenuous, and Mrs Cheevey's admission to having no knowledge of a Miss Penelope Owens seemed to rule her out as the heir, but further enquiries had led him to believe that there was more to Mrs Emma Cheevey's position than had first seemed possible.

'I have some news that I believe will settle the matter at last, Ma'am,' he said, with a gentle smile.

'I hope so, Mr Smyth,' Emma replied. 'I just want it settled now, one way or the other.' She indicated a chair to him, wondering if his news would put her life back on an even keel.

He acknowledged her gesture and waited until she had seated herself facing him before he sat down.

She looked at him expectantly, an expression he had come to know well over recent weeks when his visits here had become more regular.

'We have finally collected affidavits ruling out the other candidates as suitable heirs. Therefore, Mrs Cheevey, you are now the sole beneficiary of Deepdale Manor and its contents, together with all associated land, two home farms and two tenanted villages.' As he further itemised the properties concerned she kept her face expressionless. 'Well, Mrs Cheevey, that is the property and landholdings dealt with. Now I must clarify the monetary side of your inheritance. To put it simply, Ma'am, when all outstanding debts on the estate, including our expenses, are taken into account, you will be a very rich woman. The round figure I can give you is five hundred thousand pounds.'

As well off as she was in her present circumstances, Emma blanched and gasped at this piece of news. She gave a little shake of her head. 'I can't believe it. To think, I didn't even know this person existed.'

'She was a distant cousin on your mother's side who had never married, though I discovered that she was once engaged. Her prospective husband left her a fortune in his will, made just two weeks before he was killed in the Highlands while stalking deer there. His fortune forms the basis of your inheritance ... so now you have decisions to make. If there is any way in which I or my firm may help, please do not hesitate to ask.'

Emma Cheevey felt uncharacteristically bewildered. A settled existence was being turned upside down. She had been perfectly happy with life the way she led it, but now big decisions would have to be made and she felt very alone; her husband and one son serving in South Africa, the other expecting to be posted there before long. There was no one at hand to help her, no one to advise on the right course to take with all this wealth suddenly at her disposal. Only this attentive and rather personable solicitor.

'I will bear that in mind,' she told him. 'I have so much to think about concerning Heatherfold as it is, and now to have this thrust upon me too...'

'Don't look upon it as a burden, Ma'am. There are ways we can deal with what you have now at your disposal, and I can offer you the best advice.'

'Thank you. You sound most reassuring.'

'I hope I do, Ma'am. Don't rush into any decisions, I beg you. Keep this to yourself and your family, and take your time over deciding what you will do.'

'It is awkward with my husband and eldest son

so far away, and I really don't want to worry Matthew at this delicate stage of his career.'

'I understand, Ma'am. With the wealth that has come your way, it would be quite in order for you to keep both properties, maybe view this one as your Scottish retreat.'

'Thank you. I will think things over and more than likely seek your advice once more.'

'Contact me at any time. You have my office address in Kelso and York should matters become urgent.' When Mrs Cheevey made no further comment, he stood up. 'I will take my leave, Ma'am. Remember, no problem is insurmountable. I'm sure everything will turn out as you wish.'

Emma rose from her own chair and walked with him to the front door, where she paused and thanked him once again for his help in administering this prize that had come so unexpectedly into her life. In some ways she was thankful that Robert and their two sons had been too far away to involve themselves once she heard of it. They would have wanted to take over, or certainly Robert and Stephen would; Matthew would probably have let things take their course without any interference from him. Now she could make her own decisions and act on them as she chose ... well, maybe with some more advice from the extremely attentive Mr Smyth.

As the door was opened for him, he turned back towards her. 'I am pleased with the way things have turned out for you. I have gained great satisfaction from the outcome of this matter, and feel it deserves a little celebration. Would you do me the honour of dining with me this evening at the

White Heather in Kelso?'

She left only the slightest hesitation. 'Why not? That is most kind of you, and I accept.'

'I will send my carriage for you. Is six o'clock convenient?'

She inclined her head in acceptance and was sure his step was lighter as he went to the conveyance that one of her grooms had taken in charge.

Emma watched it depart then closed the door and leaned against it, lost in thought. A Scottish retreat, he had said. Whatever lay behind that suggestion?

2

Sam guided the carriage skilfully around other vehicles seeking to pick up their passengers outside York's busy Station Hotel. He drove over Lendal Bridge, crossing the River Ouse and passing Bootham Bar, one of four fortified entrances to the ancient city. Heading north, he settled the two horses into a steady motion to make the ride comfortable for his three passengers.

After a year's absence, Alice felt especially pleased to be returning to the countryside that she loved. It felt as if she'd been away longer than that, for her school years had always been divided between home and school, the hall and the convent. Now she anticipated a long settled period at home, a whole lifetime at Wooton stretching ahead of her. She had not yet contemplated what those years might bring, but she was certain they would include her home and all that it meant to her.

She took in the passing landscape of the flat fertile Plain of York, knowing her father owned what he described as 'some of the best farming land in the county.' Ten miles further north, with the rolling Howardian Hills and their myriad of summer greens adding variety to the view, Sam eased the carriage away from the main road and on to a lesser one that climbed steadily through the foothills. After two miles the roadway steepened, causing him to encourage the horses with soothing words. After a mile the escarpment flattened. Keeping in mind the Ware family tradition of stopping here to admire the view, he drew the horses to a halt.

'You remembered, Sam!' cried Alice excitedly as she jumped down from the carriage, not waiting to be assisted by the coachman.

Cecilia laughed but there were tears in her eyes too when she said, 'We've brought her home, Sam.'

'And a pleasure it is, Ma'am. It is always good to have Miss Alice back.'

'It is indeed,' agreed Sir Raymond. 'And what could be better than that view to greet her?'

Alice cast her eyes across the scene she had carried in her mind all this last year: the Vale of York stretching north and south and westward towards the Pennines. She glanced along the escarpment on which they were standing and then turned slowly so she could look across the farms in the small valley to the north that rose towards the moors, alluring in their wild majesty. Soon they would be a sea of purple when the heather bloomed in all its glory.

'Father, Mother, don't ever leave Wooton. Let us all be here for ever,' Alice called out to them.

They both smiled to see her so happy but, knowing life was never as easy as that, made no promises.

Within ten minutes they were turning through the gateway to the hall and along a drive that led to a cobbled courtyard overlooked by stables on two sides, one of which gave easy access for horses to be brought to the front of the house when required. Workshops occupied a third side while the fourth overlooked an inviting view towards the south, but also led to walks through well-tended gardens from which there were further spectacular views.

A groom and two stable lads hurried into the courtyard when they heard the carriage arriving. They politely greeted Alice and busied themselves tending to the horses and carriage.

'Sis! Sis! Welcome home!' shouted her brother, racing across the cobbles.

'Nicholas!' They embraced amid peals of joyous laughter.

'Sorry I wasn't at the station to greet my grown-up sister.'

'It doesn't matter, Nick. We're together again now.'

He laughed and whirled her round.

Inside the house they were met by the house-keeper, Mrs Greville, immaculately attired in a tight-fitting black dress trimmed with white lace that accentuated her slim figure and air of confidence. 'Welcome, home, Miss,' she said to Alice. She raised a finger and the two maids and a footman, who were standing by, came forward to take the outdoor wear of the new arrivals.

As she escorted them into the house, Mrs Greville informed them, 'Coffee and Mrs Gordon's homemade treacle scones will be ready in the morning room in ten minutes.'

Alice let out a whoop. 'Mrs Greville, you're a wonder! You remembered my favourite.'

'You are kind to think that, Miss, but it wasn't me, it was Mrs Gordon who remembered,' the housekeeper admitted.

'Then I shall come to the kitchen and thank her when I have tasted her delights and decided whether she still has the magic touch or not.'

'I'm sure you will find that she has,' said her mother, 'though your father and I can't confirm that about her treacle scones. Mrs Gordon said she would make no more until you returned.'

'What?' Alice laughed disbelievingly.

'It's true,' her mother assured her.

'I'm off to see my room,' shouted Alice as she ran for the stairs.

'Don't be long!' called her mother.

Shortly afterwards when Alice entered the morning room her mother was pouring the coffee.

'My room is just as it was,' Alice enthused. 'Oh, it's so good to be back.'

'Sally, there is no need for you to wait up for me tonight,' said Emma Cheevey, studying the reaction of her lady's maid in the dressing-table mirror, while pretending to adjust her earrings.

'Very well, Ma'am,' replied Sally, with no discernible change of expression. 'Will it be a cape or a shawl, Ma'am?'

Emma pondered a moment then said, 'The green cape and a matching silk scarf would do well this evening.'

Sally removed the required items from the wardrobe and stood by while her mistress made some adjustments to her hair.

Emma then shrugged herself into the cape and draped the scarf casually around her neck. One last look in the full-length cheval glass and she was satisfied. She headed for her dressing-room door. Sally opened it, saying, 'Have a pleasant evening, Ma'am.'

'Thank you, Sally.'

Emma's footsteps were light as she swept down the stairs. She felt younger, prettier – a man had invited her to dine with him. The last time must have been shortly after Steven had been born when Robert had insisted on celebrating his heir's arrival. Dining with her husband had then become a matter of course whenever occasion demanded. As the years had passed, she'd fallen into the routine required of a serving Army officer's wife.

When they first married she had supported Robert's ambitions, knowing he had set his eyes on climbing the officer rankings. Emma accepted that her luxurious life style was based on money derived from his land-owning family. She had played her part as she knew he expected her to do, providing him with an heir and a spare without allowing her figure to be spoiled. She had been satisfied to be there whenever he wanted, but where once there had been passion between them, ennui had set in followed by loneliness, particularly when Robert's Army commitments required him to serve abroad. True, she had made friends among the officers' wives, but she was tired of the Army's stranglehold on them.

Then John Smyth had walked into her life.

As he made his enquiries about her ancestors, his visits to Heatherfold Hall became more and more frequent. Emma began to wonder if this increasing frequency was strictly necessary or if Smyth was deliberately drawing out the process. She found herself not caring overmuch as the pleasure she felt in the company of this good-looking man, two years younger than her own age of forty-six, was changing her life for the better. Now as the carriage headed for the hotel in nearby Kelso, she wondered if more than due attention to a client lay behind this invitation, and if it did, how she might respond.

When the carriage drew to a halt in front of the hotel, the groom was quickly down from his seat to help Mrs Cheevey to the ground. As soon as they entered the hotel, the manager hurried to greet her.

'Mrs Cheevey, it is a great pleasure to see you.' He smiled, making a slight bow.

'It is kind of you to say so when I am not a frequent visitor to your estimable establishment.'

'That is your prerogative, Mrs Cheevey. You are most welcome at any time, I assure you. Please, follow me.' As he set off across the spacious hall he snapped his fingers and two neatly dressed maids followed them. He opened a door that led into a small vestibule. One of the girls stepped forward and said, 'May we take your cape, Ma'am?'

Emma smiled her thanks, slipped out of her cape, removed her gloves and scarf and handed them over. As the maids disappeared, the manager knocked at another door, paused, opened it and said, 'Mr Smyth, your guest is here.' He stepped to one side to allow Emma to enter the room.

John Smyth jumped to his feet and came to greet her as the manager quickly left. 'Mrs Cheevey, welcome.' John held out both hands to her. He ran his eyes over her silk evening dress, cut to display her well-rounded figure according to the fashion of the time. Its pale ice blue shade was the perfect foil for her peach-like complexion. The low neckline of the dress was trimmed with Brussels lace, and a choker of pearls completed a picture that brought a heartfelt compliment from her host.

'You look exceedingly beautiful this evening, Mrs Cheevey.'

Her smile was warm as she held on to his hands and said, 'Thank you for those kind words. This is most pleasant. I think, as it is a social occasion, you should use my Christian name.'

He nodded his appreciation and said, as if savouring the sound, 'Emma... What a pretty name. My own is dull in comparison.'

'But John has the ring of dependability, and it suits you well if I am any judge. You have dealt very creditably with the Deepdale inheritance.'

'My profession,' he replied, with a shrug.

'But you acted with consummate understanding, gentleness and charm, reassuring me from our first meeting that I was in safe hands.'

'You are too kind. We came here this evening to celebrate your good fortune so let us drink to that.' He went to a small table where glasses and a bottle of wine had been placed in readiness. He handed a glass to Emma and then raised the other, saying, 'To you. May the future bring you everything you wish for.'

'Thank you, John, that is very thoughtful of you.' She glanced round the room with its paintings of lochs and mountains hanging on three of the walls. A serving table was placed inside an alcove and a small dining table, set for two, occupied the centre of the room.

'This is most pleasant, and I like the privacy we have. It's so much easier to talk freely when one is not on public display.'

He gave a slight smile. 'We have known each other for just over a year now so I think we may allow ourselves this latitude.' He took a sip of wine, as did she. Their eyes met and held over the rims of the glasses. Each of them smiled.

Ten minutes later a knock on the door, followed by a pause, heralded the appearance of one of the maids.

'Dinner is ready, sir. Would you like me to serve now?'

'Please,' replied John, having received a slight nod of agreement from Emma.

A leisurely progression of courses beautifully presented, brought praise and thanks from them both when the meal was finally finished, leaving them to enjoy their after-dinner wine.

Their conversation strayed into new territory

once they were free from interruption, enabling them to learn more about each other in a casual way.

Then John broached a subject he had avoided until now but felt he must raise, 'Have you had word from South Africa of your husband and son?'

'News is slow in coming and by the time it is received the situation can have changed for better or worse. Like other wives, I wait. It's a solitary business for a colonel's wife. The other women form cliques around their husband's rank, but there is only one colonel in a regiment; apart from which there are no barracks in Kelso and my husband was adamant I should stay in what has always been his family home. He doesn't understand that life here can be lonely for me.'

John let this leading comment hang for a moment then said, 'I mean no imposition but if you ever want companionship, remember that I am near.'

'That is a kind thought. I may take you up on it.' Emma glanced at the clock. 'It is late ... time I was going. This has been a most enjoyable evening. I am so glad that you suggested a celebration of my good fortune.'

'My pleasure,' he replied. After a slight hesitation he added, 'Might I suggest we dine together again? That is, if you would like to?'

'I would be delighted to accept,' she replied without hesitation.

He smiled with relief. 'Then I will arrange something.'

'I shall look forward to it.'

Emma was about to rise when he stopped her. 'This has been an evening for celebration and I do not wish to detract from that, but there is one business matter I feel I must mention since a speedy decision from you is required.'

'This sounds ominous.' Emma eyed him, grave-faced.

'It is something that you may not have considered in the short time since learning of your good fortune, but something that I urge you to consider now, for your own good.'

Emma looked askance at him as he paused. 'Very well then, John, let me hear what you have to say.'

He cleared his throat. 'You now have a fortune at your disposal. I'd advise you to allow me to draw up documents protecting your wealth from outside influences. Legally it is yours, but money can bring out the bad side in people. Your husband, if he ever chose to, could lay claim to it. He could object to your having control of such wealth. He could even claim you were incompetent to handle your affairs and say your interests would be better served if he were put in charge of your assets.' John left a little pause then said, as he took her hand in his, 'Should we wish to pursue our friendship, as I certainly do, he could even seize on that to build a case against us.'

Emma looked alarmed. 'I don't think Robert would go that far.' With her grip tightening on his hand, she said, 'But I would not wish your reputation to be dragged through the gutter.'

'Please don't consider that. My main concern is that we safeguard your position, draw up documents to preserve your wealth for your sole use and forestall any intervention by your husband. The first move would be for you to sanction the necessary documentation.'

His words troubled Emma. In the short time since receiving news of her inheritance, she had not considered that there might be any adverse consequences. She pondered them now and reached a decision.

She must act to use the law before it could be invoked against her. She knew her husband, if he were so disposed, could cite the estrangement within their marriage, maybe even contest her soundness of mind, so as to seize control of her inheritance. She could not allow herself to be manoeuvred by him into a relationship in which she was a powerless dependant. The wealth she had inherited in her own name threw a different perspective on Emma's future. She needed to observe the precautions John was suggesting.

'Very well,' she said firmly. 'I will seriously consider your suggestion. Please draw up the necessary papers and we will talk again.'

Outside a gentle warm breeze stirred the trees. Stars burned in the heavens, their white light tranquil. Emma let it bring peace to her troubled mind.

John respected her silence on the ride home.

He halted the carriage close to the front door. Emma turned to him and took his hand in hers. 'Thank you for a wonderful evening, and for the offer of a friendship I shall cherish.'

He slid his hands around her waist and drew her towards him.

'I think I am falling in love with you, John,' she murmured.

Their lips met, gently at first, then hungrily. Emma wished she was just setting out on the evening again and then she would have this kiss to look forward to all night. But, too soon, a light shone inside the house. John drew away and sat straight-backed as the door was opened and a manservant came outside to escort the mistress into the house.

3

Light streaming through Emma's bedroom window awakened her to a new day. She lay on her back and stretched out her arms as if to embrace her recollections of an evening spent with John Smyth. She allowed herself to be drawn into imagining what life with him could be like

Then his words of warning came to mind and she guiltily pictured two figures in military dress, enduring searing heat and constant danger. Robert and Steven ... recollecting them, her pleasure in the preceding evening was pierced by self-reproach.

She beat at her pillows, annoyed with her own weakness in daring to imagine a life spent with John. She sobbed for what she saw as an impossible dream, and let the tears flow until they had washed away her feeling of guilt.

Finally she glanced at the clock and hurriedly

got out of bed to remove any evidence of her tears. She had no sooner returned to it than there was a knock on the door, one that she could easily identify. A moment later Sally walked in.

'Good morning, Ma'am.'

'Good morning, Sally.'

'I hope you had a pleasant evening, Ma'am?'

'I did, Sally, thank you. It was a delightful meal in agreeable company,' Emma stated calmly.

She chose her clothes for the morning: a pale blue silk skirt, gored to give it a little extra flair, worn with a cream chiffon high-necked blouse with long tight sleeves trimmed at the wrists with cream lace. Sally got them ready and helped her mistress dress. Emma viewed herself in the long wall mirror. She approved of the extra wave Sally had introduced to her hair, and thanked her. Ready to meet a new day, she went down to the dining room.

The butler and maid were attentive throughout the meal; finding the mistress appreciative of their service and considerate towards their welfare, they knew they were better placed at Heatherfold Hall when Colonel Cheevey was away on Army duties.

Emma liked to have her coffee in the drawing room so she could admire the view towards the old pele tower of Smailholme, on top of Lady Hill some five miles away. Sometimes she would decide to take a ride in that direction, but today her thoughts were filled by visions of a hot, dangerous land far away.

These were dismissed by a knock on the door. It was her butler, Dryden.

'Ma'am, I'm sorry to interrupt, but Mr Smyth is here.'

Emma felt her heart beat a little faster but gave no indication of surprise. She glanced at the clock on the mantelpiece. It was eleven a.m. 'Thank you, Dryden. Please show him in, and ask Betsy to bring another cup and some more coffee.'

In a few moments the butler was announcing the new arrival, who walked briskly into the room.

'I am sorry to intrude,' he said as the door was closed. 'I know you will be arranging things for the day with your staff but I felt it imperative to get these documents signed immediately.'

Emma waved away the apology. 'You are most conscientious,' she returned, eyes meeting his as she gestured to him to sit down.

'I have been up most of the night working on the documents I mentioned to you.'

'Ah, so that is why you are not your usual soigné self,' she told him teasingly.

He looked embarrassed by her observation. 'We should have all the documents signed, witnessed and notarised as soon as possible,' he told her.

'I am most grateful for your solicitude as to my welfare.'

The maid walked in with a tray.

'I'll see to that,' said Emma.

'Yes, Ma'am.'

John watched Emma pour the coffee, accepted the cup and took a sip, then picked up a large envelope and withdrew several sheets of paper. 'If you don't mind, I would like to discuss several points I have noted here. There may be some aspects of this documentation you would like amending or others you may wish to insert.'

'This could take some time then?' asked Emma.

'It could, yes. I want you to give every point I raise your full attention.'

'Then you will stay to lunch?'

'I should like that.'

Emma rose from her chair and went to the bell-pull beside the fireplace. In a few moments her personal maid appeared. 'Betsy, tell Cook that Mr Smyth will be staying to lunch.'

Three hours later, John made his final note, saying, 'That should counter every possible challenge you may face concerning your newfound wealth. I am not pretending that it will deter any objections from being raised, but it will give you solid ground from which to beat off any contest for control of Deepdale.'

'I am more than grateful for all you have done and are doing,' said Emma, in a tone that expressed more than mere appreciation. 'I will tell no one of my good fortune, not even my family, for the moment.'

'That is sensible,' he agreed.

'It will also give me time to view Deepdale. I know nothing of North Yorkshire. I would like to see it for myself.'

'A very good idea.'

'Could you arrange to take me there and show me what is now mine?'

'Nothing would please me more. Have you any preferences as to when?'

'None. I will fit in with your working schedule.'

He pulled a notebook from his pocket and flicked over a few pages until he found what he was looking for. 'I have to be in the York office two weeks from today. What if we travel down together by train three days before that? I will book our seats and accommodation in York. There we can hire a carriage and make the journey together.'

'How exciting,' Emma told him, unclear whether she meant the prospect of seeing Deepdale or the chance to be alone with John for several days.

'Good morning,' Alice said breezily when she walked into the dining room and found her mother, father and brother about to start breakfast.

'Good morning, my dear,' returned her mother, accepting a kiss on the cheek from Alice.

Her father did the same and asked, 'Did you sleep well?'

'I did, it must be the Yorkshire air.' She looked at her brother as she sat down at the table. 'Will you ride with me today, Nicholas?'

'Like old times?'

'Yes. We always did when I came home from school.'

Nicholas glanced at his father; there was a lot of work to be done on the estate. He liked being out in the open air, working alongside the men, who appreciated the fact that the young master did not mind getting his hands dirty when need arose. A slight nod from his father signalled approval of a day's holiday.

'The weather's just right for us,' said Nicholas.

Twenty minutes later Sir Raymond left his son and daughter to follow up their plan.

'I'll see Sam about the horses,' said Nicholas.

'Give me fifteen minutes to change,' said Alice. 'Meet you in the hall.'

As good as her word, she came down the stairs in time to hear her mother call from the veranda, 'We're out here.'

Alice found her parents and brother waiting outside for her.

'What did I say, Raymond?' said Cecilia, with a smile of satisfaction at her husband.

'You were right, my dear,' he agreed.

'I said your riding habit might be getting a little tight for you, Alice,' explained her mother.

She automatically smoothed her safety skirt. 'It's not so bad,' she said, 'but I had a little trouble with the buttons and the waistcoat is a little tight.'

'Then tomorrow you and I will go into York and get you a completely new riding habit,' promised her mother.

'Light brown, please!' Alice's eyes shone with excitement.

'Whatever you like,' replied her mother, determined to have a day on her own with her daughter, spoiling her.

Alice eyed her brother up and down. 'You don't need anything new,' she commented, admiring the cut of his black riding jacket and jodhpurs, white shirt, yellow cravat at his throat and highly polished calf-length riding boots.

'Come on. We're here for a ride not a fashion parade,' he said, hurrying her over to the steps and the path leading to the stable yard.

'Enjoy yourselves,' their mother and father called after them.

As they approached the stables, two grooms

appeared leading Beauty, Alice's chestnut Arab mare, and Firebrand, Nicholas's Cleveland bay.

Alice greeted Beauty with affection. 'My fine one,' she said, patting the mare's neck. The horse nuzzled her affectionately. Alice turned to the groom. 'Thank you for looking after her so well while I was away.'

Brother and sister rode out of the stableyard and on to the lengthy sward of grass stretching before them.

'Race you!' shouted Nicholas, just as he always did.

Alice took up his challenge automatically. Earth flew beneath the horses' hooves. Laughter came to Alice's lips.

The horses entered into the contest and sped on eagerly until they were slowed to a walking pace when Nicholas indicated harder ground ahead.

'That felt just as if I had never been away,' said Alice, running her hand through her hair, which was tousled by the wind. 'Do you like running the estate with Father?' she continued.

'Yes, I love the land. But he is set in his ways, won't readily make changes. Although he has Wooton in his heart, I can't make him see that time doesn't stand still. Changes should be made if they are for the better.'

'I'm sure the time will come when he will agree with you. Not with every one perhaps, but I'm sure he wants the estate to prosper. After all, he loves the place. Changes aren't always easy to make, especially for older people. Be patient, Nick. The time will come. After all, you are his heir.'

'Only if he doesn't cut me out of his will.'

'He wouldn't do that, Nick.'

'You never know.'

'Then you'd better walk a straight path,' Alice said, with a laugh. She pulled her horse to a stop and gazed out across the green fields in which cows grazed contentedly. 'These look a fine herd,' she commented.

'They are, and the yield is good. We could do with some more milkers but Father is reluctant to buy them.'

'Don't start again,' said Alice, and added with a note of warning. 'And don't upset him. That's one thing you don't want to do.'

'Don't worry, sis, I won't. Besides, you'll be here to keep me on the straight and narrow.'

They negotiated a small wood in single file, coming out on a slight rise. Alice brought them to a halt.

'I'd forgotten this path came out here,' she commented.

The land fell away before them, a patchwork of small woods and meadows.

'But you remember how Deepdale Manor just shows through that stand of trees?' said Nicholas.

'Yes, I do. Mother said it has stayed empty since Miss Owens died. Have you never been tempted to investigate?'

'No. Maybe I was remembering Mother and Father telling us not to go there as children, and not to bother Miss Owens. The land is being neglected now except for some tidying up around the house.'

'Mother said she thought something might be in the offing.'

'I don't know where she got that idea from. Must be wishful thinking.'

'Let's ride that way and have a look,' Alice suggested.

'There's nothing to see but an empty building. But as you wish, it's your homecoming.'

They put their horses into a gentle trot.

The house was lost to view as they moved into a small stand of oaks. When they emerged at the other side, Alice, who was surprised to see they were much closer to the house than she had expected, stopped again.

Her gaze swept across the façade. Paintwork was flaking, windows grey with dust. Curtains hung forlornly upstairs. At ground level the glass was uncovered and bore a tracery of cracks. On the stone terrace a garden seat had tipped sideways on one crumbling leg.

'It's sad to see it so neglected,' said Alice. 'It shouldn't be like this.'

'It's been let go for years. Miss Owen was a recluse, remember. I never heard of anyone seeing her, except a maid of sorts and a general factotum, though they were both mysteries as well.' Nicholas gave a little chuckle. 'Remember how we imagined she was a witch?'

Alice gave a little shiver at the recollection, but her resolve stiffened. 'Have you never been near the place, not even after she died?'

'No. I've been too busy even to consider it.'

'Weren't you curious?'

'Not really. I did ride past once, but not close by. I was taking what I thought would be a short cut to a field where some of our cattle had

41

strayed after a fence had broken.'

'And?' she prompted, sensing there was more.

'It was odd. A big house with no one living there seemed to give out a strange feeling.'

'You didn't investigate?'

'No. I rode away.'

'Have you lost your spirit of adventure?' She made it a challenge and tapped her horse forward; Nick could not do anything but follow.

Alice led the way to a small rise from which they could view the layout of the site.

The stone house stood within acres of neglected gardens. It had an imposing set of stairs before the main entrance, and a veranda which stretched the full length of one side of the house.

'I'm surprised,' commented Alice. 'It's bigger than I remember, but of course we never really knew it. It's a pity it has been uncared for, for so long.'

'I suppose Miss Owen lost interest and didn't bother as she got older.'

'Let's circle it and then take a closer look,' Alice suggested.

They found the back of the house led on to a flagged yard with access to what they judged would be kitchens and domestic stores. Standing separately across the yard they could see what had once been stables for six horses. Beyond them tumbled old stones were visible through overgrown grass.

'I'm going back to the front to take a peep through the windows,' Alice decided. Not waiting for an answer, she turned her horse and her brother followed.

When she stepped on to the stone veranda, she had the strange sensation that the house was enveloping her with a deep, comforting sense of peace.

Nicholas had walked past her and was peering through the French doors.

'This is a fine spacious hall and I like the double sweep of the staircase meeting on the first floor,' he called over his shoulder.' Receiving no answer, he looked back. 'Wake up!' he called. 'Come and see.'

Alice started. She gave her head a little shake. Standing beside Nicholas, she peered into the hall. Once again she felt the building welcoming her, holding her more and more enthralled.

'It's beautiful,' she said, half to herself, but he caught her words.

'It would be if it weren't full of dust and cobwebs,' he replied, shuddering as a spider crawled across the window.

'Use your imagination,' countered Alice. 'I can see myself dressed for a ball, with everyone's eyes on me as I sweep down the stairs and into the arms of a young man, who guides me into a waltz in the ballroom.'

'You've far too much imagination,' said Nicholas. 'There won't even be a ballroom.'

'Let's see.' She moved away from the door towards the set of windows to the right. She peered through one, ignoring the crack that ran horizontally across the glass. 'Here it is! This room's big enough for a ball,' she called in delight. 'I knew I was right.'

'I'm not sure...'

'Don't be such a wet blanket,' Alice chided her brother.

They moved on.

'The dining room ... and all the furniture is still here.'

'Solid, from what we can see,' said Nicholas, his interest mildly stirred. 'Oak I'd say. That would fetch a bonny penny.'

'There you go,' Alice rebuked him. 'Only ever one thing on your mind, money, whereas I see a festive gathering around that table, enjoying enticing food and fine wine. Maybe one day we'll see that happening again. I'd like to see this house come alive.'

They wandered round, looking in windows wherever they could.

'I'd love to see upstairs,' sighed Alice.

They were near a side door when she happened to express this wish and Nicholas, without any expectation of success, pushed at it. Much to his surprise, it yielded. He gave it another shove. 'Hey, presto!' he said, in the manner of a magician.

Alice spun round from examining a carving in the wall. 'Oh, my goodness!' she gasped on seeing the open door.

Nicholas made a little bow with a sweep of his arm as he said, 'My sister's wish is my command.' He held out his hand and led her inside.

He escorted her up the stairs on to the floor above. Each room, most of them still furnished, drew fresh expressions of delight from Alice. Looking out of the window, she saw beyond the unkempt Deepdale land swathes of well-tended grass belonging to estate owners who cared for their land.

As his gaze swept across the undulating scene, Nicholas said wistfully, 'I wish I could persuade Father to buy this place. It would be a wonderful investment for the future.'

'I let a question on that very point slip out as we were coming home and he was adamant that he wouldn't,' Alice cautioned her brother.

'I know. It's always the same answer whatever I ask him,' said Nicholas. He cast another glance out of the window and said, 'Come on, we'd best get going.'

When they went downstairs, Alice paused to examine the stone in the wall she had looked at previously.

'What is it, sis?' asked Nicholas.

'This is worn but I'm sure there are traces of carving here.'

He came over and examined the stone she indicated. After a few moments, he said, with a note of agreement in his voice, 'I believe you are right. Whoever built this house must have used an old site or else brought the stones from a derelict property.'

'I think it more likely that it is built on the site of a previous house,' said Alice. 'Let's have another look round.'

'We can't be too long,' warned her brother.

Within the next ten minutes a closer examination of the walls of the house revealed several more places where there was evidence that figures and patterns had once been worked into the stone.

'They are rather worn but I'm sure some of these are angels,' commented Alice.

On closer examination, Nicholas had to agree with her. He added, 'I noticed, where two windows had been blocked in with stone, you could make out what had once been pointed arches. Those and the carvings could signify that there was once a convent or a monastery here.'

'Could be,' agreed Alice, privately convinced this was the case – she wanted to keep the feelings she had experienced on first arriving to herself, believing her brother would only ridicule them. Instead she said, 'I've never heard our parents mention what was here before Miss Owens's time.'

'Maybe they don't know,' he said. 'Mother and Father wouldn't trespass as we have done.'

'So how do we find out?'

'We don't,' replied her brother firmly. 'It's of no interest, really,' he added. 'We are hardly likely to come here again. It would be better to stay silent on the subject.'

4

'Good day, Sir. Good day, Ma'am.' The amply built landlord of the Wild Hussar, ten miles northeast of York, knew immediately that these new arrivals were the guests he was expecting. 'I trust your journey to York was uneventful and you found your way here without trouble.' He turned to the rotund woman who had joined him; a welcoming smile appeared on her round rosy face. 'May I introduce Mrs Beckwith, my wife? She supervises the household side of our business, and also the catering. Our cook is excellent, so if you have any special requests, my wife will pass them on.'

'I am pleased to welcome you,' said Mrs Beckwith. 'Two single rooms are ready for you, one with communication to a box room for Mrs Cheevey's maid.'

Mr Beckwith gave a signal to the two 'boots' standing by to handle the luggage. Sally indicated which belonged to her mistress and those pieces that should go to Mr Smyth's room.

As they started up the oak staircase, the front door opened with a bang and four people in high spirits came in and made straight for the bar, casting glances at the people going up the stairs.

'Two local gentlemen and their wives,' said Mr Beckwith.

'I hope you will be comfortable here,' said his wife, opening a door to allow Emma to pass into her room.

She studied it closely. The bed looked comfortable; the sheets crisp and clean. Plain yellow curtains were draped at the two large windows. She could see this hostelry was well cared for.

'I'm sure we will be most content,' said Emma, 'but would you oblige me with a cup of tea now?'

'Of course, Ma'am. Would you come down when you are ready? If your maid would like one, there is a room where the servants dine. She will be made welcome there.'

As Mrs Beckwith left, Emma went into the adjoining room and found Sally already sorting out clothes.

'You'll find a servants' hall near the kitchen, Sally. There'll be a cup of tea there if you would like one.'

'Thank you, Ma'am.'

Emma washed her hands and face, patted her hair into place and checked her appearance in the mirror. Satisfied, she went downstairs where she found John in conversation with the landlord.

He broke off to greet her. 'Is everything to your liking?'

'Yes, thank you.' She turned to Beckwith. 'A very nice place you have here, well placed for York yet providing all the peace of the countryside.'

He smiled. 'A number of our customers remark on that.'

'I was just explaining to the landlord why I could not divulge the length of our stay when I made the booking,' John explained.

'You carry on. I'm going to have the cup of tea I ordered from Mrs Beckwith.' Emma headed for the dining room and John resumed his explanation.

'We are here to look at Deepdale Manor and there was no knowing in advance how long my client Mrs Cheevey would choose to spend there. Our stay in York last night was convenient for us to reach here this morning and spend the afternoon looking at Deepdale. After that who knows?'

'You are welcome to stay as long as you like, Mr Smyth. Deepdale has been unoccupied for two years, and left untended for much longer. Miss Owens was very much a recluse, as you no doubt know, and became incapable of attending to all her property, though she did keep the west wing in good condition and lived there herself. I think the whole building very fine, but I believe it will need some renovation. You will soon see for yourselves.'

'I look forward to it. Now I think I'll join Mrs Cheevey for that cup of tea.'

Half an hour later they were driving away from the Wild Hussar, the landlord having seen that the stableman had a carriage ready for them.

'This is exciting, seeing my property for the first time,' said Emma. 'I am surprised you did not view it yourself before you contacted me, John.'

'I had too much work to do, ascertaining Miss Owens's heir. Viewing the property was not a priority. I already knew the Hall to be a big house with an extensive estate, much larger than Heatherfold.'

'So here we are, wondering what surprises await us,' said Emma lightly. 'And I am pleased to be sharing these moments with someone who has helped me so much.' She gently tapped his hands, which were steady on the reins.

'Enjoy your ride this fine morning,' called Nicholas on seeing his sister ride Beauty out of the stable yard. 'By the way, your new riding habit looks perfect.'

'Thank you. I am pleased Mother persuaded me to have one made.'

'Certainly worth waiting for,' he approved. 'Heading anywhere in particular today?'

'No, just where fancy takes me. I wish you were coming.'

'Too much to see to,' he answered regretfully.

'Enjoy yourself.'

She had given him a non-committal answer but Alice knew exactly where she was going. Deepdale had occupied her thoughts for twenty-four hours after her visit there with her brother, but then it had slipped to the back of her mind as her days moved into an enjoyable pattern. She had not thought of it again until last night when, contrary to her usual habit, she had woken about three o'clock.

It was a warm night and she had slipped out of bed to open her window a little wider. The moon was bathing the fields and trees in a white light, painting a picture that held her transfixed. She felt transported into another world, not that of Wooton Hall but Deepdale... She could not imagine why but the house had lodged in her mind and now she knew she must visit it again.

She set Beauty to a lazy pace, matching the movement of wispy white clouds in the sky ahead. Alice gazed across a patchwork of grass and tilled fields dotted with the occasional barn and cattleshed. Her eyes veered to the right, following the track that would bring her to the back of Deepdale Hall.

She surveyed the building, sombre and silent, as if waiting for someone to restore the life it had once known.

Alice guided Beauty towards the back door, dismounted and looped the reins around a rusting piece of iron. She stepped inside, paused a moment, and, hearing only the sighing of the breeze, walked through the derelict part of the house. It felt different today. Annoyed with herself for not being able to decide why, she turned to go but found herself held by a compulsion to stay. Reaching the west wing, she entered the main bedroom. As she crossed over to the large window, she had the sudden feeling she was intruding on Miss Owens's privacy. A shiver ran through her and she instantly turned to leave. Before she could, her attention was distracted by the view of the cornfields, lit by the morning sun and rippling and dancing in the delicate breeze. Alice stood spellbound by the sight.

'Are you sure we are going the right way, John?' asked Emma.

'I'm following the landlord's directions to the letter,' he replied haughtily.

'It's just that I'm certain we passed that gate before.'

'If you are right then you can navigate us from now on.' He held out the reins to her in a gesture of capitulation.

Their eyes met and they burst into laughter simultaneously.

Their amusement died away a few minutes later when they caught their first glimpse of Deepdale Manor. John drew the carriage to a halt.

'Not the best view of the house, I hope,' said Emma, disappointment in her voice.

'I'm sorry. We should have approached it from the front, but I'll go on now and we'll take in the principal aspect on our return.'

'Go carefully, John, the ruts seem to be getting deeper.'

'Don't worry, I'll take it steady.'

He slightly turned the horse and carriage and started it on its way, only to stop again as soon as they entered the yard to the rear of the building.

'Someone's here!' he said in surprise on noticing the fine chestnut horse tethered by the door.

'It's a good-looking animal,' pointed out Emma, 'and the side-saddle indicates the rider is female.'

'There's only one way to find out,' said John, getting down from the carriage.

He helped Emma to the ground as he said, 'We'll do this quietly. We don't want to scare the intruder away, and she may have company.'

'You think they're inside?'

He nodded. 'I think the horse proves that. I don't suppose they would leave it there if they were going to explore the grounds.'

They moved to the back door, which John eased open. After he had closed it, he held up his hand and they both froze, listening for any sound that would betray the intruder's presence. They heard the shuffle of feet. John pointed upwards and then gave Emma a reassuring look. They both knew that whoever the trespasser was, they could not get out unless they used force to pass by on the stairs.

Gingerly, step by step, they climbed up, hoping that the age of the treads would not lead to loud creaking.

They reached the landing. Heard a footstep. John pointed to a door and Emma nodded agreement. He flung it open and stepped inside. With Emma stepping up quickly beside him, they had blocked the intruder's escape route.

'What...!' John was taken aback to see the intruder really was a young lady, elegantly attired in a riding habit that had obviously cost a lot of money.

The sound of the door opening brought Alice spinning round from the window. She was horrified to be caught intruding, and to be confronted by two people who were blocking her only means of escape.

John was swift to collect himself. 'Who are you? And what are you doing here?' he demanded curtly. Alice was so shocked she could not utter a word. 'Do you know, young lady, that you are trespassing? You have no right to be in here!'

Emma was quick to grasp the situation. Whoever this person was, she recognised breeding. She saw that the intruder was frightened but noted that she was quick to control that emotion and hold herself in readiness to explain. Emma laid a hand on John's arm indicating that he should say no more, at least for the moment.

'Young lady, I am Mrs Cheevey,' Emma began. 'I am the owner of this estate and I would like an explanation as to who you are and why you are trespassing on my property.'

'Ma'am, I am Alice Ware. I live with my mother, father and brother at Wooton Hall about five miles from here. I am profoundly sorry to have trespassed on your property. Please accept my sincere apologies. I did not know Deepdale had a new owner; it has been empty for two years. I have only recently finished my education in France and on my return felt the urge to reacquaint myself with the area in which I was born and bred.'

Emma raised an eyebrow. She liked the composure of this young stranger. 'Very well, Alice, I accept your apology. You obviously meant no harm and I can understand your wishing to revisit this place you obviously love.'

Alice brightened. 'If you live here, I am sure you will come to love it too.'

'I'm sure I shall,' Emma smiled. 'Now I must introduce you to Mr John Smyth, my solicitor, who has been handling the transfer of Deepdale Manor to me.'

'Mother and Father will be most interested to hear that I have met the new owner. No doubt they will scold me for trespassing but they will be delighted to hear that Deepdale will be occupied again. I am sure they will be pleased to entertain you at the appropriate time.'

'And I shall look forward to that,' replied Emma.

'When will you be settling here?' asked Alice, aiming to obtain as much news as possible to pass on to her parents.

Emma gave a little laugh. 'Oh, I have no plans as yet. This is my first visit to see what I now own. And there is my husband's estate near Kelso, where I live, to consider also.'

'He is not with you?'

'He is an Army man, and at present in South Africa.'

'Fighting the Boers?'

'Indeed. With Robert away I have a lot to think about, but I have my solicitor to guide me and see that I don't do anything silly with my new property.' Emma turned to him. 'Well, I think I really will tour the house and property now.' She turned back to Alice. 'It has been pleasant meeting you. I am sure we will meet again before long.'

'I hope so, Mrs Cheevey. And I hope you are going to bring life back to this house; it doesn't deserve to be neglected. Goodbye, and thank you for not prosecuting me for trespass.'

Emma and John smiled as they listened to her footsteps recede down the stairs and out by the back door.

'Our intruder wasn't at all what we expected,' commented John.

'Far from it. An elegant, vivacious young lady with poise and grace. I look forward to having her mother as my neighbour.'

This remark caught John by surprise. 'So you have made up your mind to move here?'

'Something is telling me I should.'

'You can't decide on the spur of the moment. You'd better take a good look round now and then I suggest you consider all the pros and cons before you make a final decision.'

Alice quickly set Beauty into a gallop. The news she carried was too exciting to hold back.

Hearing the pounding of approaching hooves, Sam hurried out of the stable. Alice was already bringing Beauty to a halt and was quickly out of the saddle. 'See to her, Sam, she's had a hard run.' With that she was off to the house, leaving him wondering what all the haste was about.

Alice ran through to the hall and into the main drawing room. It was empty. With a little gasp of irritation, she made for the small drawing room. Inside, she pulled up with relief. 'Mother!' she panted. 'We have new neighbours at Deepdale.'

'Alice, Alice, calm down. What on earth are you talking about?' Cecilia laid down the book she had been reading. 'I haven't heard anything. If that's the case, it's a wonder the servants haven't been gossiping.'

'It's true, Mother. I've been talking to a Mrs Cheevey, who is there now with her solicitor!'

'How did you meet her? Where exactly have you been?'

It was no good pretending so Alice confessed, 'I was at Deepdale Manor.'

'You were caught trespassing? What have I told...'

'Everything is quite all right. Mrs Cheevey was very kind about it,' Alice reassured her mother.

She gave a resigned shrug and settled back in her chair to take in everything her daughter had to tell her.

'I expect it will be a considerable time before she moves in,' commented Cecilia at last. 'The house will need to be made habitable, and if she has a home elsewhere there'll be no need to hurry.'

'Mother, I'm sure you'll find out everything when you meet Mrs Cheevey.'

'You've not been very talkative this evening,' commented John as he and Emma left the dining room of the Wild Hussar.

She gave a little smile. 'Sorry if I haven't been good company, I have a great deal on my mind.'

'That's understandable. I don't wish to intrude, but I'm here if you decide to share your thoughts.'

She hesitated for a moment then decided to

confide in him. 'Today I saw great potential in the whole of Deepdale Manor. I believe I could make it an attractive residence where I could enjoy living. I was making plans in my mind when we walked around the house.'

'And by the fourth tour you had almost reached a decision! Before you tell me it, please reflect. This could be life-changing for you.'

'I realise that, but Deepdale is mine and it is only I who can decide what to do with it.'

'So?'

'I want to make it my home, bring it to life. I want to start on some renovations straight away; I would say the west wing is the best and easiest section to make habitable. After that, the rest of the property can be restored while I am living there.'

'If you definitely want to live at Deepdale, that sounds the sensible way to progress.'

'I will want an architect. Do you know of any through your York business?'

'I have had dealings with one architectural firm, Richard Hart, Brothers and Co.'

'Can you arrange a meeting?'

'I need to go into our York office tomorrow. Would you like to accompany me and if possible visit Hart's?'

'Splendid. I want it all finished before Robert comes home from South Africa.'

Three days later everything was in place: Emma approved John's choice of architect and had discussed with him her ideas for the house. A firm of builders had been engaged with instructions to begin work within the week.

57

As they drove away from the site Emma turned to John. 'I am deeply grateful for all you have done, but I have one more favour to ask you. Can you stay on here, do most of your work from the York office and be able to supervise the progress of the building?'

'But won't you be doing that?'

'I think it will be best if I return to Heatherfold and only pay occasional visits to Deepdale. I will be happy to know it is in good hands, and, as we won't be seen returning here too often at the same time, it will avoid any scandal.'

5

10 August 1900

Dear Emma,

I hope that life at Heatherfold is more settled than it is here. It is has been an uneasy peace since I came to South Africa. The Boers hate us and we always seem to be looking over our shoulders. However, we manage a decent social life especially when we are in Pretoria, Cape Town, and other places where there is a strong Army presence, though we have to take care when we are off duty. Although I am an Army man, having been brought up with that sole end in mind, there are times when I long for the peace of Heatherfold and to be walking in the Scottish hills like we used to do, rather than patrolling the vast dry veldt.

I fear the situation between our Government and

the Boers is deteriorating so badly that nothing will prevent another outright war between us. That will be a great pity. This land will be torn apart.

I am well. Steven is too, and revelling in his Army service in this country. He is making a good name for himself and those in the know tell me he is destined for high rank and honours in a life that seems to have been tailor-made for him. You can be proud of him.

If Matthew is posted here I do not know what he will make of it, but it will make a man of him.

I trust your life continues pleasantly.
Take care of yourself and of Heatherfold Hall,
Yours,
Robert

Emma read the date again. The tenth of August? She glanced at her diary. It was September 21st. Where had this letter been? Why the delay? There could be many reasons; careless sorting, incompetent dispatch, and the threat of war; letters from South Africa had never taken as long to reach her. She folded it, placed it back in its envelope and set it in a slot in her escritoire. She sat back in her chair, contemplating a message that had brought no endearments, only a brief reminder of the past they had once shared. Where had Robert's affections gone? Was someone else, in a land far away, receiving them now? Or had Army life made showing feeling impossible? So much had happened in her life since her husband's previous letter had arrived.

She gave a little shrug of her shoulders. Once her husband's neglect of her would have caused her pain, but now John Smyth had entered her life the old feelings of boredom and neglect were giving way to stirrings of excitement and anticipation.

A knock on the sitting-room door interrupted her thoughts. Sally came in. 'The newspapers, Ma'am.'

'Thank you, Sally.'

Emma took *The Times* first and put the *Morning Post* to one side. A quick glance sent shivers through her. Britain was now formally at war with the Boers again. The implications made her fear for her husband and eldest son, with her youngest set to join them soon.

She read the reports of what was happening in South Africa and the speculation about the possible direction the Boers might take.

The predictions by some that the fighting would be over in a few weeks proved to be wrong. The Boers soon laid siege to Kimberley and outmanoeuvred the British in several encounters, their eyes set firmly on Ladysmith and Mafeking. As the weeks passed Emma felt more and more guilty that she was living in comfort and safety. To counteract that, she decided to spend some time in Yorkshire and superintend the work on Deepdale Manor herself. Three days later she and Sally arrived at the Wild Hussar.

'Is Mr Smyth in residence here at present?' Emma enquired of the landlord.

'He is, Ma'am.'

Emma was pleased by this news; not only would she have the pleasure of John's company and attention, but her mind would be distracted from those worrying thoughts of South Africa.

'He said he would be late back from the Manor, Ma'am.'

'Thank you. Please have a horse saddled for me.'

'Ready in ten minutes, Ma'am.'

She hurried upstairs, calling to her maid, 'Riding habit, Sally.'

The weather held fine but, in her eagerness to reach Deepdale and surprise John, Emma did not view the countryside with a critical eye or mind, and only slowed for a moment when Deepdale came in sight. Her sharp eyes noted the alterations she had approved and had left John to supervise. More work had been completed than she had expected. She tapped the horse forward and put it into a gallop. She could wait no longer to be in her own property.

The sound of a horse's hooves brought John on to the veranda at the front of the house. He wasn't expecting to see anyone at this time in the afternoon. He stopped in surprise on seeing Emma and then rushed forward to be down the stone steps and ready to help her from the saddle as soon as she reined in the horse.

'Emma! What a delightful surprise.' His hands were on her waist. When her feet touched the ground, instead of letting her go he drew her towards him. He looked deep into her eyes. She slid her arms round his neck and their lips met eagerly. Finally she broke away to say, 'Oh, John, it's so good to see you and to be with you at Deepdale.'

'Is that really why you are here?'

She gave a little nod as she said, 'Yes.'

'Not a guilty conscience, because of the war?'

'You are very perceptive. I have been troubled, but have come to terms with that. I was overcome by the need to see you and my Deepdale.'

'Then let me show you the progress we have made.' He took her hand and led her to the west wing. He said nothing as they entered. Emma made no comment at first as she looked around and took in all that had been achieved.

'You've done exactly what I planned ... and so quickly,' she said finally.

'I recruited a large workforce. I was determined to have your living space finished first so you could stay here while work continues on the other renovations. I thought you would feel closer to Deepdale if you saw it take shape around you. I hope that will make you feel this beautiful house is really yours.'

'It was so thoughtful of you,' Emma said appreciatively. With excitement in her voice, she added, 'I will buy furnishings in York and engage staff and be living here as soon as possible. And I'll call on Lady Ware and invite her and her family to dine with us. This is so exciting! I've never been able to do this at Heatherfold Hall.'

John smiled at her enthusiasm. Then cautiously he asked, 'And us?'

'You are part of this, John, a big part. Thank you for finding me.'

Over the coming weeks the war in South Africa faded from Emma's mind apart from the recurring question: Are Robert and Steven safe?

6

Mafeking sweltered under the African sun.

Colonel Robert Baden-Powell, commander of the British Force of approximately 2,000 men, wiped the sweat from his face. 'We will hold out,' he said with a conviction that raised the flagging hopes of his second in command. 'We must.'

He knew anxiety stalked the minds and hearts of the British military and civilians, trapped with over 7,000 faithful natives and refugees, in the small town of Mafeking. They were faced with starvation unless the siege by 5,000 Boers could be raised.

'Sir, things are desperate. There are murmurings ... the civilians are beginning to say we should surrender.'

'Never! I will not take down the British flag. We are an outpost on the edge of nowhere, but we are defending more than there appears to be out there.' He pointed through the open door, at the small town's array of ramshackle buildings. 'This is part of the British Empire. What would the world say if we capitulated to the Boers? We know they would herald it as a great triumph. The three main Boer states would then unite and become a formidable enemy. Africa would be lost to us, and that can't be allowed to happen!'

So the inhabitants of the once insignificant town had to cope with intense heat and dust or else torrential rain and cold, enduring the monotony and privation of a siege, with little to do except wait for a relief force to be sent by a world they were beginning to believe had forgotten them.

'Sergeant!' the cry rang out from a sentry on the lookout for any movement across the sun-drenched landscape. 'A runner!'

The NCO shaded his eyes against the beat of the sun. He picked out the puffs of dust. 'Corporal! Ready to escort runner to B-P.'

But their colonel had picked up the shout and was already at the door to his quarters. Could this be the news the whole town was waiting for? Word of the sighting spread like wildfire. People emerged from their shelters, ignoring the sun and heat, to hear if the runner had brought the news they all desired.

Then their hopes were deflated by rifle shots cracking across the veldt: snipers shooting at the runner. The native messenger knew how vital his role was; he was entrusted with word that heralded salvation for the trapped of Mafeking, if they could just hold out a little longer. He struck a weaving course, using any possible cover in the barren landscape to confuse the Boers who were seeking to stop him. Shouts rose from the beleaguered people, urging him on to success. The garrison, bent on protecting him, returned fire with fire. Time stretched endlessly. Then the runner staggered, his chest heaving as he gasped air into his painful lungs. Cries and gasps of horror were heard from the watchers. Was hope to be cruelly snatched away from them?

The runner summoned the last of his strength and pushed himself across the parched land. With each yard, the trenches shielding British soldiers returning enemy fire, loomed closer. A few more strides... The man made a final lunge towards the nearest trench and flung himself across the remaining feet. Two soldiers, risking Boer bullets, grabbed him under his arms and hauled him into the trench where they all collapsed in a heap, breathing heavily with the effort.

'Good on us, mate!' one soldier called to the other when he realised they had succeeded. Panting, they struggled to sitting positions with their backs to the trench sides, keeping their heads down, not allowing the snipers to get a telling shot at them.

'Get down there!' yelled a sergeant from further along the trench. 'And bloody well play little men!'

When the soldiers had recovered their breath, they conducted the runner to the sergeant, who took over and bustled the messenger quickly to B-P's quarters. Still breathing hard, the runner looked the colonel in the eye, giving a little nod when he had verified he had found the man to whom he must report. He thrust a piece of paper towards B-P, whose eager glance took in the words. 'A relief column, under the command of Colonel Robert Cheevey, is on its way.'

He hastened to spread the news to the officers and civilians who had gathered outside. Cheers rose from them and gathered momentum as the people of Mafeking heard and joined in. Deliverance was at hand! Holding out against the foe had been the right tactic. Now they must keep alert against any move by the Boers, for they must surely have interpreted the arrival of the runner, followed by the cheering, as heralding the coming of relief for the people trapped in the town.

Colonel Robert Cheevey brought his troop to a halt in a depression four miles from Mafeking. He sat for a few minutes, weighing up the possibilities before him. From information received from scouts he doubted the strength of his force to carry out their mission successfully, but he kept that opinion to himself. He had his orders and would obey them to the best of his ability. He tipped his hat off and mopped his brow with a red handkerchief, recalling the moment, after his last promotion, when he had received it from Emma, who had said, 'A lucky talisman for you.' He had carried it with him ever since. His mind drifted back to his home in Scotland, but when he found himself beginning to wonder if he would ever see it again, he pulled himself up sharply – there was a town to relieve and a war to be won. He crammed his hat back on, straightened in the saddle.

'Scouts!'

Five natives broke away from the group of twenty standing apart from the troops. They knew what would be required of them but came to receive the final details from the colonel. He spoke quickly to them, then added a brief word to their leader, who nodded his understanding before speaking in a sharp tone to the group. A moment later five men, their outer garments discarded for easier movement, were away, climbing the depression at an easy jog, stopping only just short of the top.

On a signal from their leader they fanned out. After a few yards they dropped to their stomachs to await the next signal. The leader inched his way to the top of the rise and cautiously raised his head to survey the land in the direction of Mafeking. He half turned and lifted his arm. The four runners split into two parties, one moving to the right, the other left. When they were in position their leader signalled again and they carefully judged what lay between them and Mafeking. After making their assessment they eased their way back to their leader and informed him what they had seen. He reported to the colonel.

Still taking in the information, Cheevey called his seven officers to him. 'There is a reasonable amount of cover to begin with, but less so the nearer we get to Mafeking. The runners reported that the Boers are also using that cover, so we can discount achieving any element of surprise except briefly in the initial stages. After that they will turn everything they have against us.'

'Do we know their ordnance, sir?' someone called.

'Not with any certainty. There were rumours that they had brought up some more cannon but I have no confirmation of that.' He paused waiting for any more questions. When none were forthcoming, he continued, 'I look to my officers in charge of the five wagons with supplies to do their utmost to get them through to Mafeking. The situation there is getting desperate. I have delegated two officers to lend support wherever it is needed.

Captain Pringle and Lieutenant Mosey will be at my side, ready to pass on orders as we assess our progress. You all know your duties. I look to you to carry them out to the best of your abilities. Convey my good wishes to all those under your commands. Prepare to move off in half an hour.'

With Captain Pringle and Lieutenant Mosey prone on the ground beside him, Colonel Cheevey surveyed the land ahead through his binoculars.

'I don't like it, sir,' said Mosey. 'It's too quiet.'

'The Boers will have something up their sleeve, trying to lull us into thinking they've gone,' said Pringle.

Cheevey glanced at his watch. 'Five minutes.'

Every second that followed was charged with tension. Each man felt it, despite the heat beating down on them from a cloudless sky. The colonel called out so that everyone could hear: 'To relieve Mafeking!' The cheers that rang out gradually subsided into a chant, 'Mafeking Mafeking...', until it seemed the whole veldt was echoing with the word.

Colonel Cheevey drew his red handkerchief from his pocket and glanced at his watch. Five minutes had passed. He raised his arm, waved his handkerchief and stood up, instantly moving forward in a weaving run. He was aware that the whole force under his command had been motivated by his example.

There was no Boer response. The British moved forward, puzzled by the absence of the enemy. Supply wagons were urged onward. Mafeking drew nearer and nearer. Suddenly all hell broke loose as volley after volley was poured at the relief force by Boers skilfully concealed across the terrain. Then it was man against man as the relieving force grappled with those determined to stop them. The battle ebbed and flowed. Three wagons crashed, stranding much-needed goods out of reach of the besieged.

Colonel Cheevey was running everywhere, urging his men on to greater feats until, realising victory was eluding them, he called out in despair, 'Mafeking! Every man for himself!' His words were passed on in a frenzy. Troops broke cover and, ignoring the shots that whined around them, raced for sanctuary.

Colonel Baden-Powell had been keeping an eye on the situation and, as soon as he realised the relieving force had been instructed to give way before the Boer assault, ordered covering fire for those seeking to reach Mafeking. Cheevey urged his men on. Once he was satisfied that most of the survivors of the battle were safe within the town, he sought out Baden-Powell.

'I regret my failure to relieve Mafeking,' he apologised as he shook hands with B-P.

The commanding officer of the town would have none of it. 'You did your best against superior numbers. When I saw the size of your rescue force, I knew you would be substantially outnumbered and that even the fighting spirit of the British could not prevail. You have no need to blame yourself.'

'That is generous of you, and I thank you.'

'No, Colonel, it is the people of Mafeking and I who should thank you. You got two wagons of supplies through. Only a little of what we need, but it will help.'

'I knew my force would probably be too small, but the "I am right" attitude is entrenched in some of our higher-ups.'

'My despatch will plead for the next attempt to be by a much larger force. We must outnumber the Boers; it is the only way. You can add your opinion to my report; it will strengthen my points. I am going to make a tour of the town, see that my citizens are sharing the supplies and that your men are being cared for.'

'May I accompany you, sir?' Cheevey asked.

'Of course. By the way I'm generally addressed as B-P.'

'Well then, B-P, may I request that I be given a job under your command while I am here? I will not stand on rank and will do anything my men are called upon to do.'

'Very well. I may require you to be on look-out duty. I generally post two men together so if you have any preference...'

'Captain Pringle, if he has survived injury.'

'Let us go and find out.'

They found him taking a roll-call of the able-bodied survivors, but Pringle handed the task over to a sergeant on seeing Colonel Cheevey. He could not hide his relief to see his superior officer. 'Someone reported they had seen you go down. Thank goodness you aren't injured.'

'I bear a charmed life. Someone was looking after me. What about Mosey?'

'Went down in a hand-to-hand fight with a Boer. Have you any instructions for the men, sir?'

The situation was quickly brought under control; the wounded taken to the convent now in use as a hospital, the uninjured bedded down wherever they could be and allocated duties for the siege ahead.

7

Three weeks later Cheevey and Pringle were on lookout duty together half a mile out of town.

'The devils are going to try and pound Mafeking into submission,' commented the colonel as the morning's opening barrage of shells reminded the British that they were still under siege.

'Help must be on the way, sir,' commented the junior officer as they watched the enemy through binoculars. They had sought shelter behind a low mound of boulders near the edge of the town that offered them some protection, if small, and from which they could scan the enemy positions.

'Maybe so, Pringle,' Cheevey commented, keeping his misgivings to himself.

'I hope, for the sake of the women and children trapped here, our superiors realise the strength of the opposition and that there may come a time when we are starved out,' added Pringle. They both ducked as another shell whined by overhead.

'Colonel Baden-Powell will be doing his best to keep that problem at bay. He has instigated strict rationing. I have implicit faith in his ability to see us through. He has a good military mind but also a gift for being able to keep morale high. He... Down, Pringle!'

Howard Pringle obeyed instantly and dropped beside his superior as a shell burst only a few yards away, showering them with earth and stones.

'Bastards!' snapped Pringle viciously. 'You'll get more than that before we're finished!' He started to scramble to his feet but the colonel grabbed him.

'Stay still!' he snapped. The earth shook under a bombardment that made moments seem like hours.

'They have the measure of us here, sir. Should we move further left?' Receiving no answer, Pringle rolled on to his side. He turned cold in spite of the blazing sun and his eyes widened with alarm and horror. Colonel Cheevey, his head thrown back, stared vacantly at the blue sky. One arm hung limp beside him and blood poured from a leg wound that appeared to be serious.

'Sir! Sir!' The panic in the captain's voice was drowned out by the crunch of another shell exploding close by, but the explosion gave him some relief when it caused the colonel to groan slightly.

Pringle, encouraging the wounded man, hauled him as fast as he could to the protection of a larger boulder. The captain made a quick assessment of the state of his superior officer, and realised he needed urgent medical attention. There was desperation in Pringle's eyes as he looked around the shell-torn ground. There was no one else alive, only the bodies of a previous party sent out on observation duty. Another whine and Pringle automatically scrabbled at the ground with his fingers as if he could make a hole to protect himself from shells. He heard the explosion and shuddered at the sudden pain coursing through his head; his hand came up to his right eye and felt blood running on to his cheek. He swept it away, needing to see; needing help. His blurred vision cleared and he swung his gaze across the shattered landscape. There was movement nearby. Help? It had to be. He drove away the pain and concentrated on what might be his salvation. A figure moved cautiously along the side of a mound of clay and rubble. Pringle concentrated the sight in his good eye upon it.

'Sergeant! Sergeant!' The words burst from Pringle with all the authority he could muster. He saw the man stop crawling across the earth and raise his head to see where the call had come from.

'Over here!' Pringle yelled, waving from his prone position. 'Over here!'

'Coming!'

Pringle's relief was short-lived. There was another explosion. The captain felt eternity yawn to engulf him and then, thankfully, the sergeant reached him.

'Thank goodness!' Pringle exclaimed with relief.

'Are you all right, sir?' It was an inane question but it was at least friendly-sounding.

'My colonel caught the worst of it.'

'He certainly did, sir. Are you new here?' asked the man as he began examining the colonel's wounds.

'Yes.'

'Then you can thank God tomorrow is Sunday.'

'Why?' Captain Pringle looked puzzled.

'B-P...' the sergeant started, then stopped himself. 'Sorry, sir. Colonel Baden-Powell, commander of the British garrison in Mafeking, and Piet Cronje, the Boer leader, have an agreement there are to be no hostilities on Sundays, so both sides take the opportunity to attend to their wounded then.'

'Oh, I see. Then what I heard upon reaching Africa is true.'

'Yes. You and your colonel should be receiving treatment in Mafeking tomorrow if the Boers agree to exchange the wounded.'

'Will I be able to accompany him?'

'That will depended on how generous the Boers are feeling. They generally hate us but, as everywhere, there are always those who show sympathy and compassion to men wounded in action.'

'Now sir, if you don't mind my saying so, I think we should try to make ourselves as comfortable as possible here for the night. If you were sent out on observation of the enemy then you would have been supplied with iron rations and a canteen of water?'

'Yes.'

'Ration it carefully, sir, it will have to last you until tomorrow.'

They were afforded a respite from further bombardment when the enemy guns were realigned on a different target. The booming eventually stopped; only the crack of spasmodic rifle-fire remained.

'That's silenced their guns, for the time being,' commented the sergeant. 'Our crack snipers have made it too hazardous to man them.'

'Will the colonel survive the night out here?'

'We'll do our best to keep him alive. Continue packing stones and rocks around him, and anything else we can find. It gets mighty cold out here on the veldt at night, but with their warmth we should survive. Are you all right as you are, sir?'

'As you say, Sergeant, I'll survive. Left eye bloody well hurts and it doesn't seem too good. What about you?'

'Nothing wrong, sir. Must be the luck of the Irish touching me, though I ain't Irish!'

So the hours moved on. The sun sank in the sky. The cool of the evening embraced the cold of the night. Pringle ignored his wounded eye as he tucked his commanding officer's cape more closely around Cheevey. The sergeant, thankful that he had escaped injury, resolved to see them through the night and seek safe passage to Mafeking in the morning.

The dark sky was pierced by the rays of the rising sun, bringing light to the silent veldt. Far away an elephant trumpeted and received an answer; baboons started to chatter. A Captain with a lacerated eye and a sergeant, stiff from his uncomfortable bed of stones, scrambled to their feet and immediately turned their attention to the officer lying on the ground. He stirred.

'Sir!' the captain exclaimed, relieved his superior had survived the night.

Robert Cheevey groaned at the pain which stabbed through him as he turned his head to see who had spoken. 'Ah, Pringle.'

Being recognised sent a wave of relief sweeping

through the captain. 'Lie still, sir,' he said, putting one hand on the colonel's shoulder. 'We were caught in shell-fire and both wounded. Sergeant Saunders here helped us to get comfortable for the night.' He indicated the man standing beside them.

'Take it easy, sir. Help will be coming and we'll get you into Mafeking.' Seeing doubt in the colonel's expression, the sergeant went on quickly to explain about the Sunday truce.

It was an uneasy and impatient wait until ten o'clock when signals were exchanged and the wounded were given the attention they required. Colonel Cheevey was soon made comfortable in a makeshift hospital bed in the town. Captain Pringle's answer to the news that he had lost his left eye was, 'At least I can still line a rifle on those bloody Boers.'

So lives in Mafeking settled down to their accustomed routine, commanded by Colonel Baden-Powell who still hoped another Army force would be organised to relieve the beleaguered town.

8

'John, can you be free today to come to York with me and see a decorator now that the alterations are nearing completion?' asked Emma.

'I can be free for you at any time,' he replied flirtatiously.

'Keep your mind on decoration and furnishings,' she warned coquettishly.

'I have already done that and suggest visiting Bellerby's of Petergate to handle the decorating. Their work is first class. You can't better it. Because you want everything ready before Matthew comes on leave, I checked that they are able to employ a suitably large workforce. They assured me that they can.'

'Splendid. That's the first place we will visit when we get to York. Now ... furnishings?'

'I have two suggestions for you. And if they don't come up to expectation, I have others up my sleeve.'

'Then let us go into York and settle everything. I want the first part of the house ready as soon as possible. And I must visit a reliable employment agency so that I can be ensconced before Matthew comes.'

'So you intend him to come to Deepdale? I thought...'

'I won't be at Heatherfold Hall.'

'So are you going to tell him about your inheritance?'

'Yes, Matthew and only Matthew, for now. I'll swear him to secrecy. Robert and Steven will hear on their return.'

'And us?'

'I will see how the land lies before I reveal to my son how things stand between us. In the meantime, play the efficient solicitor and keep your room at the Wild Hussar.' Emma said pointedly, 'It will be a good test of your patience. You can always contemplate the future.'

He pulled a face.

She laughed. 'Don't look so glum. Think about how different it will be when we are alone again!'

That night Emma wrote to her son.

Dear Matthew,
I look forward to seeing you on your next leave and have some news I think you should know. I don't want to commit it to paper but will give it to you face to face.
Therefore I am asking you on your next leave not to go to Heatherfold Hall but to come to an inn, the Wild Hussar, about ten miles north-east of York. Your best plan would be to hire a hansom cab at the station there to take you on.
I will meet you at the inn. If I am not there, make yourself comfortable and await my arrival. The innkeeper and his wife are good people, ready to be helpful.
I hope to see you soon.

Emma re-read her words, smiled to herself at the curiosity they would stir in Matthew's mind, then picked up a quill and signed the letter with a flourish: 'Your loving mother'.

His reply was not long in coming.

Dear Mother.
I will be with you on the 15th after following your directions from York. What are you doing there? Why aren't you in Scotland? The Wild Hussar... It all sounds very mysterious.
I hope you will reveal all when I see you.
Your loving son,
Matthew

She glanced at her calendar. Two days' time. Thank goodness all the rooms they would need at Deepdale were ready. She looked forward to having her son to herself, after cautiously arranging for John to return to Kelso for the time being.

The following morning, the landlord of the Wild Hussar prepared his horse and trap and loaded Mrs Cheevey's belongings inside. As she was bidding farewell to Mrs Beckwith, he dispatched a rider to Deepdale Manor to deliver a prearranged message to the newly engaged head butler there.

'Beckwith, this is a beautiful day on which to be arriving at my new home,' commented Emma as he guided the horse round the final curve of the drive to the front of the house. 'Oh, my goodness ... I didn't expect this!'

The complete household staff were lined up; males in one line with Bannister at the head, and females in another with Mrs Brigstock the housekeeper in charge.

As the horse and trap were brought to a stop, Bannister stepped forward, opened the door and helped his employer to the ground, saying, 'Welcome home, Mrs Cheevey.'

'Thank you, Bannister.'

'Your staff, Ma'am.' He led her along the line, introducing each man and his trade. He then walked Mrs Cheevey to Mrs Brigstock, who took over the introduction of her female staff, at the end of which the housekeeper said, 'I hope you will be very happy at Deepdale, Ma'am.'

As she walked into the west wing Emma felt

truly welcomed by the house. She waved aside the maid who came to take her cape and hat, wanting nothing to disturb her concentration as she walked slowly through the house, drinking in the changed atmosphere. Gone were the dark trappings of the previous era. Emma revelled in admiring the new decorations: warming in the dining room, gentle in the drawing room, cool in the study and light in the library, to ease the heaviness that would come with the acquisition of books to fill the bookshelves. The bedrooms were light and airy, each with a fireplace to contest the winter cold. Feeling joyful and content, she arrived back in the hall.

Mrs Brigstock promptly appeared. 'I thought you might like a cup of tea, Ma'am, so I asked Mrs Storey to have one made. It will be ready in a few moments.'

Resplendent in Army uniform, with shoulder insignia indicating that he held the rank of lieutenant, Matthew soon found a cab at York station to take him to the Wild Hussar. He was thankful that the day was fine. When they moved into the hill country north-east of York, he was able to admire the countryside from a raised vantage point.

'The Wild Hussar, sir,' called the cabbie as he stopped the horse below a sign swinging in the wind. Matthew cast his eyes over the front of the inn and gave a little nod of approval; his mother had chosen well.

He paid the cabbie, took his valise and entered the building.

'Good day, sir,' a man greeted him. 'You must

be Lieutenant Cheevey.'

'Indeed I am.'

'I'm Charles Beckwith, the landlord. Welcome to the Wild Hussar. I know you are here to meet your mother, who will be with us soon. Would you like a drink while you wait?'

'At this time of day, tea, please.'

Matthew was pouring his second cup when the dining-room door opened and Emma swept in with a flurry. A smile lit up her face as she said, 'Matthew!' and opened her arms to him. He sprang up from his chair. His expression broke into the broadest of smiles as he said, 'You look radiant, Mother. I've never seen you look so exotic.'

She laughed heartily and raised an eyebrow, pleased that he admired her trumpet-shaped skirt worn with a tight blouse with embellishment down the wrist-length sleeves.

'I like the colour ... grey-green suits you ... as does the way you have piled your hair so high.'

Emma smiled. 'My youngest has certainly grown up. Someone must have taught you to admire a lady – who is she?'

Emma caught his blush and laughed teasingly. 'I'll ask no more then I'll hear no lies.'

She stepped back, still holding her son's hands as she did so. 'How long since you were home?' she queried. 'Eighteen months?'

'All of that,' Matthew replied. 'But don't let's dwell on our separation. We've two weeks to make up for it now.' He glanced around and then met her eyes. 'Why here?'

'It was the most convenient place to meet and

take you on somewhere I want you to see. My horse and trap are waiting.' He looked at her questioningly. She laughed and said, 'I'm not telling you any more now.' She let go of his hands and turned towards the door.

In a few minutes Emma was driving the horse and trap away from the Wild Hussar. 'No questions yet, Matthew.'

Though he was aching to know what all the mystery was about, he knew better than to press the matter, so let her extol the beauties of the countryside through which they were driving.

'Those hills in the distance look inviting,' was the only comment with which he interrupted his mother's flow of words.

'The North York Moors,' she replied. 'I'm looking forward to exploring them.'

'When are you going to do that?'

Realising she had nearly given herself away, Emma tightened her lips and drove on in silence. Shortly afterwards she turned off the track. Another hundred yards on she pulled to a halt on the edge of a slope from which there was a splendid view with the North York Moors soaring in the distance.

'What a wonderful place to have a house,' commented Matthew, indicating the building on the upper part of the slope.

'I only discovered this view of it a few days ago.'

'Weren't you trespassing? Aren't we trespassing now?'

His mother smiled as she said, 'No. It's my house, and much of what you see is my land, except to the west and north-west.'

The shock brought Matthew swivelling round in his seat to face her. 'You aren't serious?'

'I am deadly serious.'

'But how...' He broke off to say, 'So this is the secret you alluded to in your letter, and it's something my father and brother don't know about yet.'

'Correct. They are too far away to concern themselves with such matters, and there are other reasons for me to keep it a secret until they come home. But you are here and someone close to me should know what has happened in my life.' She glanced at her watch, fastened to the lapel of her blouse. 'We are just right for lunch. My housekeeper will have organised it.' With that she sent the horse carefully down the slope.

'You are living here then?' Matthew queried.

'Yes, and it is your home too, of course.'

'What about Heatherfold?'

'Full story as we eat,' she said, to prevent any further questioning.

As more of the building came in sight, Matthew remarked, 'There are a lot of workmen about.'

'They are renovating the older section of the house, which I believe was part of a convent in the past. I have recently moved in to the newer, restored wing and can be here while renovation work continues.'

'I love it, and I think I will love it even more when I have seen inside,' enthused Matthew.

'Then let's take a closer look.' Emma pressed the horse on.

'There is one thing beginning to worry me,' her son said seriously. 'Where is the money coming

83

from, if Father knows nothing of this? Workmen don't work on promises.'

'All will be revealed shortly.'

9

'Welcome back, Ma'am, and welcome home, sir.'

'This is Bannister my head butler,' explained Emma. 'Ah, and here is Mrs Brigstock, my housekeeper,' she added when a slim lady in black came into the hall.

'Ma'am, sir, I am delighted to welcome you to Deepdale Manor. I hope everything here will be to your liking.'

'I'm sure it will be, Mrs Brigstock,' Matthew assured her.

The housekeeper turned to Emma. 'Lunch is ready, Ma'am. Should we serve in fifteen minutes?'

'Thank you.'

Meanwhile a footman had brought in Matthew's valise and was taking it up the curving staircase.

'Come, Matthew, I'll show you your room and then we'll have lunch before I take you to see your new home,' his mother said.

He had been impressed by the staircase with its wrought-iron rail on the inside wall and balustrade overlooking the spacious hall. He followed Emma upstairs to a door on the left of the galleried landing. She pushed open a solid oak door and stood back to allow her son to see his room.

'This is wonderful, Mother.' Light-oak panelling covered the lower half of the walls, with the top half wallpapered in a light gentle blue. The large bed looked inviting and to the right of its head stood a small table with an oil lamp on it. A wardrobe occupied part of one wall while another accommodated a chest of drawers. Easy chairs were positioned either side of a bow window overlooking a panoramic view of the countryside.

Matthew had made no comment so far but then his mother opened a door to the left of the fireplace and announced: 'The facilities.'

'What can I say?' he told her. 'I'm lost for words. If the rest of the work you've had done is as good as this, you already have a gem of a property. And if the work on the old part lives up to it, you will have created a wonder.' He heard a sigh of relief from his mother. 'Did you think I wouldn't like it or approve of your spending so much money? Who am I to criticise or doubt what you are doing?'

She noticed the worry in his eyes nevertheless and said, 'Freshen up quickly then I will tell you everything over lunch.'

Ten minutes later they were facing each other at one end of the long dining table running down the centre of the room. A lunch of cold meats and salad had been set for them.

Emma took a sip of her water and began her explanation. 'I must tell you how this came about, but first I should once again extract a promise from you not to reveal what I tell you to *anyone*.' She stared at him intently, realising this must be regarded as an unusual request.

'You said as much in your letter. I thought it

85

strange but I realised I would have to reassure you on that score, so here goes.' Matthew's expression became even more serious. He placed a hand on his heart and said, 'I promise not to reveal what you tell me to anyone, not even to Father or Steven.'

Emma explained how John Smyth had contacted her and eventually confirmed that she was the heir to Deepdale.

'Hitherto the financial side of our lives was always handled by your father, who had laid down the rule shortly after we married that I should have no say in any of it but was to live henceforth in his property. This unexpected wealth that has come to me has made me look at things differently. I could see independence ahead of me and a secure foundation for my own future. I knew your father, were he here, would regard himself as the keeper of my legacy and exclude me from having any say in it, so on advice from my solicitor John Smyth, I have taken legal steps to exclude anyone else from controlling my wealth. You probably won't understand this but I feel like a free woman at last.'

'Thank you for telling me, Mother, but perhaps I understand better than you think. I always knew Father kept close control over our lives and expected all of us, even you, to follow in his wake.' Matthew left a little pause then. Before she could speak, he added, 'On a cautionary note, Mother, is this solicitor to be trusted?'

'Yes. I have a lot of faith in him. He has explained everything very clearly to me and I am happy to have followed his advice. I am certain the documents he drew up are one hundred per cent in my favour. You can judge the man for yourself when he returns here from his practice in Kelso early next week. He has also been of immense help to me in renovating the house and ordering the estate.'

'Good. Then I look forward to meeting him. What will happen to Heatherfold?' added Matthew.

'It is your father's and will remain so.'

He nodded then asked, 'Whose land abuts yours?'

'To the west and north-west is a long-established family estate. The present incumbents are sixth- or seventh-generation, Sir Raymond Ware and his wife Lady Cecilia, herself the daughter of an Earl no less. They will be about my age. They have two children, Nicholas who is twenty-two and Alice, eighteen or nineteen. Mrs Brigstock told me they are charming people, who tend to keep their own company.'

'Have you met them?'

'Only the daughter. John and I found her wandering round the property.'

'Trespassing?'

'Well, if you like to call it that. I'd rather say she was satisfying a natural curiosity. She was surprised to see us, as neither she nor her parents knew the property had passed to me. The girl apologised, of course, and we had a pleasant conversation. She was gentle, easy to talk to, rather pretty.'

'Don't you think you ought to meet the whole family? After all, they are your nearest neighbours?'

'Yes, I do.'

'Then why not invite them to dinner one evening while I am here?'

'It's rather short notice and will go against the usual custom of allowing three weeks between invitation and meeting.'

'That is rather fading from polite usage, especially for small gatherings such as this would be.'

Emma looked thoughtful for a moment. Then she said, with a touch of excitement in her voice, 'Let's go ahead! We'll start organising it tomorrow.'

Emma penned a formal invitation and Matthew arranged for its delivery to Wooton Hall.

Over the succeeding days leading up to the dinner party, Emma was pleased with the interest her son showed in the new property and in her renovation plans. She told him the architect believed it was formerly a convent. They were interrupted one morning by a surprise announcement.

'Ma'am, Mr Smyth is here,' the maid announced to Emma, who was talking to Matthew in the drawing room.

She hid her surprise. 'Show him in, please.' After the maid had left the room, Emma rose to her feet, saying, 'John's a day early.'

'All the better for me to get to know him,' replied her son as he pushed himself out of a deep armchair.

'John, this is a pleasant surprise,' said Emma, holding out her hand formally to him as he entered the room.

He ignored it and kissed her lightly on the

cheek. It was only then that he noticed Matthew standing near the window. He glanced questioningly at Emma and, on receiving a slight nod, said, 'You must be Matthew.'

'I am, and you must be Mr Smyth.' Matthew hid his surprise to see a middle-aged man who did not fit his image of a dry and dusty solicitor.

'Oh, please, use my Christian name,' said the new arrival, his broad handsome face smiling and open.

They shook hands, each feeling the other man desired friendship.

'You managed to conclude your business in Kelso early?' queried Matthew.

'I did. I had no reason to stay on, and finding a train heading south within half an hour, I was not going to miss it.'

Matthew judged by the glance he saw John give his mother then that she was the reason he had left Kelso early.

'It is good to have you back, John,' she said. 'Will you stay to dinner?'

'If I am not intruding?'

'Of course not.' Matthew noted how quick and forthright his mother was with her reply. 'I will inform Cook there will be a guest with us this evening.'

Both men recognised that she was leaving them together on purpose when she chose not to use the bell-pull to call for a messenger, but went out to the kitchen herself.

'My mother has been telling me what a help you have been to her over the business side of her surprising inheritance,' said Matthew. 'I am grateful to you.'

'I was only too glad to help. She is a wonderful lady.'

'It is kind of you to say so.'

'No more than she deserves. She threw herself wholeheartedly into the redesigning and renovation of this part of the property. She was determined to have it finished before you came on leave. And she has good ideas for the rest of the buildings ... that is why there are so many workmen around.'

So the conversation continued between them until Emma returned with a maid carrying a tray of tea.

She was gratified by her son's remarks to her later, after John had left them for his bed in the Wild Hussar. 'I rather like Mr Smyth, and can see why you have implicit faith in him. It pleases me that you have such a man to turn to.'

'I am glad you got on so well with him. It is a comfort to me.'

'He is very different from Father. I was pleased there was no military talk for once! Pleased too to see you are happy with the gentler outlook on life that John has brought to you...' He stopped speaking briefly and with a remorseful expression on his face, added, 'Mother, I'm sorry, I shouldn't have spoken to you like that.'

She laid a hand on his arm. 'There's no need to apologise. I am glad you did speak out. I wondered how you might take my relationship with John.'

'All that matters to me is your happiness. I had

recently detected the strain between you and Father. If happiness is within your grasp, I would never condemn you for it.'

'What the future holds we will have to see, but you have given me hope.'

Emma had blushed at her son's candid analysis. Matthew had certainly grown up! She recalled the words of his father in the last letter she had received from Africa.

If Matthew is posted here I do not know what he will make of it, but it will make a man of him.

She smiled to herself. Her husband's observation had been wrong – Matthew had not set foot in Africa but had become a man in his own way, by the influences he chose to follow and in the way he behaved. Female intuition told her girls had played their part in this. She was not sorry.

Then the day of the dinner party arrived.

10

As soon as he heard the carriage approaching, Bannister sent one of the footmen to inform Mrs Cheevey and her son that the guests were arriving. Another footman was sent to inform Mrs Brigstock who alerted the staff so that, by the time Bannister escorted the Wares into the hall, the housekeeper and two maids were already in attendance as Emma and Matthew greeted the guests.

'Welcome to Deepdale Manor, Sir Raymond

and Lady Cecilia,' said Emma with a warm smile, holding out her hand to Sir Raymond and at the same time including Lady Cecilia in the sweep of her eyes.

Sir Raymond took her hand, returning her smile. 'Please, no standing on ceremony. I'm sure we shall all be friends.'

'My dear,' said Cecilia, as she embraced Emma. 'How kind of you to invite us.'

'I am more than delighted to welcome you into my home. As near neighbours, I hope it is the start of a long friendship. I am Emma, and this is my youngest son Matthew.'

'And our two children are Nicholas and Alice. I believe you met my daughter in different circumstances,' added Cecilia with a knowing smile.

'Indeed we did. Youthful curiosity... It is good to see her here this evening, as it is all of you. By the way, I have another guest, Mr John Smyth.'

'Ah, John! An admirable fellow,' said Raymond. 'He has done work for me ... estate matters, that sort of thing. I haven't seen him for quite a while; it will be good to meet up again. You remember him, Cecilia?'

'Indeed I do. A charming man and well thought of in his field. Have you known him long?'

'No. He was handling some work, which led him to contact me. It became obvious that I would need a solicitor to sort out business of my own, so it seemed right to engage him.'

'And no doubt that has proved a wise decision?' said Sir Raymond.

'It has indeed.'

Two maids had taken charge of the outdoor

clothes and now Emma and Cecilia led the way into the drawing room where Bannister oversaw the serving of drinks. He was pleased by the way the evening settled into an easy atmosphere. It was as if these two families had known each other for a long time rather than this being their first meeting.

The two ladies settled into chairs and immediately admired each other's dress.

'I am so pleased that the bustle has almost gone out of fashion,' commented Cecilia.

'So am I,' confided Emma. 'Your dress fits so well, any attempt to have made it with a bustle would have spoiled its best features. I do like that high neck and shaped waistline ... and the colour – well, it's most attractive and complements your complexion so well.'

'Thank you very much,' replied Cecilia graciously. 'If you want my recommendation, go to Leak and Thorpe in York. They have an expert tailoring department if you require anything special.' So a friendship was begun and strengthened as the evening progressed.

Alice knew she should not stare so surreptitiously but kept stealing glances at the handsome young man in uniform who had drawn her attention at the first moment of their meeting. His dazzling smile, accentuated by his blue eyes, had captivated her – and, oh, he looked so good in his red uniform! His voice was mellow but she thought that any orders he gave would be rapped out sharply when the situation demanded it.

Nicholas, Alice and Matthew sat together and made lively conversation. During the evening their talk turned to horses.

'I presume you ride?' Alice asked Matthew.

'Army trained,' he replied, 'though I did ride while at home in Scotland. I am hoping Mother will soon have stables set up here.'

'I should hope so too,' replied Alice. 'This is good riding country.'

'Maybe I could go riding with you both one day before I finish my leave?'

Alice couldn't believe her luck. 'I'd love that.'

'Then I will ask your father's permission.'

For the rest of the evening Alice was on tenterhooks, wondering what her father's reply would be. She even tried mentally to will the word yes into his mind.

She noticed Nicholas talking to John Smyth and then saw Matthew take the opportunity to speak to her father when Sir Raymond moved on after a brief word with her mother. The conversation was short. Catching a signal from her father, Alice quickly crossed over to them.

'This young man has asked my permission to go out riding with you and Nicholas before he returns to his unit. I have said yes.' Alice's heart soared but was deflated when her father added regretfully, 'But he has no horse.' He was amused by her reaction, especially the immediate change in her expression when he added, 'But Matthew had the better of me; he said he would hire one from the Wild Hussar. However, I told him he could take his pick from our stable.'

Alice's eyes lit up. 'Cally-ho will suit him.'

'Good choice,' agreed her father. 'You fix it up with Greton, Alice. He's our head groom,' Sir Raymond added by way of explanation to Matthew.

'Thank you, sir,' the young officer replied gratefully, and smiled at Alice.

As her father walked away she whispered, 'I'll soon get rid of Nick.'

'Do you think that wise?' Matthew asked, surprised by such forwardness.

Alice grinned. 'I can twist him round my little finger.'

'What about me?' queried Matthew, with a challenge in his eyes.

'I think we'll wait and see,' replied Alice coyly. 'The day after tomorrow when we take this ride.'

'Why not tomorrow?'

'Ah, that will be the day I introduce you to Cally-ho.'

'A strange name. Where did you find it?'

'I heard it one day in Whitby and found out it is sailors' slang for being free and easy.'

'And that fits this horse's temperament?' The little pause he left became further charged when he added, 'Or yours?'

Alice pursed her lips before answering, 'Now, Lieutenant, you are beginning to assume too much.'

Matthew's blue eyes still held a twinkle as he said gravely, 'Then I offer you my humble apologies. Night is closing in but I think there is still time for a stroll in the garden.' He crooked his arm and she accepted it willingly.

Cally-ho took to Matthew as soon as Alice introduced them.

As he spoke softly to the filly and patted her

glossy neck, Alice suggested, 'Let's walk her over to Nicholas in the estate office.'

Matthew was impressed with what he saw and was told about the extent of the Wooton Estate and its history. After taking Cally-ho back to the stables, he and Alice spent a pleasant couple of hours together before he announced, 'As much as I am enjoying being here, I must away home. Mother expects me to spend some time with her, and I will be back here tomorrow.'

'Of course, Matthew. I look forward to it.' There was an uneasy pause then Alice reached up and kissed him lightly on the cheek, immediately turning away and hurrying to the house.

Matthew touched his face thoughtfully. In another girl it would have seemed very forward behaviour but Alice had been living in France ... he found her spontaneity refreshing, he decided. And tomorrow he would see her again.

Alice swung out of bed and made straight for the window. A brief glimpse of the sky brought a quiet song to her lips as she dressed in her riding habit, with the help of her maid. Alice viewed herself in the mirror. The red cravat immediately drew attention to her face, just as she wanted it to do. Her long skirt was buttoned at the sides to allow quick release in case of an accident resulting in her becoming entangled with the saddle. She carried her gloves, hat and riding crop, placing them on the hall table as she went to the dining room.

'Good morning, Mother,' she said breezily. 'Please excuse me for coming to breakfast dressed like this but I thought I had better be ready.'

Lady Cecilia was surprised but waved aside Alice's apology as she replied, 'Good morning, my dear. That outfit looks good on you. I thought it was the one you were keeping for special occasions?'

On the point of saying, 'Well, isn't this one?' Alice took a mouthful of porridge instead.

'It looks as though you will have a fine day for your ride,' commented her mother. 'Matthew should enjoy seeing the area.'

'I hope so, Mother,' replied Alice, wondering what else the day would bring.

Alice was in the stables with Nicholas talking to the head groom when she heard the sound of a horse's hooves and the squeak of a trap as it was pulled to a halt. One of the stable boys stopped brushing out a stall to hurry outside and take charge of the vehicle.

Alice was only a few steps behind him, her heart beginning to beat a little faster. It raced when she saw the handsome man stepping gracefully out of the trap.

'Good morning, Matthew,' Alice greeted him.

'Good morning, Alice, and to you too, Nicholas,' he replied brightly.

'You have brought us a fine day,' commented Nicholas.

'I couldn't do other for my two new friends,' replied Matthew.

'Are we heading off right away?' queried Nicholas.

'No point in wasting time,' said Alice.

'I'll tell Greton,' said her brother, heading for

the stable.

'The horses are already saddled,' Alice informed Matthew, and added, 'you are looking exceptionally smart.'

'Mother and I went into York yesterday after I left you and I got fitted out. I had no riding clothes here and couldn't escort such a charming companion as Alice Ware in anything but the best. You see the result.'

'Very, very smart,' Alice confirmed, admiration sparkling in her eyes as she let them rove over the thigh-length tweed riding jacket with slim lapels. The two top buttons had been left undone to reveal a white silk shirt with a blue cravat tied at the neck. Ankle-length jodhpurs were slipped into calf-length highly polished black riding boots. A low-crowned black hat was set on his head at an eye-catching angle. 'You look the part. I hope your riding is as good.'

'Bring me my horse,' he commanded, smiling at her.

As if on cue the groom appeared leading Cally-ho, followed by two stable boys each leading a horse.

Within a few minutes the three riders were heading away from Wooton Hall into the undulating hills to the north.

'This is good riding country,' commented Matthew. 'Do you hunt?'

'I hope to,' replied Alice. 'I did not get the opportunity to do so while I was in France, so I plan to make up for lost time.'

'What about you, Nicholas?'

'Nothing I like better,' he replied. 'I go out with

the local hunt whenever I can. I've told Alice I'll escort her to the next meeting.'

'I regard it as a social event chiefly,' she said. 'I love an exhilarating ride with other people.'

'Then regard me as other people!' called Matthew, who, seeing a stretch of grassland ahead, urged Cally-ho into a gallop.

Laughter rang out as Alice set her horse to match Matthew's. Nicholas responded too but held his mount back a few paces. He knew what his sister was up to. He wasn't sure he approved but did not want to spoil their day. The horses' hooves drummed against the turf, their riders exhilarated by the power they controlled. After a mile Alice gave her horse its head, widening the gap between her and Matthew. The track they were on split and Alice took the branch that headed down the hillside. Matthew followed but Nicholas held to the trail that continued along the top of the hill, heading towards a small coppice. Alice's glance behind told her her brother had read her mind – she would be alone with Matthew.

The dip in the track, though not steep, demanded that they bring their horses to a walking pace to negotiate the slope without mishap.

'We've lost Nicholas,' called Matthew, breathing deeply after the exhilarating ride.

'We'll find him somewhere at the bottom,' replied Alice, showing little concern.

When the track swung round the hill it brought into view a small tranquil lake in a rocky basin fringed by a wood of pine and oak.

Matthew pulled his horse to a halt. Expecting him to do so, Alice pulled up beside him.

'Peace,' he said quietly, almost to himself, but she caught the emotion in his voice.

'You feel it too?' she asked in a hushed tone as if reluctant to disturb the calm this place offered.

'Yes.' He swung down from his horse and went to help her. His hands spanning her waist, he took her weight and lowered her gently to the ground. He did not release his hold nor did she try to ease away. She looked up at him. Their eyes met. Words were unnecessary. He kissed her, their lips lingering together. Still they held each other. Then their lips met again with renewed passion. When they eased apart his hands still circled her waist. Alice looked up at him, longing in her eyes. Matthew leaned towards her, brushed her lips with his, and then reluctantly let her go.

He looked contrite when he said, 'I shouldn't have done that, I'm sorry.'

'What do you mean?' asked Alice. 'I wanted you to kiss me. Did I not please you?'

'Of course you did, but were we merely influenced by the romance of this place?'

'Now you are talking rubbish,' Alice chided. 'I think there was more than that. Now let's walk.'

After a few steps he slid his hand into hers and, by the way he held it, she knew his conscience had been appeased.

'How long have you known about this place and its magic?' he asked.

'Since we were children,' she replied. 'Nicholas and I were great explorers.'

'I am glad you brought me here,' commented Matthew. 'I will always remember it.'

'Oh, it and not me?'

'You are part of it and always will be.'

'Flatterer.'

'No, I mean it.'

'And you for me. Now my visits here will always bring memories of the first time we came here together. It has become even more special. The magic I have always felt here has drawn us both together.' The trees swayed gently as if in agreement with Alice's words.

The air became charged afresh and they walked in silence, each lost in their own thoughts for a while. At length Matthew, wishing to dispel the heightened atmosphere, commented, 'You ride well.'

Alice inclined her head in acceptance of his praise. 'Thank you, kind sir. You don't do so badly yourself. You'll be better with the Army's rough edges smoothed away, though.'

'I know what you mean. It will happen one day.'

Alice wondered what lay behind his last sentence and could not help but seek to allay her curiosity. 'You mean, you are thinking of leaving?'

'I was never made for it nor it for me, but Army service was expected of me. That is the drawback of being born into a military family.'

'So you are sacrificing your ambitions, whatever they are, just to please your father?'

'You could say that.'

'Why don't you walk away?'

'I'd be branded a coward by my own family.'

'I don't think your mother would believe that.'

'Maybe not if she knew how I truly felt.'

'Then talk to her.'

'It would only lead to trouble with Father and

she is subservient enough to him as it is. Besides, my brother is making a successful career for himself in the Army and I mean to do the same.'

'Why, when your heart's not in it?'

Matthew gave a shrug of his shoulders and said, 'You don't understand.'

She sensed there was more to the story, but did not press him for further details.

Alice loved to lie in bed with the curtains drawn back, allowing the moonlight to stream in and fill her room with enchantment. Tonight thoughts of Matthew both intrigued and troubled her. His looks, his kisses ... he was very pleasing to her.

But then there was the matter of his subservience to his father's wishes. He hated military life but chose not to assert his own preference in the matter.

Was Matthew not the man she'd thought him to be? Didn't he know how attitudes were changing with the twentieth century? Thank goodness I spent that year in France with the Bergers, thought Alice. Now I realise it showed me a broader way of life, with more freedom of thought. How can Matthew blindly obey his father's wishes? Does he have no dreams he wishes to follow? What would my life be with a man like that? Could I bear to spend a lifetime with him? Were his passionate embraces just a diversion from thoughts of a lifetime sacrificed to the Army?

Knowing that Matthew's leave was nearing its end, Alice realised she must think deeply about all the implications of allowing herself to consider a future with him.

11

Before leaving to rejoin his regiment Matthew came to take his formal farewell of the Wares.

When the maid showed Lieutenant Cheevey into the drawing room, he hid his surprise on seeing only Alice's mother and father.

'I have come to make my goodbyes to you and your family, Sir Raymond.'

'We are grateful. And I noticed that you arrived on a beautiful grey mare.'

Matthew smiled. 'My mother's new acquisition. She allowed me to give Peg her first run.'

'Well done, Mrs Cheevey! I hope the horse will give your mother much pleasure.'

Before Matthew could enlarge on this the door opened and Alice walked in.

'Good morning, Matthew.' She met his answering smile with marked coolness.

He gave a little frown that disturbed Alice for a moment. Had she been too harsh towards him?

'I have brought my mother's new mare for you to inspect.'

Weakening on seeing those blue eyes of his eager for her approval, she nodded and said, 'I would love to.' She glanced at her father and received his nod of permission.

'This is Peg,' said Matthew, introducing the thoroughbred.

'She's beautiful,' said Alice as she stroked Peg's

neck, but Matthew noticed a reluctance to exhibit the admiration he would have expected.

'Is something wrong, Alice?' he asked. 'Have I offended you?'

'No, Matthew. Perhaps it's because you are going away and I don't know when I will see you again. I would like us to remain friends, though. Let us both see how we feel when we meet again.'

Matthew reluctantly replied, 'If that is your wish. You'll be in my thoughts, as I hope I will be in yours.' He bowed to her, and as he did so Alice said quietly, 'God go with you, Matthew.'

'Mother, I would rather you did not come to see me off at York,' Matthew insisted one more time. He knew it would mean tears if Emma accompanied him. 'You'll have more to occupy you at Deepdale than in York. I will be happier knowing you are here.'

Eventually Emma gave way. Even so she allowed a tear to trickle down her cheek as she watched the trap turn the final bend in the drive.

On reaching his depot near Salisbury Matthew found his regiment still on standby for South Africa. Hoping to obtain news of his father's, he sought out the adjutant.

'News is sparse, Cheevey, but we do know your father led a brave attempt to break through at Mafeking. We also know that the attempt failed, largely due to the force being too small to contest the strength of the Boers, but your father and what remained of his men were welcomed by Colonel Baden-Powell. We understand that in a subsequent bombardment by the Boers, your father and his captain were both injured while acting as lookouts.'

Concern immediately enveloped Matthew. 'How badly, sir?'

'We don't know the full extent of their injuries but we understand they are being well looked after in Mafeking.'

When the same news was received at Army Headquarters in Bloemfontein, Captain Steven Cheevey immediately sought an interview with his commanding officer.

'Sir, as you know, my father was in charge of the relief attempt. I only hope his failure will force our superior officers to learn from it in their next attempt to relieve the town. Rumours are now spreading that a new and larger force is planned.'

His superior held up a hand to stop him. 'Cheevey, don't believe all the things you hear. I know you are concerned about your father, however, so to ease your mind I will tell you in strictest confidence that a larger expeditionary force is indeed being assembled. It will be a coming together of various commands throughout South Africa in a once-and-for-all attempt to bring this conflict to an end. It may not be quick, but it has to be successful so must be planned in detail, which takes time. To you progress may seem agonisingly slow, but I assure you the plan of campaign will be thorough in order to achieve success.'

'I thank you, sir, for easing my worries on this point. As you will appreciate, my chief concern is for my father. With this in mind, sir, may I request that if part of the plan involves an onslaught on

Mafeking, which I expect it will, I am included in some capacity in that particular engagement?'

His commanding officer looked thoughtful. 'I appreciate your request, Cheevey. It is commendable. I have no knowledge of the plan our superiors are considering. All I can do is forward your request to higher authority, which I will do immediately. You have an exemplary record, one which must make your father proud. I wish we had many more officers as devoted as you.'

'Thank you, sir.' Steven saluted smartly and left, feeling very satisfied with the interview and the praise from his commanding officer. The prospect of advancing to higher rank was alluring. Nothing must be allowed to mar it. Maybe he should control his drinking and visits to unsavoury houses more carefully. Steven had always been discreet in such matters but there was the chance that some of those who accompanied him on the outings might let something slip. He needed the calming influence of a wife, but for now his mind was filled only with thoughts of his father.

Then he received the call.

Under the blazing South African skies the inhabitants of Mafeking went about their lives in the way to which they had become accustomed since the first day of the siege, trying to live under the threat of outright attack while suffering recurring outbreaks of bombardment from the Boers' limited artillery. At times it was effective until snipers forced the cannons to be moved to a different site.

Rumours reached the besieged town that two

British forces, each pursuing its own part in an overall plan, had connected to form a stronger contingent, but Mafeking had heard all this before. Scepticism hung heavy over the town. After their deprivations of the past months, dare they hope that this report was true? Even if it was, they had better be prepared for another attack by the enemy attempting to engineer the escape of Boer prisoners.

Lookouts were charged to be extra-vigilant. Arms and amoury were checked and double-checked. Baden-Powell rehearsed his officers in his strategy to counteract the likely direction of the Boer attack. Then...

'They're coming!'

A figure in tattered trousers and jacket raced through the streets, shouting the same words over and over until a soldier grabbed him. 'Who's coming? Tell us, man, who's coming?'

'Relief! Relief! It's got to be,' he yelled and, wide-eyed, tore himself out of the other man's grip and ran off, still shouting. His first call had brought people streaming from their houses. Others were opening windows to hear the news, more climbing on to roofs to get an early glimpse of the force coming to relieve them, but all they could see was a dust-cloud. Was it British or Boer made? The query spread from mouth to mouth until the announcement rang out: 'The Boers are retreating, running away!'

The good news swept through Mafeking like veldt fire.

The people of the town ran wild with joy. Their seven-month ordeal of danger, rationing and further privation was over. Tears of joy were shed. People shouted and danced in the streets, hugged strangers, welcomed the troops that marched into Mafeking. The African recruits danced for joy and filled the air with celebratory chants and songs.

'Away with you, Cheevey,' Steven's commanding officer called, his voice barely audible above the din that filled the air.

'Sir!' Steven gave him a quick salute and broke into a run in the direction of the convent, all military decorum forgotten.

The door of the makeshift hospital had been opened at the first sign that Mafeking was on the point of being relieved. He reached the entrance just as a matronly figure stepped out.

'Colonel Cheevey?' shouted Steven above the din.

'First floor front, second door on the right.'

'Thanks!' Steven darted past her and was on the stairs as the nurse was saying to herself, That must be the colonel's son. He's very much like him.

Steven flung the door open and pulled up short when he saw two beds were occupied.

'Steven!' The familiar sharp commanding tone was there but he detected weakness in it.

'Father!' Steven crossed to the bed quickly. He wanted to show his delight at seeing his father by embracing him, but knew that Robert would recoil from such a show of sentiment, which he would regard as weakness. Instead Steven held out his hand. His father took it in a firm grip but Steven, knowing how strong it had once been, realised his father was attempting to show him that his being in bed meant nothing. Robert could not, however, disguise his thinness and pallor. Trying hard to conceal the shock he felt, Steven glanced at the man in the other bed.

'This is Captain Pringle, injured alongside me when we were helping here as lookouts,' his father explained. 'Bloody Boers hurled a cannonball at us. Ruddy good shots too. Put us in here. I requested that Pringle should share a room with me. This is tiny, but they did well for us, particularly as space is at a premium.'

'How bad are your injuries, Father?' asked Steven anxiously.

'Left leg hurts like hell at times, especially when dressings are changed. Medical supplies have been in short supply, but hopefully that'll change now.'

'It should do. Medical teams are part of our relief force.'

There was a sudden outburst of determined firing. 'You'd better get back out there, Steven.'

Knowing his father's outlook, Steven took that as an order and hurried from the room, calling over his shoulder, 'I'll be back.'

By the time he'd linked up with his unit the firing had died to a desultory nuisance. He quickly assessed where the trouble was coming from. A sergeant and three privates were close by. 'Follow me,' Steven called. Crouching low, he sped for the next cover, a low wall. Rapid rifle fire broke out but the sergeant and his men reached the cover without mishap. Steven split his small group, indicating what he wanted them to do. His next signal sent them into action with himself at the forefront. The small group of Boers was so overwhelmed by the suddenness of the attack that they had no time to shoot in retaliation. They dropped their rifles and revolvers and raised their arms in surrender.

'Take 'em in, Sergeant.'

'Sir!'

The Boers were led away to swell the ranks of the prisoners.

With the relief of Mafeking, an important step in the South African campaign had been taken. News of the British success resounded around the world. The people of Britain, seeing it as a glorious military triumph, took to the streets in celebration.

Emma was elated by the news, but as she read about it in the press a stark truth became plain to her. Robert would be coming home, maybe not immediately, possibly not until some sort of unification of the states within South Africa had been established, but his return was clearly signalled.

She awaited further news while contemplating the future. She had found a new life for herself in Yorkshire; Deepdale remained unknown to Robert and Steven while Heatherfold was occupied only by servants. And there was John. She expected Steven to stay in the life he loved, whereas Matthew was only serving as a soldier to please his father; to her that was not a good basis for a happy future, though it was something she had not as yet been able to do anything about. Now, with her changed circumstances, could she help Matthew defy his father and find his true path in the world?

Then communications arrived from South Africa.

12

Two letters were delivered. Emma recognised Robert's and Steven's writing. Her heart missed a beat. Although she'd known this would happen, she was still unprepared for the news they would bring.

Under instructions, any correspondence that was delivered to Heatherfold Hall was forwarded by the staff there to Deepdale Manor. The house-maid who had taken delivery of the letters placed them, as usual, on the small mahogany table in the entrance hall at Deepdale.

On seeing them, Emma felt a chill sweep over her. She stared at the letters as if that would send them away so that her life here could continue as it was. But she could not leave them unread. She walked slowly into the study and sank on to a chair in front of her escritoire. Opening a drawer, she took out a silver letter opener and slit the envelope she knew she had to read first.

Dear Emma,

My good news is that I will be on my way home soon after you get this. I look forward to seeing you and to being at Heatherfold again.

The not so good news is that I was badly wounded at Mafeking. I was well looked after there but inevitably with the conditions that existed, shortage of medical supplies, etc., I have not recovered as I had

hoped. Because I can get better care in London, I am
being shipped home earlier than might have been the
case. One good side to this is that Steven, who has
served in exemplary fashion throughout this whole
campaign, is being allowed to accompany me as an
aide. He will also be carrying dispatches and reports
for higher authority in London, who, of course, will
still be directing the war to its successful conclusion,
which is expected to be within the year.
   Sincerely,
   Robert

Emma was left under a cloud of uncertainty as to
the extent of her husband's wounds, what his
being in London entailed and why was he being
accompanied by Steven under the guise of his
aide? Only one thing was certain: her husband
would be back on these shores soon.

   Maybe Steven's letter would shed light on the
ambiguity of his father's message.

Dear Mother,
   Even as you read this you may already know that
Father is being sent home for better care after being
wounded in action, and I am to accompany him to
England. I don't know to what extent he has made
known to you the seriousness of his injuries.
   He had reached Mafeking leading a relief force that
was lamentably too small to achieve its objective con-
sidering it was hugely outnumbered by a well-armed
Boer force. He fought valiantly, and was lucky to
survive and reach the town. Typically he set aside his
superior ranking to serve under Colonel Baden-
Powell, commanding officer of Mafeking. It was while

Father and a fellow officer, Captain Pritchard, were acting as lookouts that they suffered heavy bombardment from the enemy, resulting in their both being severely wounded.

I will not go into details but the final outcome was that it was deemed wisest to return Father to London for better treatment. Typically, he insisted that his fellow officer should also have the benefit of treatment in London alongside him. What will happen when they reach England I have no idea, we can only wait and see. The ship will be leaving a week tomorrow so you will get this before Father arrives. I know no more about his health; that will have to wait until medical officers have made their examination.

I look forward to seeing you soon, Mother.
Keep a brave heart,
Steven

Emma laid the two letters side by side on her escritoire and looked at them in dismay. Though they told her little about the true condition of Robert's health, she felt that both communications carried the threat of upheaval, if not disaster.

When John arrived later in the afternoon, he was met by a housemaid who seemed concerned. 'Sir, Mrs Brigstock said to tell you as soon as you arrived that Mrs Cheevey has been alone in the study ever since two letters were delivered shortly before noon.'

'And has anyone tried to talk to her?'

'Yes, sir. But she refused Mrs Brigstock's attempts to persuade her to come out for luncheon or tea.'

'I'll go to her now,' he replied, shrugging off his overcoat and dropping it on a chair near the front door. 'Tell Mrs Brigstock I am here.'

'Yes, sir.' The maid hurried away to find the housekeeper.

John was quickly into the study. He found Emma sitting at her desk, two sheets of paper in front of her. She did not move. He couldn't decide whether she had heard him come in or not. He went to her and placed one hand gently on her shoulder.

She gave a little start, raised her arm and placed her hand on his, as if the touch of it would bring relief to her troubled mind.

He kneeled down beside her. She turned her head to look at him and he was startled by the mixture of expressions he saw in her face: fright, helplessness, despondency. 'Emma, what is it? What's troubling you?' he asked.

She did not answer but allowed another tear to fall.

'Tell me what has brought this on?' She gave a little shake of her head as if it was useless to explain. 'Please let me help you. Tell me what has caused this change in you since I left this morning?'

Still she hesitated, but John saw her lips tremble as if she was trying to force words out but had no idea what they should be.

'Tell me,' he whispered persuasively. 'A trouble shared is a troubled halved. Let me help.'

She looked hopefully into his eyes as she reached out to the two sheets of paper and slid them towards him.

'Are these the cause?'

She nodded. He read them without saying a word, but the arm he had slid around her tightened in reassurance.

As he finished reading, she cried out, 'Oh, John. What am I to do?'

He stood up. Taking her hands in his, he brought her to her feet. 'We will cope with this. We have much to consider but we will find a way through it. First of all, my dear, the maid tells me that you have been sitting here since the letters arrived and have had nothing to eat or drink. So you are going to eat now with me, and don't say otherwise. I am hungry and am not prepared to eat by myself.' He steered her towards the door. As they went into the hall the housekeeper appeared.

'We'll have something now, Mrs Brigstock,' John told her.

As they ate he chatted lightly about his day, interspersing it with some amusing events he had witnessed in York. He was pleased to see this was having some effect as he noticed Emma relax and manage to eat a little. Afterwards they went into the drawing room.

'I'm sorry, John, for causing you such concern, but I saw my whole world threatened by those letters and couldn't imagine how to prevent disaster. Everything they reveal and imply runs counter to what I hoped our future might be.'

'Before we go any deeper into this, answer me one thing, Emma. What do you wish our future to be?'

'I've never said this to you but when Robert came home, I was going to ask him for a divorce. I was waiting to see when the time would be favourable.'

'Though divorce is now legal it still carries a stigma, and it is always the woman who suffers most,' he warned.

'I could have dealt with that, but now things will be worse. The wife of a wounded hero ... mud would be slung at you too. Your business could suffer. There would be...'

'Stop, Emma,' he said sharply. 'We don't know all the facts as yet. That might not happen; Robert might not be a hero.'

She gave a little laugh. 'There is evidence that he is, in Steven's letter. If there is a grain of truth in that, Robert will milk it for all it's worth.'

'Even if it is true, it needn't dent your determination to get a divorce.' He saw doubt in her expression.

'And there will be Steven to contend with,' she said. 'He will be expecting to go to Heatherfold. He's going to have to be told, and he'll have to see Deepdale too. I don't think his attitude will be as accepting as Matthew's.'

'Let us wait and see. We might be meeting all our troubles in advance. They could all vanish into thin air.'

Emma gave a tight smile. 'How I wish they would.'

'We'll give them a little shove to get them out of the way.' As John was speaking he took her hands and drew her to her feet. 'And here is the start of it.'

He drew her close and gave her a kiss that drowned her misgivings; she knew it would only be for a while but she let herself forget her troubles and resigned herself to wait.

Then another letter arrived, one that chilled her to the heart.

Dear Mother,

Father and I arrived in London yesterday. I thought it best not to write until I knew more about his situation. I have just received news about that so I am writing to let you know.

It was thought in Africa that he could only survive if he agreed to the amputation of his left leg. He stubbornly refused to let them operate even though he was in a lot of pain. He has proved to be right. On arrival here he was taken immediately to the London Hospital in Whitechapel where he had an intensive examination. The examining surgeons now believe amputation will not be necessary, but he will still require an operation and long-term treatment, both here in hospital in London and afterwards at home. The outcome could be one of four possibilities: 1. Do nothing and he would gradually be left completely incapacitated. 2. Partial incapacity, in which he would be able to manage only with assistance. 3. A recovery in which he is able to do much for himself but will be left with a troublesome limp that will impose limited activity. 4. The possibility that during the long operation he could lose his life.

Father insisted that he be told in full the options that faced him. He met them exactly as I had anticipated. He has insisted that the operation goes ahead.

The surgeons then consulted me and agreed with my opinion that you should see Father and them before anything further is done. Therefore they have asked me to contact you and tell you it would be advisable for you to come to London as soon as possible.

That is the reason for this letter. Anticipating your arrival, I have booked you a room and accommodation for your lady's maid at Claridge's as from tomorrow. I think at a time like this you should have the best. You are not to worry about the cost; I will attend to that. When you arrive in London, take one of the new taxi cabs to the hotel. I have certain appointments to fulfil in London but will keep in touch with the receptionist to learn of your arrival.

There will be much for me to see to, as I am due to return to South Africa four weeks from today. That, I'm afraid, cannot be changed.

I am sorry this is a gloomy letter but, to end on a better note, I look forward to seeing you and hopefully Heatherfold Hall, even if that has to be a brief visit. It will do Father good to know I have been there.
Steven

Emma felt a stab of guilt. She had been in the arms of another man while her husband had been suffering, and facing a possible amputation that could wreck his life, leaving him dependent on others among whom he would expect to find his wife.

She could not escape the summons to London. She rang the bell for Sally.

When they reached their destination, Emma called over a porter. 'A taxi?' she enquired.

'Follow me, Ma'am.'

Within a few minutes the porter had them

installed in the horseless vehicle, and passed on their destination after receiving it from the lady, who also gave him a generous tip. The taxi driver set his cab in motion.

'Oh, Ma'am, what's happening?' cried Sally above the engine's thudding and the rattling of the vehicle.

'Everything will be all right. The driver knows what he's doing,' Emma reassured her.

But Sally was unconvinced and held on tight to the seat until the taxi slowed and finally stopped at Claridge's.

'There, that wasn't so bad, Sally, was it?' said Emma, though she herself still felt shaken by the ordeal.

'Ma'am, we have a message from your son Captain Cheevey. He will dine here with you this evening at six,' a receptionist announced on her arrival.

Emma glanced at the wall-clock. Four o'clock; just time to get settled in and compose herself for what might well be a difficult evening.

She found her rooms to be the height of luxury, with every aspect of the decoration and furniture complementing each other. Sally soon arrived to help her dress for the evening and prepare to meet Steven.

He was not late. Emma was nearing the foot of the stairs when he came in at the front entrance. He stopped and looked at her with admiration. He came over to her, took her hands and kissed her on both cheeks. 'You look wonderful, Mother. I have never seen you...'

He hesitated so she finished for him, with a little laugh, '...like this before?'

'Well I...' He stuttered to a stop.

She linked his arm with hers and started for the lounge. 'You have been abroad so long you have forgotten. Much has happened in that time. I have a lot to tell you.'

He saw her comfortably seated and signalled to a hovering waiter.

'You have a lot to tell me?' prompted Steven when their order was given.

'Yes, but first give me news of your father.'

'He is in good hands. You should not worry. He was badly wounded but there is every chance he will recover, though he may be left with some disability that could restrict his active life.' Steven gave her as much detail as he knew. As the story unfolded, Emma realised that the outcome could develop in a way she had not envisaged. Fear gripped her but she fought against her misgivings.

The moment's silence that followed was broken by Steven.

'You do realise that Father will need a long period of rehabilitation and special care, but his determination to return to Heatherfold could help his recovery so you will have a great deal to do.'

His words sounded to her like nails being driven into her coffin at a time when she had been seeing her future as filled with other possibilities. Thoughts of Deepdale and John shone brightly in her mind. Was her future to be destroyed by a war in a land far away? Her husband had loved it, loved the Army regardless of the risks attached, but must she be forced to suffer the consequences of war too?

Emma stiffened her spine and replied firmly. 'I may not be able to do that.'

For one moment it appeared that Steven had not heard, but then came the realisation that she was going against his wishes. 'What?' he exclaimed. People turned to stare at them both.

Emma was embarrassed. Her son glanced apologetically at the people sitting at nearby tables and then leaned towards Emma, whose expression reprimanded him.

'I'm sorry, Mother, I apologise for my reaction. Your statement was so unexpected that I didn't know what I was doing.' Then he looked at her askance. 'You surely don't mean what you said?'

'Oh, but I do,' replied Emma, her voice steady so that there was no doubting her declaration.

'But ... I don't understand?'

'I said I had much to tell you. I think you had better hear me out before you say any more.'

He nodded. 'Maybe I'd better.'

'I will come straight to the point, Steven. I am now a very rich woman in my own right.' She deliberately emphasised every word of her statement so there could be no mistake about what she was saying.

He stared at her with a blank expression.

'It is true. I am completely independent. I have property and money.'

'But how? Where has this come from?' he asked, still looking bewildered.

She told him the whole story, except for the details of her relationship with John.

It was only natural for her son, as her story ended, to pose the question, 'Do you truly trust this John Smyth to handle all your financial affairs?'

'I do. I have never once doubted his honesty. He has been the foundation of my new life. I could never have handled the complications of inheriting so much money and the property I now occupy in Yorkshire without his support and wise counsel.'

'Yorkshire? What about Heatherfold? That's our home.'

'It is no longer my home, Steven. I have my own now. Heatherfold is your father's. It always has been and always will be.'

'So you have been living in Yorkshire since you learned of the inheritance?'

'Yes. I want no part of Heatherfold any more. Steven, I want you to come and see my new home. I think Deepdale will help you understand some of the things I have been talking about.'

He hesitated, frowning as if trying to make sense of what he had heard. 'All right, I'll do that, but I won't come north with you until I know Father is comfortable and being well looked after here.'

'I entirely agree. We won't move until we know his condition is stable.'

'Very well. Hopefully that will be before I have to return to Africa in four weeks' time.'

'Whatever the situation is when he leaves hospital, I won't go to Heatherfold. The full household staff is still there. He can be put in their care, with the addition of a professional nurse. Steven, I think you should know that I am tired of being taken for granted by your father. He has constantly done that over the years but has been very clever in hiding it from you and other people. I will

122

contribute financially to his care but I will not move from Deepdale; I cherish my newfound independence too much. I will not surrender it now.'

13

The next morning Emma entered the hospital wondering what she would find. She had seen her husband the last time just over two years ago. She recalled the fine figure of a man he had been then, ramrod-straight, dark-haired, strong-jawed, all of which reflected his resolute, unbending will-power. Robert was not a man who would allow his judgement to be questioned. People said how lucky she was to have such a husband beside her but Emma had soon found out that his apparent generosity ran skin-deep. From her he'd expected complete subservience, and no doubt he still did.

Robert appeared to be sleeping when she approached his bed, Steven beside her. Emma was shocked to see how thin her husband's face looked, and how exposure to extreme heat and illness had given him the look of tanned leather. There were streaks of white in his hair.

'Hello, Robert,' she said quietly.

He grunted and muttered in reply.

Emma repeated her words.

He turned his head on the pillow. 'Good Heavens, woman, what are you doing here?' he demanded in a stronger voice than she had expected.

'Have you left Heatherfold to God and Providence?'

'Mother has come to see you, Father,' interposed Steven.

Colonel Cheevey's eyes focused on him. 'You should be in Africa, get yourself back there.'

'All in good time, Father. There are Army matters I have to see to in England first. But Mother and I are here in search of news of you.'

Robert scowled. 'Ask him.' He indicated the man who had just come into the room accompanied by a nurse. Introductions were quickly made to Dr Ferby.

He announced, 'I and several colleagues who examined you on your arrival, Colonel Cheevey, have come to the conclusion that we should operate immediately to reduce the possibility of amputation.'

Robert tightened his lip for a second then burst out, 'All right, man, get on with it!'

'Just as soon as we can,' replied the doctor, 'Nurse Jordan will be looking after you, overseeing all the preparations for your operation and during your recovery afterwards. There are certain things I need to discuss with you, Colonel, so I must ask your wife and son to leave now. I'll give you a few moments together. Nurse Jordan and I will be outside.'

As they both left the room Robert's lips tightened. 'Damn those Boers who put me here!' His eyes fixed on his son. 'See you make them pay when you get back to South Africa.'

'I will, Father,' replied Steven with an air of resolve he knew would satisfy his father.

Robert turned to Emma and reached out for her hand. 'Sorry about this,' he said, sounding reluctantly apologetic. 'I know it has been rough for you, our being apart for so long, but that's the lot of a soldier's wife. Bear up. I'll be all right when this damned op is over. Now you two had better be off.'

Taking this for an immediate dismissal, Steven shook hands with him and left his mother and father alone.

Emma stood for a moment looking down at her husband. She remembered again the handsome, loving man with whom she had walked down the aisle, and thought she saw the same recollection in his eyes.

Robert drew her hand closer. Emma felt his grip tighten.

'I know that as I have grown older,' he said, 'and we have been apart, I have become less affectionate but I still think a great deal of you.'

Tears came to her eyes as she bent and kissed him on the forehead.

He gave a little smile and requested gently, 'Mind you look after Heatherfold well. I might soon be spending a lot of time there.'

Words sprang to Emma's lips but remained unspoken. It would not be kind to speak them now. Besides, who knew what the immediate future held – perhaps those words might never be needed. Instead she kissed her fingers, pressed them to his cheek and followed Steven from the room.

Dr Ferby came forward and said gently, 'A word, before you leave, Mrs Cheevey. I must warn you that this is a big operation to repair your husband's leg. We won't know until we start to operate the extent of the damage suffered. Also there is a lot of shrapnel in various parts of his body ... in fact, we are amazed that none of that proved fatal to him. Now, I suppose you are wondering about visiting. Your husband will need time to get over the shock of the operation, and that means time without any disturbance. I have noticed that Colonel Cheevey is highly strung so I would recommend no visiting for a week, but do call in the morning when I will be able to tell you how the operation has gone.'

After giving the doctor their assurances of co-operation, Emma and her son left the hospital. It was only when they stepped outside into the sunshine that Steven took hold of his mother's arm and stopped her.

'In those few minutes with Father, I recognised the attitude you spoke of to me.'

'What you saw was mild compared to some of the treatment I have had to take, without daring to say even one word back.'

'When did it start?'

'Only gradually, and not at all until ten years ago.'

'Why do you think it happened?'

'Let us find somewhere for lunch and I'll tell you about it,' Emma suggested.

Within twenty minutes they had found a restaurant that was to their liking. Once they were seated and had placed their order, Steven looked expectantly at his mother.

'I have gone back over the years myself, trying

to discover the reason for your father's behaviour, but I failed. I do not believe I provoked his treatment. I have tried to be the wife he wanted. All I can blame is Army life. I never questioned what he did while away from home ... that was never part of my life. Maybe Heatherfold had something to do with it. He was obsessed with the place, and woe betide me if I ever did anything to question his authority regarding life there. You saw, just now, what he expects of me.'

'Surely you'll take him back there?' Steven asked, a touch of sharpness in his voice.

'I'll see he gets there and has the medical attention he needs, but I will not be there with him.'

'You can't just desert him!'

'Steven, I have told you what I will do. I know you are closer to him than to me.' She saw a protest forming on his lips. 'Don't deny it. You were always the apple of your father's eye. I never minded; you were happy together. It was only natural, because of that closeness and what you inherited from him, that you would follow him into the Army and make him proud of you. I also know that you are like your father in loving Heatherfold. I don't hold that against you, it is the only home you've known, but I would like you to see Deepdale.'

Steven hesitated then said, 'All right, Mother. I'll come there with you after Father has had his operation and we are able to see how things will be for him.'

'I would expect no other.'

On their way to the hospital the following morning Steven asked the taxi driver to call at the War Office. Reaching that imposing building, he instructed the driver where to park and said to his mother, 'I should be no more than ten minutes, possibly less. Will you be all right waiting here?'

'Of course.'

Steven hurried inside, receiving salutes from the two privates on sentry duty at the door. With his credentials accepted he was allowed inside, where his enquiry after Brigadier Samson brought a swift reaction and an escort to the brigadier's office. He handed over a large envelope, which the officer accepted thankfully. 'Cheevey, I understand you have brought this from Africa while escorting your father home for medical reasons?'

'Yes, sir.'

'I am told he served gallantly in attempting to relieve Mafeking.'

'Yes, sir. It was there that he was badly wounded.'

'How is he?'

'He will have had his operation today. My mother and I are on our way to the hospital now.'

The brigadier nodded. 'I'll just check the contents of this and then you can be away.' He opened the envelope and ran his eye over the pages it held.

He frowned and muttered, 'Bloody typical. They always send half the story... How am I to plan this damn' conflict that's draining our coffers without better intel than this?' He looked thoughtfully at the papers then at Steven.

'Have you been in action over there?'

'Yes, sir.'

'Then you should be able to give me some useful background information.'

'Well, sir, I can only state what I personally know to be true.'

'Come on, Cheevey, you'll have made up your mind what should be done to see off this war.'

'Yes, sir, all serving officers have their own ideas about that.'

'Sometimes they can prove valuable, especially from someone like yourself who has seen action recently, providing first-hand information on which we can base the suggestions to go to all the leading officers in the field. Without proper input they'll look like bloody ignorant fools.' He didn't give Steven time to reply. 'I'll have six copies of these reports made for the officers making a judgement of the campaign and suggestions for the future conduct of the war. I would like to surprise them with some personal testimony from you. Could you write something and let me have it by this time tomorrow?'

'Very well, sir.'

'Good, Cheevey, good. When are you returning to South Africa?'

'Because of my father's condition, plus some personal issues, I was given permission, before I left South Africa, to extend my leave in England by six months, provided I presented reports about troop training in South Africa. I am dealing with those but I was told the envelopes I have just handed to you were to be given priority.'

'And you have duly done that. They must think you badly need to take some leave. Thank you, Cheevey.' He stood up and shook Steven's hand. 'Good luck in your Army career. I hope the personal issues are not too serious. They can be if they are wife trouble. Often happens when husbands are abroad.'

'It's not that, sir. I'm not married.'

'What? A fine fellow like you, not married? Marriage can further an Army career if you find the right girl, so keep your eyes open and your wits about you!'

'I'll do my best.' Steven saluted and marched briskly from the office.

As he walked out of the building his mind dwelled on the brigadier's final comment, and he marvelled at the coincidence that it matched his own thoughts shortly before leaving Africa.

Maybe I should find myself a suitable wife while I'm here, he decided.

14

Three days later, Emma and her eldest son were settled comfortably in a first-class compartment of the train bound for York. They were leaving in the knowledge that at this stage Robert's operation seemed to have been successful. Dr Ferby reassured them that, 'All will be well, provided there are no unforeseen complications. We have taken every precaution, but sadly there is much in such cases that we still don't understand. I would like no more visits to the patient for a month. After that, as far as I and my colleagues can assess, we expect him to remain in hospital for at least four months.'

Commenting on this as the train rattled its way north, Steven said, 'Things here have worked out well for me. I dealt with the military reports easily...'

'Even the one you said Brigadier Samson asked you to write?' his mother asked.

'Yes, I made sure I delivered it promptly. I saw it as an opportunity to impress and maybe further my career.'

Emma nodded but made no comment. She thought how like his father he was, ever ready to seize an opportunity that would enhance his standing with anyone in authority.

'I'll stay with you a couple of nights and then leave for Heatherfold,' Steven suggested.

'I'd hoped you would stay longer at Deepdale.' She gave a little shrug of her shoulders. 'But if that's what you want, who am I to stand in your way?'

'I'll see you again before I leave for Africa.'

He picked up his newspaper and Emma, taking this as a sign that he did not wish to talk, let her mind drift, speculating about his reaction when he saw Deepdale Manor and John. Would he view either as a reason to stay longer with her in her new home? Knowing the hold Heatherfold had on her son, she thought not. She led the way out of the station at York and they engaged a motorised taxi to take them to Deepdale.

Steven said little until the land began to rise, causing him to remark on the ever-changing views.

'Do you like them?' queried Emma.

He gave a little smile. 'Anything would be better than the flat veldt but I suppose even that has its own drama and beauty, very different from this.' He paused in thought for a moment then added, 'But Heatherfold country beats them both.'

They had been climbing higher as he was speaking. Emma said nothing.

A few moments later, as the track levelled out on the edge of the escarpment by now familiar to Emma, Steven sat upright and called out, 'Driver, stop!'

Her son was out of the taxi almost before it came to a halt. Emma smiled to herself at his reaction, which was just as she hoped it would be. She stepped out without saying a word and came to stand beside him. She respected the silence until Steven broke it.

He spun round and looked accusingly at his mother. 'You didn't tell me Yorkshire was like this!'

She laughed. 'You thought it was just mills and coal mines!'

He ignored her pleasant jibe. 'Are we far from Deepdale?'

'See that wood,' she nodded in its direction, 'you can just glimpse a house among the trees. That is where I live; that is Deepdale.' She said it forcibly so he would link it with her earlier determination to stay there.

'Unbelievable! You must have inherited a fortune.'

'I told you I had.'

'But I didn't realise the extent of it.'

'You'll realise a bit more when I tell you that the land we have travelled through for the last

132

two miles is all mine, as is practically all that you can see now.'

'Good God, I never imagined... But how do you manage it?'

'With the help of reliable staff and a very good friend, John Smyth, the solicitor who discovered I was the rightful owner. He has practices in Kelso and York. When I told you earlier how I came to inherit Deepdale, I only mentioned John in passing. I have asked him to be at the house today when we arrive.'

Steven made no comment; he sensed there was more to this story than he had been told.

The taxi took them down the track that joined the gravelled drive to the front of the house. Steven's concentration on the unfolding landscape was only broken when he saw two men come out of the main door on to the stone veranda.

'That is John on the right; the other is our head butler.'

Steven was quick to pick up on the word 'our' and immediately raised his eyebrows.

'I could say I am referring to the family, but I won't. I think you have surmised, even from the little you've heard, that there is more than a professional relationship between John and myself. I will not deny it, and will tell you now that when your father is well enough, I shall seek a divorce.'

Steven looked shocked. 'Mother, you can't! Think of the scandal.'

The taxi was beginning to slow down.

'There's no time to discuss this now. We'll talk about it later. Don't jump to too many conclusions, and please be civil to John. It would mean so much to me.'

Steven nodded but did not commit himself in words.

The taxi came to a halt. The butler was quickly at the door of the taxi. 'Welcome home, Ma'am. You too, sir.'

'Thank you,' replied Steven.

The butler raised a finger and two footmen, who had been standing by, came forward to take the luggage.

John greeted Emma and turned to Steven. John held out his hand and felt it taken in a firm grip.

'I am pleased to meet you, Steven. I hope I am going to hear good news of your father?'

Steven was momentarily taken aback that the query had been directed at him and not his mother, though at that moment John had linked arms with her.

'The operation has been successful so far as can be ascertained, though a long recovery time is anticipated.' After a brief pause Steven added, 'So it may mean my mother has to spend some time away, but thank you for your concern.'

They had reached the steps to the veranda where Steven stopped. His gaze swept across the front of the house. 'This is a very imposing building,' he commented.

'All thanks to your mother's vision,' revealed John. 'The work you will have noticed being carried out on the older parts of the property is all based on her ideas.'

'Because I want it to be *my* home,' Emma interposed. 'I hope you will like what you see when we show you the inside.'

'If it is anything like the exterior then I'm certain I will.'

'You know, you are welcome to live here. There is plenty of room.'

Steven gave a gentle, considered smile. 'Heatherfold will always be home to me.'

Emma gave a little nod of understanding.

The rest of the day passed off well, with Steven learning about the Deepdale Estate from his mother and John. After an early-evening meal, John left mother and son together and returned to room at the Wild Hussar.

When Steven and Emma had settled in the drawing room, he queried her plan for a divorce. 'You're set on going through with it?' he asked, eyes seeking out any chink in her resolve.

He did not find one and could not doubt the firmness of her reply: 'Yes.'

His lips tightened. This was not what he wanted to hear. 'Mother, think of the scandal; be aware of what other Army wives will think.'

'Army! Army! Army! Why should I consider what the Army thinks? And as for other officers' wives, why should I care what they say? I have never been close to any of them. In any case, they and the Army will soon have to get used to the idea of divorce. It's here to stay, no matter what the Establishment thinks.'

'But what about Father? He's going to need you.'

'Need me to look after him? But I'll do that in my own way. I'll pay someone to be with him, and that will mean he'll receive better care than I could give him. He can live in his beloved

Heatherfold, have his own friends ... without having to refuse me mine.' She left a little pause and when no response came from her son, added, 'That is the situation, Steven. Your father will not suffer because of me. I do owe him some consideration in respect of our earlier life together, but I see no possibility of my returning to a miserable existence from which I have so recently escaped.'

'I don't agree with everything you say in favour of divorce but I respect your right to say it. I noticed how the situation between you and Father had deteriorated, and I thank you for your explanation, but the way everything has unfolded, I had hoped it would draw you together again.'

'That is not going to be possible,' Emma said resolutely. 'I am sorry, Steven.'

Silence fell. Steven stood up, sat down again beside her and kissed her on the forehead.

'Just one more question. Does Father know about your good fortune?'

'No. Knowing how he would try to use it in his own favour, I took legal measures to prevent that. When he learns of it, I'll be surprised if he doesn't try to contest what I have done. Well, he will find that door closed and bolted. He will have to realise that the days of a husband having rights over his wife's possessions are gone. I have found a new independence that I mean to hold on to and enjoy.'

Steven could not deny the determination in his mother's voice, but he felt he must say, 'I found John pleasant enough and au fait with the situation, but do you trust him in every way?'

'Absolutely!' Emma returned with conviction. 'He and I love each other, Steven. With such a vast fortune to protect, he helped me take every precaution and I am satisfied that no one can benefit from my good luck but myself.'

'Very well, Mother, I am happy with your re-assurance.'

'Thank you. I have had the same caution from Matthew. I would like you both to keep this confidential. I will tell your father myself when I think the time is right.'

When Emma had settled herself in bed that night her mind was too full of the day's events for sleep to come easily. She was reasonably content with Steven's attitude to her changed circumstances but was also aware of his reservations. The thought of Robert's suffering was painful to her. She had seen a strong man brought low by injuries sustained in the service of his country. She could tell they had softened him somewhat. But the thought of what she had endured in the past hardened her resolve not to give way and lose the independence her inheritance had brought her.

The following morning, while mother and son shared breakfast, Emma made a suggestion. 'It is a glorious morning. I would like you to see more of Deepdale. Will you ride with me?'

Steven could not refuse the hopeful look she gave him.

'Of course! You have a stable then?'

'Yes, one of the things I was determined to acquire when fortune smiled on me. There are four horses. Bonny should suit you.'

'Good. I look forward to it.'

So it was that he accompanied his mother on a ride that would change all their lives.

15

'Perfect, Mother, perfect,' called Steven, as he settled comfortably in the saddle. He leaned forward and patted his horse's neck, imparting his confidence that they would suit each other well. He straightened up.

'You sit the horse well,' commented Emma admiringly.

'I was taught young by a good teacher,' he replied, putting thanks into his smile.

Curious about the estate and what he was seeing, Steven kept up a flow of questions, which pleased his mother for she had feared his love of Heatherfold would drown out any affection he might develop for Deepdale.

'Those are good-looking cattle, Mother, though I'm no expert.'

'Since I know little about farming, I appointed a farm manager as well as an estate manager and they seem to be working very well together. They have assembled a good herd of Friesians.'

They rode on until Emma drew her horse to a halt. 'The next field is part of the Ware Estate. Tell me if you see any rails or hedges that are faulty. I would hate to have any of our cattle stray on to their fields. Not that they would object, they are a very kind family. I would have asked them to dinner if you had been staying for a few days.'

'Sorry, Mother.'

She shrugged. 'One of those things; can't be helped, I know. You want to be off to Heatherfold.'

They rode on in silence, eyeing the hedges for any breaks that needed repairing. They were nearing the stretch they had made their target when they heard the sound of a horse being ridden hard.

'It's Alice!' called Emma. 'Alice Ware.'

'She rides fast and furiously,' said Steven.

'She does,' agreed Emma, and waved down the rider.

Steven watched the girl bring the horse round in their direction and hold it in a trot towards them. He saw the joy she felt at being at one with her mount. Her features were bright from the enthusiastic gallop; her hair, which she had freed from its tie, fell loose to her shoulders and contributed to an air of carefree boldness.

'Good morning, Mrs Cheevey,' called Alice as she brought her horse to a halt. Her eyes had already taken in the young man with her neighbour, an imposing figure astride his horse.

'Good morning, Alice,' Emma returned. 'This is my eldest son, Steven.'

'Hello, Miss Ware,' he said, sweeping his gaze across her in such a way that she felt he was taking in much more than a polite glance would have afforded. 'It is good to meet one of my mother's new friends.'

'You should meet the others. Mother and Father are at home. My brother Nicholas would have been with me today but had important work to see to on the estate.'

'I would like that. Pictures to carry with me in my mind when I return to South Africa.'

'When will that be?' asked Alice.

'Not for about five months,' he replied.

'Well, that gives you plenty of time to meet my family, as your brother Matthew already has. I'll mention it to my parents.'

'And I'll look forward to meeting them.'

'Goodbye for now,' said Alice, turning her horse but letting her eyes meet his for a moment longer. 'Goodbye, Mrs Cheevey.'

'Goodbye, Alice.'

They watched her ride away for a few moments until Emma broke the silence.

'Come on, it's no good sitting here, there is still much more I want you to see.' She set her horse forward and Steven fell in beside her. After a few minutes, during which not a word passed between them, Emma said, 'You are looking very thoughtful, Steven.'

'Well, I was just working out what I have to do before returning to South Africa and I was wondering if you would mind if I stayed on a bit longer with you?'

Emma's lips twitched a little. 'Of course not! I would more than like you to spend time with me. But I thought you wanted to get off to Heatherfold?'

'I needn't do that just yet. And besides, if I stay with you the trains would be more convenient for reaching London to see Father again.'

'And I suppose also it offers more possibilities of

seeing a certain young lady who has just left us,' added Emma, a twinkle in her eyes. Seeing he was going to refute her observation, she countered quickly, 'It's no use denying it, Steven. Remember, I was young once. All I'll say is, she's a nice girl and you are returning to South Africa. Don't break her heart.'

Alice had a pleasant ride home filled with thoughts of the handsome man she had just met. She put a query to herself and answered it almost immediately. Yes, Steven was more handsome than Matthew; a better build too, which hadn't been disguised by the casual clothes he wore. Matthew had cut a fine figure in his new riding attire, but Steven had an air about him, one that had captured her attention. No doubt he could switch into formality when required to, smart beyond measure in his officer's uniform. In the few exchanges they had had, she had detected a more forceful disposition than that of his brother.

She tightened her lips and put her horse into an earth-pounding gallop, as if thundering hooves could destroy the recollections of two young men, vying for supremacy in the turmoil of her mind.

When at home Alice casually mentioned that she had met Mrs Cheevey and her eldest son Steven, who was on leave from Africa, her mother did not hesitate: 'We went to the Cheeveys' to dine. With Steven at home, it would give us a good opportunity to reciprocate.' Gaining her husband's agreement, she penned an invitation to dinner one evening the next week and included John Smyth, though he had to write a polite refusal because he had work that would take him to Kelso.

Two days after receiving Mrs Cheevey's acceptance of the invitation, Cecilia was informing Mrs Brigstock of the coming dinner when the housekeeper mentioned they had been told in the village of the unexpected arrival of Lieutenant Matthew Cheevey at Deepdale.

'Thank you for informing me. I will invite him to join us too. Please arrange for one more guest.'

When their butler announced the arrival of the guests, Sir Raymond and Lady Cecilia, Nicholas and Alice, greeted them in the drawing room. Alice stifled the gasp of surprise that threatened to ruin her decorum. Steven and Matthew were both resplendent in uniform so that she could not decide who was the most handsome, but there was a confidence about Steven that was immediately apparent.

After a most enjoyable meal, digestifs were served in the drawing room. With the evening agreeably warm and the moon bright, those who wished were able to make use of the veranda. Seeing his brother and Nicholas deep in discussion with Sir Raymond, more than likely about the South African War or perhaps the bothersome Irish question, Matthew seized the opportunity to invite Alice to stroll with him on the terrace.

'That would be pleasant,' she replied, feeling a little nervous after their last meeting.

'I'm sorry this is only a brief visit,' he apologised, and quickly added with regret, 'and that I shan't see more of you.'

'The life of an Army officer,' she sympathised.

142

'But it has at least enabled you to see your brother.'

'We've been apart for two years and, with postings to South Africa held up, I was granted a special short leave to see him. I wasn't going to miss the opportunity of seeing you again either. You promised to write to me,' Matthew reminded her.

'I know, I'm sorry. Things got in the way. But I will try to do better.'

Alice was relieved when their two mothers, deep in conversation, stepped outside to enjoy the evening air.

Seeing Matthew with Alice, Lady Cecilia said, 'I told the butler we would manage the drinks ourselves this evening. Matthew, would you be so kind as to arrange them for us? My husband is seeing to those inside.'

'I'll come and help.' Alice headed for the table on which glasses and decanters had been set but then noticed Matthew's attention had been diverted by Nicholas. She was left to place the brandy glasses on a tray and pour out some Napoleon brandy.

Steven, who had seen his brother waylaid, said, 'Excuse me, gentlemen,' and rose to help her. 'Pour another glass and let me carry the tray for you,' he offered.

She returned his smile and said, 'Thank you. A gallant officer to my rescue.' She led the way to their mothers. Steven placed the tray on the small table beside them, held a chair for Alice, and as he placed his hand on another, said, 'May I join you?'

Emma left it to their hostess to reply, 'Of

course, it will be our pleasure.'

They settled down to enjoy each other's company and the conversation flowed pleasantly without the war in South Africa being mentioned once, though Steven's uniform was a constant reminder. Again Alice was struck by how handsome he looked in it.

After their glasses were emptied Lady Cecilia said, 'I think I will see how Raymond is getting on.'

'I'll come with you. We'd better inject some feminine charm into that all-male gathering,' said Emma. She smiled and added, 'They may not enjoy that.'

The two women walked away, leaving Alice and Steven still enjoying their brandy.

'I'm pleased our mothers seem to be getting on so well together,' he commented.

'So am I,' said Alice. 'It is good for Mother to know she has a neighbour again and that Deepdale is coming back to life.'

'I am grateful that your mother has not shunned mine because of her present situation with Mr Smyth.'

Alice quickly changed the subject. 'What are your plans for the rest of your leave?'

'Well, I will have to visit Father, but we were prevented by the doctors from seeing him for a month, so, when that time is up, Mother and I will be going back to London. How long we stay will depend on what we find there. Also I feel it my duty to check the Heatherfold Estate in the next few days so that I can report on it to Father. I had several jobs to see to at the War Office but I have done most of them and can finish the outstanding ones when we visit London. As for the rest of the time, I'll be with Mother at Deepdale. When I return maybe we can meet, go riding together, even visit York. But only if you would like to?'

'I would be delighted.'

'Then I'll ask your parents' permission as soon as I am back.'

16

The next morning when Steven came down for breakfast he found his mother already in the dining room.

'Good morning, Mother. Did Matthew get away on time?' he said brightly.

'Yes, he left at first light.'

'That was a splendid evening,' added Steven, 'and I found it reassuring to find you have such pleasant neighbours.'

'I'm happy you got on well with them.'

With breakfast under way, Emma put a question to him. 'Have you made any plans for your leave yet?'

'I gave them some thought before I went to bed. I'll make use of the time when we are not allowed to see Father to go and check on Heatherfold. He's sure to ask about it when we see him. So, Mother, if you'll inform the staff there, I'll head north in three days' time, see how things are with the servants there and make sure they are happy to stay on and remain in Father's employ when he is allowed back to Heatherfold.'

'I would be grateful if you could secure re-assurance on that point from Mrs Hewlet, who is doing a good job keeping in touch with me about the present running of the house.'

'I'm sure everything can be arranged. When are you going to inform Father of your plans?'

'As soon as I judge the moment to be right.'

'I hope that will be soon.'

'It's not going to be easy...' Emma cut her words short when she judged that her son was about to interrupt in an attempt to prevent the rift in his parents' marriage.

'Don't, Steven, don't,' she said purposefully. 'I am not going to reconsider.'

'I know, Mother. And I will give you my support in the best way I can.'

Her mind warned her, Remember, he was always his father's boy, but she pushed that aside, telling herself Steven was now a man.

Steven was thankful that the train north arrived on time at Edinburgh's Waverley Station, which enabled him to reach Heatherfold before daylight was beginning to surrender to twilight. The butler was taken aback when he answered the doorbell and found Steven on the doorstep.

'Captain Cheevey, my goodness! We were informed Mrs Cheevey's son was coming and presumed it was Master Matthew.'

'Hello, Dryden. It's good to see you.'

'Good gracious, sir, I thought you were still in South Africa.'

'I was but I'm here now. For three days maybe.'

'Well, sir, I'm pleased to see you in good health after being in that godforsaken country.'

Steven smiled, 'It's not all that bad, Dryden.'

'I'll find Mrs Hewlet and tell her you are here.' He started to bustle away then stopped and looked back. 'Mr Steven,' he mumbled. 'In person!'

He departed and a few moments later Steven heard Mrs Hewlet's voice saying, 'Stop joking, man! He's in South Africa. You're a wicked tease.'

Dryden's voice rose in exasperation. 'He's here, woman. He's here!'

There was the clatter of shoes on the stairs. They fell silent when Mrs Hewlet stepped into the hall with Dryden beside her.

Her eyes widened. 'Oh, my goodness, it's true! Mr Steven, sir!'

'Yes, it's me,' he laughed. 'You haven't seen a ghost.'

Then it was all activity as Mrs Hewlet took charge. Orders flew, bedclothes were brought to what had always been called 'Mr Steven's room', and now the dining room became a centre of activity. All-in-all the staff seemed to be enjoying having someone living in the house, albeit for only a short time.

It wasn't until Steven was sitting in the dining room, empty plates and dishes cleared, that he felt relaxed. He nodded to himself; it was good to be back at Heatherfold again and he looked forward to tomorrow when he would walk the estate in the morning.

After breakfast he called Mrs Hewlet into the

dining room where he was having his second cup of coffee.

'Mrs Hewlet, please tell Cook I won't be in for lunch today.'

As he was setting out on his walk Steven called at the stables and asked the head groom to have a horse and trap ready for him at eleven-thirty. He discussed a few points about repairs to part of the stables as well as the fitness of the six horses. He visited the estate manager on his return and congratulated him on the condition of the land.

'I'll be seeing my father next week. I know he will be pleased by my report of how well everything is looking at Heatherfold.'

Steven called in at the house, changed clothing and then, with overcoat and deerstalker on, collected the horse and trap and drove to Kelso. He left them with the stablemen at the Hart Hotel and enquired the location of the office of John Smyth, Solicitor. It was only five minutes' walk away, in a street of large Georgian houses, all of which he judged from their condition to be cherished by their owners. He was surprised that one of them was being used as an office but there was no doubt about it when he saw the highly polished brass plaque with John Smyth's name on it at the front door.

He rang the doorbell and a few moments later the door was opened by a middle-aged man, with hair greying at the temples. He stooped a little, giving the impression of frailty, but his voice was pleasantly toned with a slight Scottish intonation. He was dressed in black trousers, black jacket, white shirt and stiff winged collar.

'Good day, sir,' he greeted the newcomer at the door.

'Good day to you too,' replied Steven. 'If Mr John Smyth is in, I would be pleased to see him.'

'Have you an appointment, sir?'

'I'm afraid I haven't. I am only in this area for two more days and made a very recent decision to come to Kelso.'

'I will see if Mr Smyth can see you. Please step inside. Your name, sir?'

The clerk ushered him along the corridor to a room on the right. Steven had already noted how smart the entrance looked, spacious with two highly polished small oak tables and comfortable chairs. On one of the walls was a large mirror and opposite a painting of the Highlands.

'I'll see Mr Smyth right away,' said the clerk and left the room, shutting the door behind him.

Steven thought he had never seen a solicitor's office as opulent as this. He strolled over to the painting but had little time to study it closely before the door opened and the clerk announced, 'Mr Smyth will see you now, sir, please follow me.'

He led the way along the corridor, opened a door at the end, announced, 'Captain Cheevey,' and stood back to allow the newcomer to enter.

Steven was taken aback when he saw the room. Though he hadn't a moment to take in any details, he was immediately aware that it was large and welcoming.

John rose from behind a desk neatly laid out with stationery and writing implements. He held out his hand, and, as Steven took it, said, 'This is an unexpected pleasure.'

He indicated an easy chair to Steven and took a similar one himself.

'I hope I'm not interrupting anything,' said Steven.

'There is always work, but if I can't stop and give some time to friends, it is a poor lookout. I knew there was more than a likelihood of you visiting Heatherfold Hall but I did not know when.'

'Nor did I. I only decided the other day that this would be the best time. I came up yesterday. I have looked round the estate this morning, and have come into Kelso hoping you would be able to accept an invitation to dine with me tomorrow evening at the Hart Hotel.'

'That's very civil of you, I would be delighted. Please call here at six-thirty. We can take a quick tot together before we go.'

'Here?' queried Steven.

'Well, not here but next door, where I live.'

The following evening Steven was admitted to 'the house next door' by a maid in a calf-length black dress, trimmed with smart white lace cuffs and matching collar.

When he gave his name, she said brightly, 'Come in, sir. You are expected.' She took his overcoat and led him through.

When he entered the parlour, John sprang to his feet. 'Welcome,' he greeted Steven. 'You are very punctual.'

'Army training,' he replied.

'Of course.' John turned to the maid. 'You can go, Maisie. I don't know what time we will be back. I'll lock up.'

'Thank you, sir.'

John poured two glasses of whisky. 'Single malt,' he said, handing one to Steven. 'To see us to the hotel.'

Steven took a sip. 'Excellent,' he approved. 'I hope I haven't upset any plans you had for this evening.'

'You haven't. I probably would have spent the time reading.'

Steven cast his eyes round the room, which was a little larger than John's office and very tastefully furnished with heavy pale-blue velvet curtains drawn across the windows. He went to look at two paintings and, seeing they were by the same artist, asked, 'Do you collect his work?'

'Yes, Hornel, one of the Kirkcudbright artists; I have two other paintings by him.'

Steven turned to face him. 'With what I see here and in your offices previously, you have created a very elegant and comfortable home,' he commented.

'Thank you. I was given this property and a moderate but useful income by a bachelor uncle, brother to my mother. I did not create what you see, my wife did, so I am pleased to hear you say that.' He caught the look of on Steven's face and added, 'Ailsa died six years ago.'

'Oh, I am sorry to hear it.'

'Maybe I had better explain a little more as I believe you are here not from idle curiosity but rather concern for your mother. That is commendable. I also believe you are very much your father's son, and that too is commendable. When I made contact with your mother regarding Deepdale, she brought joy back into my life. Not that she supplanted my wife, but she made me see, without any intention on her part, that I could still enjoy life. We formed a friendship that worked for both of us because we made an understanding that, if either of us had to walk away from the other, for personal reasons, we would remain friends. I am a wealthy man in my own right ... but I have probably said enough now for you to appreciate what there is between your mother and myself.'

'Although I cannot condone all that has been happening between you, I thank you for your frankness. It has made me understand a few things better and will enable me to return to South Africa easier in my mind, especially if my father makes a good recovery.'

John nodded. 'Another time, another place,' he said wistfully.

'True,' agreed Steven. A painting of an attractive young woman caught his attention then, reminding him of Alice Ware. There was a young lady who might repay closer acquaintance, he decided.

17

Satisfied that he would be leaving Heatherfold in the care of its devoted staff, Steven headed south for Deepdale with much on his mind; his father's condition, unknown at this time, and his mother's relationship with John. He felt reassured on that score, though he could see trouble ahead if his mother was determined on a legal separation. These thoughts began to pale, though, as the train heading south beat out a rhythm on the rails: Alice, Alice, Alice, Army, Army, Army. The words drummed their way into his mind until they were inexorably imprinted there, offering a solution to the way in which his Army career should develop, bringing him promotion and respect, eventually taking him to the pinnacle of the service before a comfortable retirement.

Steven took a taxi from York to Deepdale, where his mother greeted him with the news that the surgeons were satisfied with Robert's condition but no visit was possible until the date they had been given.

'Was everything in order at Heatherfold?' she enquired.

'Everything is in order and the staff are happy to carry on under the supervision of the housekeeper and estate manager.'

'Good. That's a weight off my mind.'

'I saw John while I was there. Tracked down his office and took him to dinner at the Hart Hotel.'

'That was kind of you.' Immediately Emma was on a knife-edge awaiting her son's reply, for she guessed that this had been a deliberate investigation on his part.

'You did not elaborate about his business.'

'John did not want me to,' said Emma.

'He doesn't mind the outward show of his office and his house next door – they were certainly eye-openers,' Steven commented.

'It was a condition laid down by his uncle that John should live and work from those properties otherwise they would be forfeit. That would have been a shame so he geared his business accordingly.'

Steven nodded. This information added so much more to his knowledge of the man. Emma, for her part, was pleased that her son had visited John and hoped that the relationship would remain steady whatever lay ahead.

Determined to ease his concerns for his father, Steven decided to let the freedom of a ride help him. He rode at a leisurely pace, not really paying much attention to where he was going until he was aware of the distant roof line of Wooton Hall appearing among the trees. He halted his horse and sat, considering the Wares' home for a few minutes before he moved on.

Alice, sitting at her bedroom window, reading and enjoying the sunshine streaming in, caught a glimpse of him while he was still some distance away. Her heart speeded up; she laid her book down and stepped back into the room. She did not want Steven to see her there and presume she was waiting for him to call.

Her impatience mounted but she resisted taking a peep through the curtains. She would have to move them back to do so and she did not want him drawing conclusions, no matter how right they might be.

Time seemed to drag. Noises came from the hall but she could not make out what was being said or interpret the movements until she heard muffled footsteps on the carpeted oak stairs. Expectation gripped her as footsteps came in the direction of her room. Then came the longed-for knock on her door. She gulped then immediately took herself in hand. She must appear calm.

'Come in,' she called.

The door opened. 'Miss, your mother would like to see you in the drawing room.'

'Very well, Liza. Thank you.' Alice checked her hair and smoothed her dress, allowing the maid to be clear of the hall.

Alice's heart beat faster and her footsteps were rapid as she went down the stairs. She wanted to race down but curbed the desire so that she would be outwardly unruffled and composed by the time she reached their visitor. She paused a moment before the door, drew a deep breath, expelled it, and walked in.

'You sent for me, Mother?' Then she let her gaze take in Steven. 'Oh, hello, Captain Cheevey.'

'Good day, Miss Ware.' Steven made a little bow.

'Captain Cheevey has asked our permission to call on you while he is at Deepdale,' said her father. 'Would you like that?'

'Yes, Father, I would,' replied Alice, attempting to sound calm.

'Very well.' He turned back to the visitor. 'Captain Cheevey, you have our permission to do so.'

'Thank you, sir,' replied Steven. Seeing his time with Alice shorten with every passing second, he thought the boldness expected of an Army officer should be employed now. 'Miss Ware, with your parents' permission, would you care for a stroll in the garden before I return to Deepdale? My mother is expecting me in just over an hour.'

'Thank you. I'll just get a shawl to throw round my shoulders,' she said, and hurried from the room. On her return she broke up the stilted attempt by three people to make polite conversation, having met unexpectedly.

'Ready?' Steven asked her with a smile.

'Yes.'

He turned to her parents. 'Sir, ma'am, I won't disturb you again.'

He made his goodbyes and opened the door for Alice to step out on to the terrace. Steven followed her and crooked his arm to help her down the steps to the garden path.

'This is an unexpected surprise,' she said.

'For me too. When I saw the roof of Wooton Hall I decided on impulse to pay you a visit.'

'Then I'm glad you found me at home,' said Alice, implying that she did have interests outside it. In case he was wondering, which was by no means clear. He'd left it a while to contact her after the dinner party.

There was a moment's pause. Alice softened her tone. 'I hope the latest news of your father is good?'

'We will know more when we visit but so far he is making a reasonable recovery. He'll survive,' said Steven confidently. 'Father's tough. They did not give much for his chances at Mafeking, where he was wounded, and he survived.'

'Were you there too?'

'Not during the actual siege but I was part of the force that finally brought about the relief. I saw Father immediately we secured the town and, quite frankly, I didn't hold out much hope.'

'I hope you find him feeling much better when you return to London. Have you any other plans

156

while you are in England?'

Steven bent his head closer to hers. 'Yes. To see as much of you as possible. I love Heatherfold and thought I would be spending most of my time there, but my priorities have changed unexpectedly.'

'Why? I should think you'd get more joy from your home that you would from me!'

Steven smiled at her. 'I think you are fishing for compliments.'

'I'm not!' protested Alice, and then burst out laughing when he started shaking his head at her, slowly and deliberately.

'I'll believe you, if you will agree to this suggestion. Tomorrow I'll have the horse and trap. Shall we find lunch somewhere?'

She hesitated for form's sake, which he easily saw through. 'Don't say no to a lonely soldier who will be leaving for Africa all too soon.'

'If I say yes, will it help you when you are far away?'

'Definitely. It will enable me to remember both your beauty and your kindness.'

'Then I will agree to your kind invitation.'

His face lit up in a broad smile. 'You are already making a new life for a soldier in need.'

It was a remark that made Alice wonder if more than gallantry lay below the surface.

When Alice looked out of her bedroom window early the next morning, she breathed a sigh of relief. The early morning mist overlying the fields and hills was being urged away by the warming sun. She swung round from the pleasing view, her mind full of the prospect of being with Steven again. Nothing could mar her day unless a message came from him cancelling the outing.

Stella, her personal maid, liked helping Alice dress when she was in this sort of mood. By the time her mistress had enjoyed breakfast, Stella had laid out her most suitable clothes for a late-summer morning.

Alice thanked her and slipped out of her house dress. Stella, knowing the procedure her mistress preferred, assisted her with the sky blue skirt, the white blouse, and beautifully cut dark blue jacket. When Alice was satisfied with their fit, she sat down on a straight-backed chair and slipped her feet into her highly polished shoes. She stood up and stared at the ensemble in the mirror. 'Just right, Stella.' Pleased by the praise, the maid smiled.

Alice sat down at her dressing table for one last view of her hair, and Stella held a mirror so that her mistress could view it curling at the nape of her neck. Alice nodded her approval. The maid moved away to begin tidying up.

Alice remained seated, recalling that the last time she had worn this particular outfit it had been to impress Matthew. How quickly things could change. She liked Matthew, had even thought she might love him, but Steven's arrival had made her question that. His natural charisma had helped him put his brother in the shade, but would it still be the same when Steven had returned to South Africa and Matthew remained in England? Alice met her own bewildered gaze in the mirror. Only time would tell, she decided.

A knock on the door disturbed her. Stella was coming into the room. 'Captain Cheevey has arrived, Miss. He has been shown into the small drawing room.'

Alice's heart began to race. Would it have reacted in the same way if this had been Matthew calling on her? She pushed the awkward question from her mind.

'Enjoy your day, Miss,' said her maid.

'Thank you,' replied Alice, thinking, There'll be something wrong if I don't.

From the galleried landing she saw Steven waiting for her in the hall below. As she walked in stately fashion down the stairs she saw him catch her movement, glance up and smile when he saw her.

'Good morning, Alice,' he said as he held out a hand to help her down the last two steps. 'They put me in the company room but I couldn't wait to see you.'

'Good morning to you,' she returned. 'Mother and Father had an appointment in York and apologise for not seeing you. They hope to do so before long.'

'I hope so too. If you are ready we may as well start now.'

He escorted her to the trap and, after seeing her comfortably seated, with a rug over her knees, climbed up beside her and took the reins. He steadied the horse with gentle pressure then turned his head to look questioningly at Alice, 'Well, young lady who is looking very smart this morning, where are we going? It is your choice.'

'If we take the minor road to Coxwold it will be

159

a pleasant ride, and we'll have some wonderful views towards the Hambleton Hills and the moors beyond. We could take lunch in Coxwold and return afterwards by the foot of the hills and pass by Deepdale.'

'It appears that you have thought this out?'

'When you suggested bringing the trap, I did put some thought into what to do. Knowing that you were not really familiar with this area, I decided this ride might impress you.'

'Very good. Let us away.' He flicked the reins and the horse started forward. Steven kept it to a walking pace; there was no need to rush, he wanted to spend as much time with Alice as he possibly could.

She guided him on a course that caused him to stop frequently to admire the views across gentle undulations and sharp inclines, revealing landscapes that stirred the imagination. At one point the land fell away from their vantage point into a wide valley before climbing again to an escarpment with moors beyond.

'Is that a white horse cut into the hillside?' he asked.

'Yes,' she replied. 'The idea of a native of the village you see at its foot; he made his fortune in London and wanted to leave his mark where he was brought up. I believe it was the village schoolmaster who promoted the idea of the horse as a memorial.'

'What a splendid idea,' Steven approved. He was about to move on but stopped and concentrated his gaze again.

'What have you seen now?' asked Alice with a

little chuckle.

'Is that an old ruin I can just distinguish against the hillside?'

'Yes, those are the ruins of Byland Abbey, an old Cistercian monastery that fell foul of Henry VIII like so many others did. We will be going that way so you'll be close to it.'

'You have done your homework,' said Steven as he flicked the reins and signalled the horse to walk on.

'Well, I've always liked knowing things about the places where I am, so when I came back here after my year in France I refreshed my knowledge of the area.'

'Do you do that wherever you go?'

'Yes... Well, if an area is interesting and I can make the time. Don't you?'

'Not in the way you seem to.'

'Why not? I would imagine from what I've read that Africa is a fascinating place.'

'Yes, I suppose it is, but I'm viewing it most of the time with the Army's demands foremost in my mind. Because of the war I look at Africa differently.'

'Surely something of it has rubbed off on you? Aren't there things that have made unforgettable impressions on you, not of the war's making?'

He was silent for a few minutes. 'Yes, I suppose there are, now you've made me think about them.'

'So what are they? Tell me about them.'

'I suppose there are two things that have made an impression on me, though I had not seriously considered them until you prompted me. First there are the native people I have met... I am not talking about those who have come to Africa from outside like the Boers. The tribespeople are generally friendly and happy-go-lucky and will respond to you if you show them kindness.' He paused.

'And the other thing that has impressed you?' she prompted.

'The African nights, when stillness spreads across the veldt and the western sky is aflame with colour ... red, orange, yellow. They seem to bring a special sort of silence, and yet there is noise everywhere if you care to listen; you will pick up all sorts of animal sounds as they call to one another, and drums sending rhythmic beats across the darkening veldt, while stars twinkle overhead like diamonds in the vast impenetrable void.'

'You make it sound so romantic,' said Alice, swept away by his description.

Not realising how moved he had been by his own words and thoughts of the land so far away, Steven gave a little start, 'Oh, do I? I suppose it is romantic ... funny, I had never thought of it that way.'

'Well, now you can.'

'I will. And it will bring thoughts of you and how you have given me a new perspective on Africa.'

'I'm glad,' she said.

'We'd better move on.'

Alice said nothing but wished they had stayed there longer. She guided them along between broad vistas. They topped a rise, which turned into a gentle downward slope.

'A little further to the village where we can seek lunch, but before that we'll stop briefly.'

'Are we on the edge of a big estate?' asked Steven, indicating the well-constructed stone wall to their right.

'Yes,' she replied. 'Newburgh. You'll get a good view of the front of the house. It was once a priory but during the Dissolution Henry VIII gave it to one of his ardent supporters, who turned it into a country house. That is what it has remained ever since.'

'Interesting,' commented Steven. A few minutes later he was pulling the horse to a halt at the point from which he could see the house through the main gateway. 'Impressive but not spectacular,' he judged.

'I rather like it,' commented Alice. 'It looks comfortable, well settled.'

He considered her judgement. 'Yes, I see what you mean.'

He drove on only to stop again when they came to a small but attractive lake, its waters lapping at the wall close to the roadside. On the far side of the water were well-kept lawns.

'Very nice. It looks so cool – something else to recall in the heat of the African sun. Where now?' asked Steven.

'Just drive on. When we turn that corner ahead you'll see the village. We should be able to get a meal at the inn there.'

He negotiated the corner. The view of the village caused him to stop and gasp. The road dipped, flattened for a short distance then climbed as it passed between two rows of houses, to be crowned at the top by the village church.

'You have certainly provided me with some

wonderful views today, Alice. I am very grateful for that, and of course for your company. You must show me more before I return to my unit,' Steven said.

'I would love to show you more.'

'Then I will ask your parents to give me permission to keep calling.'

'I would like that.' She laid her hand on his arm. 'But I do understand that you have to be in London to see your father.'

They had reached the inn. When Steven helped her out of the trap, he held her close for a moment. 'You are a very thoughtful person, Alice, and I admire you greatly.' He gave her a gentle kiss on the cheek and escorted her into the inn.

18

Steven rode fast. He hadn't much time. He didn't slow until he was pulling his horse to a halt in front of Wooton Hall. He was out of the saddle almost before the horse had stopped. Knowing the animal, he threw the reins across its neck, leaving the horse to regain its breath while he raced up the steps to the front door. He heaved the bell pull and tapped his leg with his whip impatiently while he waited.

As soon as a footman opened the door Steven was asking, 'Is Miss Ware at home?'

Recognising him, the footman said, 'Step inside, sir.' Seeing Steven's agitation, he added, 'I'll see if

I can find Miss Ware.' He stepped briskly across the hall to the drawing room.

He reappeared a moment later, gave a little shake of his head and hurried to the stairs.

Lady Cecilia appeared from the drawing room, 'Hello, Steven.'

'Good morning, Ma'am. I'm sorry to burst in like this, but we have just heard that from tomorrow we have permission to visit Father. I wanted to see Alice to let her know that we can't meet today.'

'It must be good news that your father's immediate convalescence is over,' said Lady Cecilia.

'It would seem so.'

'Ah, here is Alice,' said Lady Cecilia, seeing her daughter appear at the top of the stairs.

Alice, concern in her expression, came quickly down to the hall.

'Steven has had good news about his father,' said her mother.

Alice looked relieved as she turned to him.

Her mother started for the drawing room, then, after a few paces, realising the two younger people were not following, stopped and looked back. 'No doubt you'll be seeing Matthew, if only at your father's bedside. If you do, give him our best wishes, won't you?'

'I will, Ma'am.'

'And good wishes to your father for a speedy recovery, of course. Goodbye, Captain Cheevey. Give us the news when you return to Deepdale, won't you?' She walked away.

'I'm sorry about this, Alice,' Steven began to say.

'It can't be helped. You must go. Is your horse at the front?'

'Yes.'

'I'll walk you to it.'

The silence between them was filled with regret.

'Come back soon,' said Alice when they reached the horse.

'As soon as it is possible.'

Steven swung into the saddle and reached down to squeeze her hand. She watched him ride away until he turned a bend in the drive and disappeared.

When Steven reached Deepdale he found his mother had everything ready, her valise and his packed; all he had to do was gather together anything personal that he wanted with him. The coach was waiting. There was nothing else to do. They reached the station with ten minutes to wait for the train to London. On its arrival at York, the porter who had taken charge of their luggage found them an empty first class carriage.

At the hospital in London the nurse on duty welcomed them, checked a list of families who were allowed to visit at any time and then announced, 'I have instructions to let Matron know of your arrival. I will do so. Please take a seat, she will be with you in a few moments.' The receptionist had given a hospital porter a special signal. He hurried away and a few minutes later the matron was greeting them.

'Mrs Cheevey, Captain Cheevey. Dr Ferby instructed me to inform him when you arrived and to see you comfortably placed in his waiting room, so please come with me.' They started along the corridor. 'Colonel Cheevey has done very well, but I'll leave all the details to Dr Ferby. Suffice to say the colonel has not been the easiest of patients to deal with, but I expect you know what he is like.'

Reaching the doctor's waiting room, she saw them comfortably seated before taking her place behind a small desk. She unlocked a drawer, took out a bulky file and placed it before her in readiness.

Dr Ferby breezed in. 'Good day, Mrs Cheevey, and you, Captain Cheevey. Please come into my office.' He started towards the door, calling over his shoulder, 'You too, Matron.' When everyone was seated he said, 'Matron, what is the latest on Colonel Cheevey? That is the late-afternoon report, I take it.'

'Still the same as this morning.'

'So everything is as stable as it was then?'

'Yes.'

'Good.' He looked at Emma with a little smile. 'Your husband was causing some anxiety yesterday; not because of his illness but because he was becoming somewhat unruly, giving orders here, there, and to everyone, even our matron, and let me tell you, that is bordering on a criminal offence.' She blushed. 'So what have I to tell you, Mrs Cheevey? Your husband is doing very well but these outbursts could be dangerous to him. We are giving him some tablets to help calm him down and hopefully they will do the trick, but really what he needs is some stability back in his life. Relaxing the embargo on visitors should help but it would be better if you were here for a while. Is there any chance of your staying in London for some time while we monitor his progress?'

Emma hesitated but only for a fraction. 'I will see what can be arranged.'

'Good. Now, as to his physical condition, most of his wounds are healing well, except for those to his arm. They are causing some concern but hopefully will start responding soon to treatment. We have had to operate several times on his left leg, hoping we would be able to put everything right again, but we can't. It means that he will have a limp, one that he will find awkward, necessitating the use of a walking stick.'

Emma glanced at Steven. 'He won't like that,' she said.

'He certainly won't,' agreed her son.

'I haven't told him yet. I wanted to see you first,' explained the doctor. 'It would be best if you could be here when I break the news. It might be more calming for him.'

Emma was on the point of disagreeing but withheld her opinion; she could do nothing but agree.

'Very well,' she said. 'When would you like me here?'

'Shall we say ten in the morning, the day after tomorrow? You as well, Captain Cheevey. Now, let us go and see your husband.' He led the way to Robert's room.

'Visitors for you, Colonel.'

'About bloody time you rescinded that ridiculous rule!'

Emma and Steven walked in.

Robert visibly brightened. 'Hello, you two.'

Then his face soured a little as he barked, 'Where's the other one?'

'Matthew is with his unit in the south of England,' Steven explained. 'I have managed to get in touch with his immediate commanding officer who, fortunately, knows you of old. He was very sympathetic about your condition and said he would immediately issue a pass to Matthew, who should also have received my message telling him to meet us at Claridge's. So he will be with us tomorrow.'

Robert grunted without further comment.

'Well, how's life at Heatherfold?' he demanded.

Emma spoke up quickly as she and Steven exchanged a quick glance. 'Everything is in order awaiting your arrival.' Her expression was guarded and non-committal.

'Well, get me there quickly,' he snapped. 'I'm fed up of lying here. The sooner I'm on my feet, the sooner I'll be better.'

'Father, be patient. You were in a bad way. The surgeons have done wonders. Don't undo all their efforts by rushing things.'

Dr Ferby had noted Robert's demeanour during these exchanges and now backed up Steven. 'Your son is right, Colonel. Rush things and you could slow your recovery. Now I'll leave you to have some time alone with your wife and son.'

Emma and Steven stayed an hour. Then, realising from his behaviour that Robert was tiring, they made their excuses and left.

Neither of them spoke until they had left the confines of the hospital.

'Coffee, now, Mother.' Steven took her arm and

guided her to the nearest café. 'I saw that the visit was becoming a strain for you.'

'Yes, it was. This coffee will be a godsend.' She gave her son a wan smile.

'I know what is bothering you ... how you will tell Father of your decision.'

She raised a hand. 'Not now, Steven.'

'You are going to have to face it some time.'

'I know, and I will. Let's get tomorrow over with first.'

Emma and Steven were pleased when Matthew arrived at Claridge's in time to take dinner with them that evening, His first concern, after the greetings were over, was for his father, but that was eased a little when they told him of the arrangements for the day after tomorrow.

It was during dinner that the subject of Deepdale came up. After an exchange of views about its continued development, Matthew asked after the Wares.

'They are all well,' Emma replied, and added as part of the ongoing conversation, 'Steven had a lovely ride with Alice to familiarise himself with the area.'

Matthew stiffened at this but skilfully hid his reaction. Nevertheless Steven caught the flash of annoyance in his brother's eyes. It was there, it was gone, but it spoke volumes to Steven, a man of the world who had experienced more than he would care to admit. With his eyes set on those Army promotions and a wife who could help him in his ambitions, he must not let Alice escape him, he vowed.

Emma and her sons, each with problems of their own, spent an uneasy time until the morning of Dr Ferby's assessment of Robert's physical condition. They were guarded about their own difficulties, recognising that the outcome for Robert might affect their decisions.

They were shown to the waiting room, but fortunately Ferby did not delay them for long.

'Colonel, we are going to have you out of bed for the first time since your arrival here,' he said brightly as they all walked into Robert's room.

'About bloody time too,' he snapped.

'What do you expect to happen when we get you out of bed?' asked Ferby.

'I'll walk out of here and get myself home, where I should have been long before now.'

The doctor nodded. 'Just what I expected you to say. Well, Colonel, you are going to have to think again. Apart from the lingering after effects of the operation, your legs will have weakened from your being in bed so long. I want to see how strong they are and judge what exercises will be necessary.' Without waiting for the colonel's reaction, he signalled to the matron and nurses.

They took up their positions, each knowing exactly what to do as they eased the patient round ready to make the first effort to stand. The doctor noted Robert wince during his first attempt.

'Now, I want you to sit up with your legs out of bed but *don't* attempt to stand. I will tell you when.'

The colonel tightened his lips with annoyance. 'Get on with it, man!'

171

The doctor ignored him but addressed the others. 'Matron, Nurses, you know the procedure.'

Everyone got into position.

'Now!' said the doctor firmly. Then, as Robert attempted to push himself up, they all saw the wince of pain that contorted his face. 'Stop!' The colonel sank back into a sitting position. 'Not as easy as you expected?' said the doctor. 'Relax for a few minutes and we'll try again.'

After two more efforts, he called a halt. 'That's enough for the first time.'

Even though he was breathing hard and his expression showed he was still feeling the strain, Robert cursed the doctor and added, 'No! That's not the end!'

The doctor glared at this defiance. 'I'm in charge here, not you. You will do as I say! What would you do to a soldier who disobeyed you?'

Robert's moment of rebellion dwindled. He heaved a deep submissive sigh and allowed the nurses to make him more comfortable in his bed.

'Right, Colonel Cheevey, it was a good effort for the first time. I expected no better. We will try again this afternoon at three o'clock. You can see your visitors now, Colonel.'

When they gathered again in the afternoon, Emma and her sons learned that the nurses had been flexing Robert's feet and moving his legs gently every fifteen minutes in readiness for his second attempt to stand.

'Let me see you move them on your own,' Dr Ferby ordered when he arrived for the afternoon session. This one was more successful and when it was over the doctor told Emma there were encouraging signs.

But when they arrived the next day they sensed panic as they neared Robert's room. A junior nurse stood on duty at the door. She stopped them from entering. 'I'll let the doctor know you are here.' She disappeared into the room, to reappear a few moments later and say, 'Dr Ferby will be with you shortly. Please take a seat.'

His serious expression set alarm bells ringing.

'What's my husband done?' Emma asked with despair in her voice.

'He got out of bed before the hospital was really awake. When a nurse came to check on him she found him on the floor, struggling to get to his feet. How long he had been like that we have no means of knowing, but certainly he was in bed when the previous hourly check was made. I've looked him over. He has some bruising, a couple of the old wounds have reopened, but worse than that ... he has damaged the leg on which I had operated.'

'What does this mean for his recovery?' asked Steven.

The doctor threw up his hands in despair. 'It has set it back. Colonel Cheevey will have to stay here longer than I had hoped. In all probability, it will mean his limp will be worse and I doubt he will ever be able to discard a stick completely.'

'What does this mean in the short term?' asked Matthew.

The doctor thought for a moment. 'I think it best if you resume your own lives, but remember your encouragement will help him even if it does not appear so.'

'Are you implying restricted visits or no visits at all?' asked Emma.

'By all means visit, that depends on you. If you are at home, write to him. It's a waiting game still, I'm afraid.'

'Thank you for making the situation clear, Doctor, and I am sorry for the upheaval my husband has caused you and your wonderful staff.'

They left the hospital feeling troubled by Robert's foolish and headstrong behaviour. They all agreed that returning to Deepdale was the wisest course in the meantime.

'I'll check train times,' Steven offered when they reached Claridge's. He sought the help of the friendly receptionist and soon realised that it was not worth departing then but would be better to wait until the next morning.

They had a comfortable journey back to York where they took a taxi to Deepdale, arriving in the early afternoon. The servants had the house running as if they had never been away.

While housekeeping arrangements were being discussed, Matthew, without making it known, went to the stables and had a horse saddled for him. Within a few minutes he was leaving Deepdale. He did not see Steven behind him running to the stables.

'A horse!' he called out. His voice was so full of authority that two grooms jumped to do his bidding. 'Did my brother say where he was going?' he demanded.

'No, sir.'

'Come on, come on.' Steven urged on every action of the harnessing. The very moment they

174

finished he was into the saddle and setting the animal into a gallop along the same track as that taken by Matthew.

The grooms raised their eyebrows at one another. 'Must be something in the air,' commented one.

Steven urged on his horse until he caught up with his brother.

'I'm going to see Alice. She declared her love for me the other night. Where are you going?' he asked.

'I was going to let her know about Father. She's been asking after him.'

'Well, I can tell her for you,' said Steven, to outflank him.

Matthew knew he had lost the point but said, 'I may as well come and say hello.'

Steven glared at him in annoyance but curbed an outburst by putting his horse to a gallop. Matthew followed suit. Steven knew he had overstated the state of his current relationship with Alice, but it was imperative that his brother did not cloud matters between them before Steven could bring them to a successful conclusion. Matthew had to be made to give way.

Alice, who was returning from her daily ride, heard the pounding of hard ridden horses. She pulled to a halt and scanned the landscape.

'Goodness,' she exclaimed. 'Those poor mounts!' She tried to identify the riders who had turned in her direction but they were still too far away for her to be certain. She sat still and waited. Then, 'It can't be. They are in London!' Even as she doubted what she was seeing, she realised it was so. The brothers were racing towards her full tilt. Matthew will never catch Steven, she thought.

Steven was panting hard as he swung his horse around in the dust and brought it to a sudden halt beside Alice. Furious with his dangerous manoeuvre, she steadied her horse which threatened to be spooked by the commotion. Matthew burst upon them then, adding to the turmoil.

Alice glared at them both. 'You two ought to be ashamed of yourselves, making your horses gallop like that, especially along this rutted track! Look at them ... they've not enjoyed the run!' She was so indignant on the horses' behalf that both young men felt belittled.

'I'm sorry,' muttered Matthew, full of repentance.

'But I wanted to see you,' said Steven, with a touch of defiance. He did not like being criticised.

Was this the real Steven? she wondered. Matthew had been humbled and had shown proper remorse, but his brother...

Alice controlled her temper enough to play down the worry she felt. 'I thought you two would be at your father's bedside. What brings you back so soon? I hope the news is good.'

'It is,' said Steven.

At the same moment Matthew said, 'It is and it isn't.'

'Make up your minds!' snapped Alice, still annoyed by their precipitate arrival.

Between them they related the facts about their father.

'A pity he wanted his own way. Natural, I suppose, but he shouldn't have taken things into his own hands. I hope the damage can be repaired.'

'He's a strong old cuss,' said Steven. The words were out before he could rephrase them. He looked repentant when he saw Alice's frown of disapproval. 'Sorry. I don't mean any disrespect.'

'Understood,' she said coolly. 'Army phraseology, I suppose.' She looked both men over and said, 'Now we have met, I'll allow you both to escort me home. But there'll be no more galloping. You've already put your horses through enough of that.'

Shamefaced, they obeyed and ranged themselves one on either side of her. They said nothing, each waiting for the other to speak first. Alice smiled to herself, her poise boosted by the power she held over them, something she was experiencing for the first time.

After about a hundred yards Steven could stand it no longer. 'Do you have any plans for visiting your friends in France?' he asked, speaking merely to break the uneasy silence.

'Not at the moment,' she replied. 'I keep in touch with them by letter. One day I will pay them a visit, or maybe they will come here. They were very kind to me.'

'Did you like France?' Steven enquired, thankful that he had got her attention.

'Yes, I did. I enjoyed the different way things are done there.'

Alice noticed that Matthew had eased his horse back a pace or two. She did not remark on it, but had a very good idea why he had done so; she had felt his eyes concentrating on her as if he wanted to remember her, as if he were about to say goodbye for ever.

When they reached Wooton Hall, she stopped before the stable yard. She included them both in her gaze as she said, 'Thank you both for your escort duties.' She forestalled any further remark with, 'I'll bid you good day,' and rode into the stable yard.

For a moment the brothers sat still, taken aback by the unexpected dismissal. Matthew accepted it at face value but Steven read more into it than there was. He yanked his horse round and dug in his heels with an urgency that sent the animal surging forward. Matthew let him go and rode steadily home, wishing he had the same length of leave as his brother. But all too soon he must abandon Deepdale and any chance of a reconciliation with their neighbour.

That night, settled comfortably in her bed, Alice's thoughts turned to the brothers. She wondered if there was anything significant in the fact that Matthew came into her mind first. She realised he had changed since their first meeting. Now he was more confident even though he still had a vestige of reserve which held him back from commanding centre-stage as his brother naturally did. Even that held a charm that was not lost on her, but as his image began to assert itself Steven thundered in, with all the charisma of a dashing Army officer who never doubted himself or his effect on her. Comparisons made her restless, knowing that she would come face to face with both of them again. Eventually she fell asleep.

When she came down to breakfast next day her

father announced that he had had a telephone call from his brother in Cornwall inviting them to visit for a fortnight, which he had accepted.

That decision signalled frenzied activity and by midday they were leaving to catch the train to the West Country.

Anticipating that she would have two callers, Alice found time to write two short notes, with instructions for them to be delivered after she had left.

Matthew received her message with disappointment for it left him in limbo, not knowing when he might see Alice again. Steven took his with regret but saw beyond it. This would cut down his time with her before he must return to South Africa. Very well, he decided. He would just have to act decisively when they did meet again.

19

When Emma and her sons arrived they found Robert had not damaged his leg as badly as the doctors had first feared. Nevertheless he must remain at the hospital for some time in order to regain his strength and be secure on his feet again, albeit with the aid of a stick.

Dr Ferby had held that news back from Robert until Emma and their sons were there. For a moment it seemed that he had taken it calmly, but then when he realised the full implications he exploded with rage. 'Stick! Stick! I'm damned well not having a stick. A soldier can't have a stick!'

'Father, it is a case of having to,' put in Steven trying to stem his ranting. 'You'll never manage without one.'

'Have to! How the hell can I march? How the devil can I lead men into battle?'

'You won't be doing either, Father,' put in Matthew.

'What's a whipper-snapper like you know?' Robert glared at his son.

'They are right,' agreed Dr Ferby. 'You must heed what I tell you and what they are saying. You will always have to use a stick. You will have to accept that. If you don't and just sit around feeling sorry for yourself, you will become useless.' He saw Robert's rebellious instincts stir at that word. Before his patient could protest again against what lay ahead, the doctor went on: 'You wouldn't want to be useless, would you? You can still have a long and active life. You have your estate to run; your family around you. Set your mind on that. The rest of your life is in your own hands.'

On Dr Ferby's last remark, Emma, who had remained silent throughout her husband's outburst, stepped closer to the bed and took hold of his hand.

'Don't get yourself worked up,' she said soothingly. 'We are all here to help you. You are strong enough to cope with this and, as the doctor has pointed out, you have Heatherfold to run. You can't turn your back on that.'

Her words, spoken gently, seemed to have their effect because he relaxed back on his pillows with a deep sigh. No one was taken in by this; they knew Robert Cheevey's temperament too well. Over the next few days this hospital room would be a test of his character and ability to cope with the life to come.

He looked round at everyone and said, quietly but firmly, 'Leave me now. There is much for me to think over.' He then directed his gaze at his wife. 'Please come back soon, though.'

Once outside the room, Emma sought to have a word with the doctor. Steven and Matthew were about to move away and let her do so in private, but she stopped them. 'Stay. You should hear the replies to my queries.'

Dr Ferby led them into his room.

'First,' said Emma, 'will Robert definitely have to rely on a stick for the rest of his life?'

'Yes,' came the reply. 'How much use he makes of it is up to him. It can make a great deal of difference to his life, but he's got to be content to use it and not consider what other people may think.'

'But he'll need someone with him too, even if he is just in the garden?'

'It would be advisable, certainly in the early days until his confidence in his own ability strengthens. But the important thing is his mental attitude. Running his estate will be an ideal way to keep him occupied. All of you should encourage him to be in charge of any new developments taking place there. His whole outlook will hinge on what he is capable of doing.'

'And the immediate medical situation?' asked Emma.

'Nothing too complicated. Wounds need to be

dressed and kept under observation. If you are worried about it, I can give you the name of a private nurse who once worked alongside me. I can put you in touch with her, if you would like me to.'

'Please, Doctor.'

'I'll have the information ready for you tomorrow.'

'Thank you. And you already have my gratitude for all you have done for Robert.'

'It has been a pleasure, Madam.' Dr Ferby smiled. 'Your husband was a bit of a cantankerous customer at times but he's an interesting character.'

It was a silent trio who left the hospital, each dwelling on what had happened that morning and the implications for the family. They decided to go to Deepdale for the last few days of Matthew's leave and return with him to London when he was due to rejoin his unit.

That evening, newly arrived in Yorkshire after a long journey, they received a surprise visitor.

'Mr John Smyth,' announced Bannister.

John walked in briskly. 'Hello, everyone,' he said pleasantly. The two young men reciprocated his greeting.

Emma's smile was warm if surprised. She raised her hand, which John took towards his lips. 'This is unexpected,' she said. 'You knew we were going to be in London.'

'Yes, but I had an uneasy feeling that I should be at Deepdale so I acted on it. It has proved to be correct.' He looked keenly at her. 'Is everything all right?'

'Yes.' She waved him to sit down. 'Robert had attempted to get out of bed on his own during the night and fell. Fortunately he was soon found and mercifully they now realise there is no serious damage, but he is being kept in hospital for another week. We decided to come back here for Matthew's last few days.'

John nodded. 'So my feeling that I should be here to see you was right. May I speak with you in private, Emma?'

When her sons made to rise from the table, she quickly gestured to them and said, 'No, no. We can use the small drawing room.'

'John, what is it?' she began with alarm in her voice after he had closed the door.

He waited while she sat down then asked, 'What are your feelings towards Robert now?'

Anguish came into her expression. 'Oh, John, what can I say? How can I explain?'

'Maybe there is no need to. I have a suggestion to make. But first, please answer my question truthfully.'

'I loved him once, but as you know we grew further and further apart thanks to his domineering ways. But now he is badly hurt and...' Tears came into Emma's eyes.

'And now you have doubts about us because you have seen that Robert needs you?' queried John. She gave a little nod. 'And you fear that your helping him will drive us apart?' She nodded again. He continued, 'That need not happen unless we allow it to. I think you and I together are strong enough to see this through. You suggested divorce. I have thought hard about that and believe it is not the answer. I fear it would eventually drive us apart, and the disgrace would compromise Robert's Army career. Can you honestly do that to a man who has served our country well as a courageous and brave officer, and who is the father of your two sons?'

The tears were rolling down Emma's cheeks by now. The question brought an anguished cry from her 'Oh, John, what are we to do? I've found you. You make me happy; you treat me in a way I have not been treated for a long time. John, I love you. Don't try to downplay that because you can't. Please don't walk away from me because you think I should be loyal to Robert. I told you I would divorce him but now you say that could drive us apart.'

'Then are you committed to continuing to live as we do now for ever, with me dividing my time between Kelso and Deepdale? Think carefully about what that would mean.'

Emma looked at him determinedly and said, 'This way means we need not drag our names through the courts. We can keep our arrangement private. Obviously the servants here know our situation, but they are loyal. We don't have many mutual friends who question our way of life and I don't know many people in this area. As for those who do know about us, like the Wares, they seem already to have accepted, up to a point, what we choose to do, so long as we remain discreet.'

'What about Robert and your sons?'

'I think in time they will accept our relationship and things can remain as they are now.'

John replied, 'If you handle things the right way

with Robert, and let him see that your suggestion regarding Heatherfold will work to his advantage, he will accept it because of his love for the house and estate. He will see that Heatherfold will always be in Cheevey hands so long as Steven keeps the line going.'

Emma sat back in her chair reflecting on John's words. So she could never be his wife, something she had longed for. Fresh tears welled in her eyes. He watched her with sympathy and understanding. He knew the enormity of the commitment she must make, to keep things as they were and to let go of her dreams; so many lives would be affected by her decision.

She said quietly, 'John, come here.'

He rose from his chair. Emma remained seated. She held out her arms to him so that he had to kneel in front of her to receive her loving embrace; she held his head close and then released her hold so that he could look into her eyes. He saw love there and a reflection of his for her. Their lips met, sealing the bond that had brought them together and would keep them together but apart for the rest of their lives.

John rose to his feet, held out his hands and helped her from the chair. 'Let's tell Steven and Matthew,' he said. She hesitated. He gave a little smile of encouragement.

'I'll tell them,' Emma said quietly as they crossed the hall.

When they entered the drawing room they found the two young men listlessly playing cards. They stopped immediately, sensing uneasiness in their mother. She sat down on the sofa and John joined her.

'There are several things you ought to know,' Emma announced to her sons. 'I indicated that I would ask your father for a divorce. Though you were shocked, you did not attempt to dissuade me, for which I am grateful. You should now know I will not seek one.' She could sense relief in them both. 'I must tell you that it was John who persuaded me not to. But, I repeat, I will not live at Heatherfold again. John and I will remain together as we are now. Deepdale will be our main home but he will keep his house and office in Kelso. If I need a change of scene I will stay with him there when he is working in Scotland.'

She felt her sons' shock at this announcement but quickly went on to explain their reasoning for choosing this path. They did not relish the idea but knew they would have to accept it if they wanted to see their mother happy.

Emma finished off by saying, 'One thing remains – to tell your father. I will do so when we next visit him. I would like your support. I will also reveal to him the plans to take him home to Heatherfold and the arrangements that will be in place when he gets there.'

Steven raised his head. 'I'll travel back with Father and see him settled.'

'Thank you,' said Emma. 'It will help your father feel that he has not been abandoned completely. Your presence will reassure him, Steven. Be sure to tell him that Matthew supports all the arrangements. I wish both of you still to look upon Heatherfold as your home, though you will always be welcome at Deepdale also.'

As much as she had primed herself for the next visit to Robert, Emma felt a hollow sensation in the pit of her stomach as they travelled to the hospital. She linked arms with Matthew, seeking to bolster her confidence, while Steven paid off the taxi. They were informed at reception that Colonel Cheevey had had a good night.

Emma hoped it was an encouraging sign, but would it make it easier for him to accept what she was about to reveal?

'Good morning, Robert,' she greeted him, trying to make her voice light and easy.

'Good morning, Emma,' he returned politely, but she could not detect any warmth in his expression. 'And to you two.' He nodded to his sons as the three visitors sat down, Emma on the chair closest to her husband.

'You are looking much better,' she observed. 'I think, from what Dr Ferby has said, that you will be able to leave hospital this week.'

'Indeed I shall, if I have anything to do with it,' Robert said. His visitors caught the acerbic note in his voice that was typical of him. 'So please will you get everything ready for my return to Heatherfold?'

Emma recognised this as her cue.

'Everything is in hand,' she said.

'Good, good,' he replied.

'But I won't be coming with you,' she added quietly.

There was a charged silence. 'What! Of course you are!'

'Robert, I am NOT!'

'Don't talk rubbish, woman!' He glanced at his sons as if posing a question, 'What's going on?'

'It is right, Father,' said Matthew. 'Mother has spoken to us about this and we think it is best for both of you,' Steven added.

Robert glared at his son and then directed his gaze on Emma. 'Explain!' he snapped, his eyes bright with hostility.

'I am not coming to Heatherfold. I will never live there again.'

'What the devil...?'

'It is your home, always has been and always will be, but it has never really been mine. For a few fleeting years before the boys went to school, I tolerated it. After that, because of the way in which you wanted me to live, the house became the shell that confined me while you were away with your beloved Army.'

'But...'

'Stop, Robert!' He was jolted into silence by the sharpness of her tone. 'Hear me out and don't make one interruption until I finish! Then you will have the full picture, the reason for what I am doing and how I am able to do it.'

She noted Steven and Matthew edging towards the door and waited until they had left the room, silently thanking them for their discretion in allowing their parents privacy for what was to come. As the door closed, Emma went on to tell her husband what had happened, to allow her to break free and take up a life of her own choosing.

He glared at her. 'When word gets out about that fortune, you'll have opportunists flocking round you. You need me to look after things for you then.'

She gave a little smile. 'Oh, no, Robert, because that means you would take every penny under your control. I would never be any better off; freedom would still be denied me. And don't think you'll ever be able to contest it. I have tied up everything, money and property, so that no one but I can control them.'

'What do you know about doing that?' he asked contemptuously.

'I had good advice from a solicitor, John Smyth, who has offices in York and Kelso. It was he who traced me and told me about my inheritance.'

Robert grunted, 'He'll be lining his own pockets, no doubt.'

'No, he is not. The documents he has drawn up have been vetted by a third party and are water-tight in my favour. No one else can touch any part of my fortune.' Seeing her husband about to protest, Emma stopped him. 'Hear me out,' she said with such urgency that he was silenced. 'There is more you should know because it concerns John.' She went on to tell him of their relationship, of how she'd wanted a divorce but John had talked her out of it.

When she had finished her husband said, 'You have it all worked out, Emma, you are a much more resourceful woman that I had ever imagined.' He sank back on his pillows with a sigh of resignation that spoke of his acceptance of all he had heard. There was nothing he could say to change her mind.

Emma was pleased by his capitulation. But then his tone became harsher.

'Your John,' he said sarcastically, 'has thought everything through so very carefully. Follow his suggestion by all means. But be warned, tongues will wag and the truth will come out. Are you ready to face that?' She nodded. He paused and added softly, 'I tried to give you the kind of love my father gave my mother, and that was good enough for her. I am sorry if there have been times when I was not the husband you wanted me to be.'

Emma leaned closer to him. 'But you never asked what I wanted. I wanted you to love me … really love me.' She took hold of his hand as tears started to pour down her cheeks.

Robert forced a smile. 'Stop crying, Emma,' he told her mildly. 'I tried to love you the only way I knew how. Before you go, let me see you smile like you did on our wedding day.' She did, thinking sadly of all the lost opportunities behind them now.

Then he asked uneasily, 'Our boys will be free to visit both Heatherfold and Deepdale?'

She replied, 'You and I will not intrude on each other's property or in each other's lives, but we are free to write, especially concerning Steven and Matthew.'

There was a short silence until Robert nodded his head in acceptance.

'I see this arrangement is best for all concerned, so the matter is settled. Let us have the boys in again.'

Emma opened the door and signalled to Steven and Matthew to come back. They looked questioningly at her as they walked past, but wanting the next few moments to be Robert's, she gave nothing away.

Their father held out a hand to each of them. When they took it they felt a warmth in his touch they could not remember feeling since childhood. The military aura had for once been subdued. He looked at both of them and said, 'All is settled between your mother and me. Look after her.'

'Yes, Father.'

'Make sure that whenever you marry, you don't make my mistake. We were so happy once. Now it's too late for us.'

Emma had never thought to hear her husband speak like this.

Matthew broke the moment. 'Father, I must say goodbye for the present.' He gripped his father's hand. 'I will think of you in your recovery. No doubt I'll be on my way to Africa before long.'

'Be a good soldier, my son.' His hold on Matthew's hand tightened and he drew his younger son to him. Matthew hid his surprise at this unexpected gesture and returned his father's embrace.

As the door closed behind him, Robert said, 'Now, you two, be off. I need time to think.'

'If that is what you wish.'

'It is. And no doubt you will have much to organise for my move to Scotland.'

Emma assured him, 'We'll organise your journey to Heatherfold, on which Steven will accompany you.'

'Very well. Now off with you.'

As they left the hospital, Steven remarked, 'Father took that better than I thought he would.'

'Being dependent on people, rather than always being in charge, has perhaps opened his eyes to another outlook.'

'But will he remain like that or will Colonel Cheevey return?' queried Steven.

'I think he will now be strong enough to accept there must be changes made in his life. A good start at Heatherfold will make all the difference to his future. See that he settles in well, Steven.'

'I promise, Mother.'

So it was that Steven escorted his father north and found him a good travelling companion, even though at times pain caused Robert to curse what had happened to him in South Africa.

'Home, son, home,' he would sigh when Steven asked if they should pause a while for him to recover.

They had hired an open carriage in Kelso to take them to Heatherfold. When he caught his first glimpse of the house, Robert called to the driver to halt. He sat letting the ecstatic feeling of homecoming fill him and resolved never to leave Heatherfold again.

Three days later Steven sensed his father was ready to be left in the capable hands of Dryden and Mrs Hewlet as well as the nurse Dr Ferby had recommended. Their parting was emotional but accepted by Robert as necessary.

As he returned south to Deepdale, Steven hoped that nothing had prevented Alice from returning to Wooton Hall.

20

Emma was enjoying an afternoon cup of tea with a slice of Cook's fruitbread when there was a knock on the door. The parlourmaid, flushed with excitement to be usurping the butler's job, hurried in.

'Mr Steven is just arriving, Ma'am!' she announced. 'I was crossing the hall and saw him through the window. I thought you'd like to know.'

Emma's heart lifted with elation but she kept her reaction under control. 'Thank you. Please bring in more tea for him.'

She held out her arms to Steven as he came through the front door. He dropped his valise on the floor and embraced her.

'You are looking very chic,' he said as he stepped back to survey her.

'Thank you.'

He shed his overcoat and dropped it on a chair, knowing it and his luggage would soon have been whisked away by one of the footmen. Emma linked arms with him and led him to the drawing room.

'You're just in time for a cup of tea,' she said. 'Did everything go well? Did your father settle?'

'It was a near-perfect trip,' he replied, which brought a sigh of relief from his mother as she sank into her chair. As he enjoyed his tea and cake, he gave her the details of getting Robert settled at Heatherfold.

'Dryden and Mrs Hewlet were a godsend with their welcome and getting him installed ... well, all the staff were, and that made it much easier for me. I took him round the estate by trap. He enjoyed that and enthused about the "old home". It surprised me how readily he took to the change and, although I could tell he was in pain at times, I saw he was resolved to master it and put his disability out of his mind.'

'Good, good.' Emma smiled with relief. 'And the stick?'

Steven laughed. 'He was treating it as an old friend before I left.'

'Excellent! It will be such an asset to him if he continues to use it.'

'I'm sure he will.' After a pause Steven asked, 'How are things here?'

Emma knew that that simple question carried a multitude of enquiries. She quickly enlightened him that all was well between her and John; that life at Deepdale promised to be plain sailing for them as the renovation work was progressing to their liking and John had had a number of new customers, enabling him to take on two more staff in the York office.

'If only Matthew hadn't gone back to his regiment and you were not going to South Africa,' she added.

'I wish it weren't so,' Steven replied, hoping that would bring her a degree of comfort. 'But I'll be back as soon as this war is over. Oh, by the way, are the Wares at home?' he asked, trying to make his question sound casual.

Emma smiled. 'I think you mean, is Alice back?' She added with a little laugh, 'A soldier shouldn't blush.'

'I'm not,' Steven replied indignantly, and then grinned.

'Go and get changed and then off with you. Yes, all the family are back, have been for a few days. Incidentally I met Alice while I was out walking and she asked after you. Very casually, of course. So go at once and let her know you are home.'

'But I've just got back, Mother,' he protested, immediately adding, 'Are you sure you don't mind?'

'Make the most of your time here before the Army whisks you away again.'

He hurried off, light of heart and mind. Steven hummed gently to himself as he rode to Wooton Hall and was even more pleased when the butler announced that only Miss Ware was at home but he would let her know that Captain Cheevey was calling.

Alice greeted him with a smile of pleasure. 'It is lovely to see you again. I understand from your mother that you have been getting your father settled at Heatherfold. How is he?'

'Very well considering the circumstances. His leg played up at times but that was to be expected. It will take time to heal, but he was in good spirits when I left.'

'I hope everything goes well for him.'

'I'm sure it will if he is prepared to let recovery take the time it needs.'

'When did you get back here?'

'About an hour ago.'

'Then shouldn't you be with your mother?'

'Having told me that you had enquired when I would be home, she encouraged me to let you know I'm back, so here I am.'

'That was kind of her.'

'You think you are stealing time that should be my mother's so to ease your conscience I'll leave in a few minutes, after I have asked you if you will have lunch with me in York tomorrow?'

'Tomorrow? Let me think.' Alice pretended to consider, though secretly she was delighted. 'Lunch? Well ... yes, tomorrow will be most acceptable.' She smiled to herself seeing the way relief swept over his face.

'Wonderful! I look forward to it. And now I must away and do your bidding. Farewell.' Steven swept her a bow and she laughed as she waved him off.

Alice's life took on new meaning in the weeks that followed. Steven played ambassador to her court, always attentive to her needs. He was careful to show his consideration for her in the presence of her parents and Nicholas, whom he knew were very protective of her. Steven discovered an exclusive inn in York where they dined on more than one occasion. They explored the countryside of North Yorkshire, walking its lanes hand in hand, wishing that this life would go on for ever. They never mentioned the day of parting, which relentlessly drew nearer.

One day they had had a particularly enjoyable ride together, culminating in a viewpoint on the edge of moorland that stretched ahead of them for miles. Steven swung out of his saddle and held his arms out to help her to the ground.

'What a wonderful vista we've discovered,' Alice commented as she stood beside him.

'Wonderful,' Steven agreed. He leaned closer to her and slid an arm around her shoulders. He bent down, bringing them even closer as he pointed into the distance. 'Look through that tiny gap. Is it the sea?'

She peered in the direction he was pointing. 'Yes, I believe it is.'

They remained as they were for a few minutes, each aware of the strong physical attraction between them.

'I'm burning this place into my mind so I will remember it as the one where I asked Alice Ware to marry me.' Steven did not move for a moment, allowing his proposal to sink in, and then he turned to her for her answer, only to find such a mixture of expressions on her face that he could not define them.

'Well, will you?' he asked. The spell was broken.

'Yes,' answered Alice. She threw her arms around him. 'Yes, Steven, I will, I will!' Her eyes sparkled, dazzling him with her joy.

For one split moment the world stood still, then a torrent of emotions swept over them in a way they had never before experienced, but not a word was spoken; instead, their kisses spoke of a never-ending love.

21

'What do we do now?' asked Alice, still lost in a world of wonder.

'First I must ask your father for your hand.'

Alice's face took on an expression of deep concern. 'Oh, Steven, we won't be able to make all the arrangements in time for us to be married before you return to Africa.'

He held her at arm's length and looked at her earnestly, 'Then come with me and we'll marry there.'

The idea, suddenly sprung on her, took Alice's breath away. She was stunned into silence, pictures of all it would mean racing through her mind.

He took this as a chance to press his case. 'It would be so wonderful, my love. Africa has a magical charm. It would be the perfect setting for our wedding. Our love would blossom like the most delicate flower on the veldt, for you to remember for ever.'

'Oh, Steven, you make it sound breathtaking, how can I resist?'

'Don't. Come with me.'

'Even if I say yes, I don't think my parents would agree. They will want us to wait until you are free from this war.'

'There is only one way to find out.' He took Alice's hand and led her to her horse. He kissed her then helped her on to the saddle. He went to his own horse then, patting it and whispering, 'Bring me luck.'

They rode at a steady pace to Wooton Hall, barely speaking, each lost in this heady experience that would need careful handling if it were to end happily.

A groom came forward to take charge of the horses and the young couple, full of excitement, hurried into the house.

Alice's mother and father looked up from the papers they were reading. 'Hello, you two, did you have a pleasant ride?' asked Lady Cecilia.

'Yes, thank you,' replied Alice. 'We could just see the sea in the distance,' she added in what seemed to be an inane observation considering what was really occupying her thoughts.

Steven, believing it was no good avoiding the moment, said, 'If Lady Cecilia would excuse me, sir, I would like a word with you in private.'

Raymond gave a little cough and said, 'Very well, young man, let us go into the other drawing room.' He stood up and started for the door. Steven cast a hopeful glance at Alice, but all she could do was give him an encouraging nod.

When the door clicked shut behind them, Sir Raymond indicated a chair to Steven, who, although trying to summon his Army training, was feeling nervous. He knew Alice's father had felt his apprehension when he said, with a hint of sympathy, 'Can I get you a whisky?'

'Oh, sir, thank you.' He took the glass gratefully and immediately plunged on. 'I have asked Alice to marry me and she has said yes. I hope, sir, you will give us your approval?'

Sir Raymond did not reply immediately but took a sip of his whisky, watching Steven as he did so. He cleared his throat to reply. 'This is something of a bombshell you have thrown at me. Have you both considered your situations very carefully?'

'In our hearts we know what we want, sir.'

'In other words, neither of you has considered the future as carefully as you should. Steven, you are an Army man, destined soon to leave these shores for Africa. This is a major step in both your lives, but probably more so in Alice's than yours. After all, you are a serving officer; Alice is barely out of school. She is a mature girl but I would have liked her to know and see more of life before she marries. It is only natural that, in this heady time, your judgement is glossed over by your emotions. I think you should wait and see how you both feel when you are separated by the necessity of war.'

'Sir, I love your daughter very much. If that needs to be proved by our enduring a separation, then I am willing to comply with your terms. May I suggest that after three months apart, if you feel Alice and I have fulfilled your wishes, you then give us your blessing?'

Sir Raymond pondered for a few moments before he said, 'Very well,' and extended his hand, which Steven took to seal their agreement.

'Treat her well and look after her when the time comes,' said her father.

'Do not doubt me, sir, I will.'

Raymond nodded and met Steven's steady gaze

with a smile. 'Now drink up and we'll join the ladies.'

Alice had been on tenterhooks ever since Steven had requested the interview with her father.

Lady Cecilia watched her as Alice ceaselessly straightened the fingers of her riding gloves. She looked at her daughter with a wry smile after the door had closed. 'Is that request leading to what I think?'

Alice blushed and nodded. 'I have no doubt your supposition will be correct.'

'Have you thought it through, Alice? You are so young.'

'Mother, how old were you when you married?'

Lady Cecilia gave a little smile. 'You have me there, Alice, no older than you. Even so, consider it carefully. My circumstances were different. You will be marrying an Army man and, if I sense correctly, that career is of great importance to Steven. Army service can lead to long separations.'

'Mother, we love each other so deeply that we can cope with that. It will be a matter of adapting our lives to cope with what is in store for us.'

'That is a sound philosophy but you have to work at it, remember.'

'I know, Mother. We will.'

'Steven will soon be returning to South Africa. We can't get everything arranged for a wedding before then. But let us hear what your father has said to him.'

The moments were tense until the men came in. Alice and her mother looked anxiously at them but could not glean anything from their expressions.

When the two men were seated, Sir Raymond spoke. 'As I expect you know, Steven has asked me if he can marry Alice. I have said yes, but with the proviso that they wait to see if their love will withstand the rigours of the parting that faces them when he returns to Africa.'

'You mean, we have to wait until the next time Steven comes to England on leave? But I want to marry him now,' Alice protested.

'We haven't time to arrange everything before then,' her mother pointed out again. 'It will be far better if you wait.'

Seeing a nervous expression come into Alice's eyes, Steven guessed that she did not want to voice the suggestion he had already made, so he stepped in. 'Sir, Lady Cecilia, because of the time element concerning my return to Africa, I had thought of the possibility that Alice might come to South Africa after a suitable interval and we could marry there.'

They were both thunderstruck by this bold proposal.

'No. Quite impossible,' said Sir Raymond, envisaging the problems and seeing the protests rising to his wife's lips. 'Alice is our only daughter and none of our family could be there; it would a great blow and disappointment to us, especially to Nicholas. And if we said yes, there would still be the problems with getting a passage for her, and you certainly could not make the journey unescorted, Alice.'

'I'm not a child!' she protested, though she

202

knew they were right.

'We know you are not but we have to look at every angle, and I don't think it wise for you to travel all that way alone.'

'Sir,' put in Steven, 'if I could find a way round the problem of the passage, would that enable you to agree to our marrying in South Africa?'

'I am not promising anything. Don't misunderstand us, Steven, we have nothing against you; it is the circumstances that worry us. I'm sure waiting a while longer won't destroy the love you have for each other. In fact, it may strengthen it. Go away and think things over. I believe that is the best course for both of you, and I think you should look to marry on your return to England, Steven, when this war is over. From reports, I believe that won't be too long.'

Recognising the stance her mother and father were taking, without its being an outright refusal, Alice knew it was no good trying to persuade them further. She glanced at Steven and gave a little shake of her head.

'Sir, Lady Cecilia, I thank you for your consideration. May I ask for one concession? If the war looks like lasting longer than expected, would you sanction our marriage then and allow it to take place in South Africa? In our love for each other we don't want to wait, we wish to be married as soon as possible, so that not one minute of our life together is wasted. As a soldier I hope I will live to see the war draw to a close, but if not Alice would be well taken care of with regards to money.'

The silence that followed this was broken by

Alice's, 'Please. Oh, please, say yes.'

The anguished pleading in her tone tugged at her mother's heartstrings. Lady Cecilia also saw, in her husband's expression, his desire to bring happiness to their daughter. She gave an almost imperceptible nod, which only he could interpret.

'Very well. Your mother and I will agree to that, so long as we may stipulate the timing.'

'I agree to that, sir,' said Steven quickly, not wanting to jeopardise his case.

'Very well,' returned Sir Raymond.

Steven stepped forward and they shook hands, sealing the agreement.

Alice, with tears of joy streaming down her cheeks, embraced her mother. 'Thank you, thank you, for making me so happy.' She turned to her father then. 'You are the best father in the world, I do love you.' At the same moment Steven was saying, 'Lady Cecilia, thank you. I will be certain to make your daughter happy.'

She smiled. 'Be sure that you do. We want Alice to be safe as well as happy.'

'I know. I promise she'll be both with me.'

Steven held out his hand to Alice. When she took it, he drew her to his side and gave her a quick kiss. 'Sir, Ma'am, I thank you for your patience and understanding. Now I will take my leave and break this wonderful news to my mother. I must write to my brother too.'

22

After Steven had left, Alice did not waste a moment before she said, 'I must tell Nicholas!'

'You'll probably find him in the glasshouse,' her father called after her.

Her parents laughed at Alice's quick exit.

'We certainly made her happy in spite of our stipulation,' said Lady Cecilia, 'but it was a sensible thing to do. I hope the war ends soon and that our troops are brought home, then we can have the wedding here.'

'I entirely agree with you but don't pin your hopes too high yet,' Raymond warned. Seeing a thoughtful expression come over his wife's face, he asked, 'What now?'

She considered a moment longer, then said, 'If it comes to it and we have to keep our promise to allow the wedding to take place in South Africa, we could send Nicholas as Alice's escort. That would mean our family would be represented.' A silence settled over them, to be broken by Lady Cecilia's question: 'That is, if you can spare him?'

Startled out of his thoughts, Sir Raymond said, 'Er … yes. Yes, of course. It's a good idea. Nicholas and Alice have always been close. Certainly he can be absent from the estate. I can take on some of his work and the rest can be shared among the staff. Splendid, splendid! But we will keep this idea to ourselves for the time being, until we see how our stipulation is working.'

They had just made this agreement when the door was flung open and Alice and Nicholas rushed in.

'Alice has told me her exciting news,' said Nicholas. 'I'm so pleased for her. I do like Steven; they make a splendid couple. Are we having a celebration? Of course we are! We must! Before Steven has to go back...' Nicholas's enthusiasm boiled over, bringing laughter from them all.

'All right, we will,' his father agreed, calming the excitement.

'I'll see Mrs Cheevey and arrange for the family to come here when it is convenient for us both,' said Lady Cecilia.

Meanwhile at Deepdale Steven went to his room and wrote a letter:

Dear Matthew,

No doubt after recognising my writing on the envelope you wondered why I was writing to you. You and I have not been very good correspondents, only just managing to keep in touch. I write now because I have some exciting news to tell you – Alice and I are engaged to be married!

No doubt you've read those words again to make sure you weren't dreaming. I assure you, it is true. You are probably saying to yourself, 'There's so much to do before a wedding, they won't have time to marry before he has to return to South Africa.' That is also true, so we have decided to wait a while. Mother and Alice's parents wanted us to wait until the war is over, but without going into detail, sufficient to say that we came to an understanding that, in certain circum-

*stances, we could marry in South Africa. That is how
the situation stands at the moment. We are all happy
about it.*

*Be glad for us, Matthew, and wish us all the luck in
the world for a long life together.*

Steven

For a considerable time Matthew sat staring at
the words his brother had written. His mind
ranged back to the days he and Alice had shared
before Steven had arrived from South Africa with
their father. Steven had no doubt seized his
chances while his brother was tied up with duties
dictated by the Army life he did not like, and
which he had only entered to satisfy his father's
wishes. He cursed his own negative attitude;
always standing back and letting others seize the
chances life offered. He had let Alice dictate the
terms of their romance. Why had he not made his
deep feelings for her known? Tight-lipped, he
walked out of the house, leaving a sealed envelope
on the hall table, ready for posting.

'What's worrying you, my dear?' asked Raymond
as he and his wife prepared for bed that same
night.

Seated, she looked at him in the mirror of her
dressing table as she paused with the hairbrush
held in the air. 'It's not really worry, so much as
disappointment.'

'Disappointment?'

'Yes. I always dreamed of a big society wedding
for my children. I imagined a glorious sunny day,
a beautiful bride dressed in the finest silk and lace,

207

bridesmaids in pink and blue, the men smart in their frock-coats or uniforms, everyone in a happy mood as they came out of York Minster with its bells loudly ringing. All of us ready to be driven away together, everyone mingling happily. Now the arrangements that are the prerogative of the bride and her mother may have to be rushed, and our only daughter is more than likely to marry, with little celebration, thousands of miles away.'

Raymond came behind her and slipped his arms round her shoulders. He bent down and kissed her neck. 'Don't fret, my love. You may yet get your wish. We will just have to make the best of whatever happens.'

She rose to her feet, turned to him and slid her arms round his neck. Her eyes, fixed on his, made no attempt to disguise the deep love she felt for him.

'You are a wise man, Raymond.'

'No,' he replied, 'maybe sensible, but far from wise.'

'However you see yourself, I think I know you better. And I love you very much.'

'You look as if you've got the cream instead of the milk this morning,' said Emma as she came into the dining room and found Steven already at the table.

He blew her a kiss. 'Haven't I a right to? I'm about to go and see the most wonderful girl in the world.'

'How would I know if Alice fits that description?' laughed his mother as she sat down.

She accepted the bowl of porridge that the

maid brought her. Steven helped himself to warm kippers from the chafing dish.

'So you are going to see Alice?'

'Yes, Mother. Isn't that natural?'

'Of course it is, especially as it won't be too long before you are leaving us. I have had one thought that you might consider: maybe you should think about going to tell your father of your engagement. He shouldn't be left out of any family matters such as this.'

'Of course, you are right, Mother. I must arrange it.'

'I'll have a word with John if you would like me to. I know he is going to Kelso in the next day or two. I'm sure you could stay with him. It would be very convenient especially if you're taking Alice for your father to meet his prospective daughter-in-law.'

'I'll do it myself. You're still trying to hold my hand.' Though the rebuke was mild it stung, but his mother held back the retort that stirred her thoughts. She had been surprised by Alice's choice, having expected her to choose the gentler, more easy-going Matthew, but who was she to interfere?

Emma smiled apologetically. 'I'm sorry. I'm your mother. I suppose I always shall.'

After getting Sir Raymond and Lady Cecilia's approval, Alice and Steven accompanied John to Kelso two days later. They were greeted by John's butler and housekeeper, who saw to having three beds made up and the house settled for their short stay.

Waking the next morning, Steven was pleased to find the weather good. He wanted Alice to see Heatherfold Hall looking particularly attractive; after all, as eldest son he would inherit, and one day she would live here.

At breakfast John informed them that he had hired a trap for them. 'I did not engage a driver. I thought you would remember the way from your last visit, Steven, and that you would rather be on your own. Use this house as you will and come and go as you please. Any questions?'

'I think not,' replied Steven. He looked enquiringly at Alice.

'None from me either,' she said, 'but I would like to thank Mr Smyth for his hospitality and generosity.'

He waved away the thanks. 'My pleasure,' he said. 'I will be in Kelso the rest of the day and all tomorrow. The next day I will be back to Deepdale. Now, if you'll excuse me, I will be away to meet my client. I'll see you this evening.'

An hour later, Steven took the reins and drove the trap until their progress was stopped by ornate iron gates suspended from two sturdy pillars surmounted by stone eagles.

'They are magnificent,' commented Alice as they awaited the gatekeeper.

'Father had them carved by a local stonemason for my tenth birthday.'

'What a wonderful present.'

The gatekeeper appeared from the lodge and swung the gates open. He touched his cap and called out, 'Welcome home, Captain.'

'Thank you, Mac. Only a short visit this time.'

Steven set the trap in motion, calling out, 'One day we'll be back for good.' Mac's eyes took in Alice. Steven smiled at her. 'That will set tongues wagging.'

The snaking drive took them between thick banks of rhododendrons, unfortunately no longer in flower.

'When are we going to see the house?' asked Alice.

'Two bends and it will burst upon you,' replied Steven.

Alice realised how telling the phraseology he used was because, when they negotiated the second bend, the sight of the red sandstone house hit her full force even though it was still a little way off. Alice felt it was reaching out to her, inviting her to embrace its serenity. The mullioned windows told of age and, coupled with the solid strength of the walls, of a determination to remain impregnable.

'I love it,' she said quietly.

He slid his arm around her shoulders. 'I'm glad you do.'

She turned her head towards him. 'I'm pleased you are glad.'

'And that makes me happy.' He leaned over and kissed her. As he started to break the kiss she held him back, tempting him to linger. He needed no further bidding and passion heightened.

'We should go,' gasped Steven, making the first move.

'No!' Her voice was sultry and charged with tension. He could not resist and was soon lost again.

211

When he parted from her, he gasped, 'I love you, Alice Ware. I'm so pleased you are to be my wife. It can't come soon enough for me.'

'Be patient, Captain. It will be worth all the more for waiting.'

He picked up the reins, flicked them and sent the horse forward.

A man leaning on a stick stepped out of the house on to the flagged terrace and moved forward to rest against the balustrade.

'Father!' said Steven.

'Oh, my goodness. Steven, do you think he could see...'

Steven cut the question off with a laugh. 'What does it matter if he did?'

'But what would he think of me?'

'I don't suppose he'll ever say.' Steven called to the horse and they drove on, knowing all the time that the nearer they drew, the closer the scrutiny became.

As Steven drew to a halt his father straightened up and called out, 'Now, who have we here?'

'Hello, Father.' Steven jumped to the ground. He turned to help Alice from the trap. 'Father, I want you to meet my fiancée, Alice Ware.'

'Oh!' Robert Cheevey's surprise was evident, not only in his tone of voice but also in the expression that had come over his face. 'Do I know her?' he blustered.

'No, sir,' put in Alice quickly. 'We have never met. You may well have heard of our family name, Ware. We have the Wooton Estate that borders Deepdale in North Yorkshire.'

'Yes,' he said sharply as if he wanted to dismiss

thoughts of that from his mind. 'My wife acquired it when I was in South Africa fighting the bloody Boers – oh, sorry, Miss. I apologise for my language, but they left me having to use this.' He shook his walking stick.

'I'm sorry about that, sir,' replied Alice calmly. She gave a little smile. 'I was convent-educated, I've heard worse language from my fellow pupils.'

Robert laughed. 'No doubt! Now come along inside. We'll let my housekeeper know you are here and how long you are staying.'

'We are not staying, Father,' put in Steven. 'We arrived yesterday, are visiting you today and re-turning home tomorrow. We did not want to cause any upheaval for you when you are just getting settled. Mr Smyth was coming to Kelso on business so we took his offer of accommodation.'

Robert grunted and accepted the explanation. Seeing his frown, Alice stepped closer to him and linked arms. 'There'll be another time,' she said gently. 'Let us make the most of today.'

He smiled and patted her hand. 'A wise girl.'

The rest of the day went well. Though it was a struggle for him at times, Robert enjoyed show-ing Alice his ancestral home and, using their trap, letting her discover the beauties of the area in which he lived. As the day went on he could not disguise his growing admiration for the girl and chose a moment when he and Steven were alone to say, 'You have found a remarkable fiancée, Steven. Treasure her.'

When the time came for them to say goodbye, he added to this earlier declaration. 'Steven, tell your mother that I approve of Alice.'

213

'I will, Father.'

He turned to Alice. 'I hope I have not bored you with our tour of Heatherfold?'

'Of course you haven't. It was good to see how much you love it.'

'I hope that my love for it continues to thrive in you, because one day Steven, as my eldest child, will inherit and it will be your home.'

Alice glanced at Steven, read his expression, then said to his father, 'You can be assured Heatherfold will be safe in the hands of the Cheeveys for a long time to come.'

There were tears in Colonel Cheevey's eyes as he watched the trap drive away. He remained standing there long after it was lost to view.

23

Two days later an Army dispatch rider arrived at Deepdale Manor.

'Is this Captain Cheevey's residence?' enquired the corporal.

'It is,' replied the butler.

'Is he at home?'

'He is. Step inside and I will tell him you are here.'

In a few minutes, Steven came hurrying into the hall. 'Good day, Corporal.'

The man came to attention.

'Stand easy,' said Steven.

'Sir,' the corporal acknowledged Steven's order

and started unfastening a pouch that was fixed to a belt around his waist. He withdrew an envelope and held it out. 'I had to deliver this to you personally, sir.'

Steven took it with mixed feelings. The envelope must contain something of importance for a dispatch rider to be sent with it. He took the envelope, opened it and moved nearer a window to read it. He did so quickly, frowning with annoyance. He looked at the corporal. 'Anything else?'

'Just for you to sign this order to say that I have delivered and you have read it, sir.'

With annoyance running through him, Steven scribbled his name and handed it back. 'Corporal, you must be thirsty. Take the door in the corner.' Steven nodded to it. 'Then down the corridor, second door on the right, take the steps and you'll find the kitchen. Tell them to give you a drink and whatever else you'd like.'

'Thank you, sir.' The corporal turned smartly and headed for the door Steven had indicated.

He read the communication once more. 'Damn, damn, damn!' he declared, then hurried to the drawing room.

His mother looked up when the door was flung open harder than usual. 'Good gracious, what's bitten you?' she said, hoping the dark cloud that covered his face would be driven away.

He said nothing but crossed the floor to hand her the piece of paper he had just received. She read it quickly, then looked at him and said quietly, 'Steven, what will be, will be. You've just got to accept it. It's no good letting it get to you.'

'I know,' he said petulantly. 'But wanting me on board ship in two days' time is rather short notice, and coming now, just when Alice and I have got engaged...'

'I know but you have some consolation in that letter – notification of your promotion to major.'

'Dead man's shoes, no doubt,' offered the peeved, newly promoted officer. He shrugged his shoulders. 'I suppose I'd better go and break the news to Alice.'

'The sooner the better, then you can plan your time together before you have to go.'

'Miss Alice is on the terrace,' the butler told Steven when he arrived at Wooton Hall.

Steven found her leaning on the balustrade, looking across the fields deep in thought. She turned on hearing footsteps.

'Steven!' Her face filled with brightness, but it faded quickly when she added, 'What's wrong? You look so grumpy.'

'So I should!' He thrust the envelope towards her.

Puzzled, she took it and extracted the sheet of paper. A cold finger touched her heart when she saw the message was on official Army paper. As she read it the chill spread over her. 'Oh, no!' she whispered. 'Why do they want you in Africa so soon?'

'How do I know?' replied Steven, an edge to his voice.

'Is it to do with the fact that you are being promoted to major?'

'It could be, if the casualties have been higher

than expected.'

'Well, over that we have no control. I can only say, "Congratulations, darling."' She ran her hands up to his shoulders and kissed him. 'Well done.'

He held her to him and looked lovingly into her eyes. 'I was hoping for a lot more of those, Alice, but this damned recall has put paid to that.'

'I'm disappointed too, but...' Then she added brightly, 'It might enable our marriage to take place earlier rather than later.'

'I don't see how. After all, your mother and father were more than keen to put a time limit on when our wedding could take place.'

'That was just to test us – make us think about how being apart would affect our love for one another.'

'Well, I can tell them that it won't change anything for me, but now I'm having to leave you to try and convince them...'

'And that task is in safe hands,' she replied with conviction. She stopped his retort with a kiss. 'We can't change the military mind nor your orders, so let us make the most of our time together. Forget about the separation to come. I'll think of some way to break down Mother's and Father's reservations.'

'It will have to be something pretty powerful,' said Steven gloomily.

Neither of them could have anticipated exactly how Alice would come to gain her wish.

Steven came to make his goodbyes at Wooton Hall. Everyone tried to make light of it but with the shadow of war hanging over them all, it was not easy.

Steven and Alice managed to snatch a few minutes alone. He took her in his arms. 'No tears, my love.'

She nodded but had to fight hard to hold them back. She bit her lip and said brokenly, 'Take care, Steven. I'll do my best to make Mother and Father see things our way and let me come to you soon.'

'I know you will. Look after yourself. Think of me. Remember I love you so much. The world will stand still until we meet again, when I will hold you in my arms and say three little words that mean so much.'

He held her tight and let his lips reveal everything he felt. They parted and he strode away. Sir Raymond and Lady Cecilia with Nicholas came out of the house to join Alice. Not wanting to intrude on her sorrow, no one spoke.

Steven reached his horse, turned and raised his hand. They all waved back. Alice caught her mother's whisper, 'God go with you.'

Two days later Steven stood on the deck of the *Thelma*, a passenger ship leaving Southampton or South Africa, and watched England being left behind as she sailed down the Solent and the English Channel. He raised his hand in salute to an imaginary Alice watching him depart as he saw the coastline disappear beyond the white-flecked waves. A deep sigh escaped his lips. He left the rail and walked slowly back to his cabin.

Twenty days later, after spending much of his

time between the deck and the lounge, he stood in the same place and watched Table Mountain rise majestically from the shore, throw off its early-morning misty shroud and reflect the glorious sunshine. His lips tightened as he wished Alice could have seen this majestic display as an introduction to her new life here beside him.

As a military man, with documents showing that he was heading north to Pretoria, he was escorted quickly, through the crowds of people milling around the station, to a reserved compartment in a waiting train.

Knowing that the development of a rail network had been slow and hampered by the war, Steven settled himself to a slow journey. It proved a wise attitude but nevertheless he was thankful when he reached his destination, the busy expanding town of Pretoria.

Here, after reporting to Army headquarters, he learned that the war was turning very much in Britain's favour and that the conclusion was stacked heavily against the Boers, though many of them were still determined to fight on. Life in the countryside and towns could remain dangerous especially as Boer feelings against the British still ran high. It made him wonder if Sir Raymond and Lady Cecilia had been right in wanting him and Alice to wait until the war was over and he was back in England. He quickly dismissed that thought however. Encourage it and how long would it be before he and Alice were married? Besides, there were military wives already here in South Africa and he was finding them resolute in the opinion that they should be beside their husbands.

He wrote to Alice:

My darling,

At last I am settled in Pretoria and, at the present time, it looks as though my duties will keep me here in Army Headquarters for this region. The fighting against the Boers is very much in our favour now, and I see no reason to doubt that you will be safe here. There are a number of wives at this place and they seem to get on very well with each other. They know the dangers of war but here in Pretoria those are not countenanced and they lead a very active social life. I am sure you will settle very quickly into it and, as the war progresses in our favour, you will have more freedom to pursue your own likes and interests.

I hope these words will help you in your effort to persuade your parents to allow you to come here to be married at the earliest possible time.

I need you here, my love. The distance between us is too great. We should be together.

You are ever in my thoughts.

I love you,

Steven

P.S. I have just heard that our leaves to England are being cancelled for the foreseeable future. As well as that, my case was deemed exceptional. The fact that I accompanied my father to England and was there for a considerable time has been counted as leave, so that means it will be two years before I will be in England again, unless circumstances change and they may not. Even if the war is over, this land will still need the presence of a military force. I point all this out to

provide you with additional means of persuasion.
Again,
Love,
Steven

Nicholas came in via the back door so that he could change his outdoor working boots before going through to the dining room to have lunch with Alice, their parents having gone into York. As he came through the hall he stopped to examine the letters that had been left on the table. Recognising the writing on the envelope that he now held in his hand but not finding Alice awaiting him in the dining room, he looked out on to the terrace.

His sister was engrossed in a book. He called out, 'Alice, lunch.' She gave him a little wave of acknowledgement without looking up. 'There's a letter for you!'

He sounded so convincing that she dropped her book as she sprang up from her seat. Then a thought struck her and she challenged him with an emphatic, 'if you are teasing, I'll get my own back!'

He laughed. 'Would I do that when it's from *him?*' He waved the envelope in the air.

She rushed to him and grabbed at the envelope but Nicholas pulled it away. She stamped her foot and glared at him. 'It's mine!'

'Say please!'

She tightened her lips in exasperation then said, 'Come on, Nicholas. It's the first letter from Africa, the one I've been waiting for.' Laughing, he handed it over. She flopped on to her chair at the dining table and slit the envelope open. She read quickly and avidly, ignoring for the time being the oxtail soup that had been placed in front of her by the maid.

'Well?' he enquired.

'It was a long journey. Steven's well and is in Pretoria.'

'Is there anything about the war?'

Alice glanced at the letter. 'Yes. We are winning but Steven hints that it might be a while before peace returns fully. He has added something afterwards.'

She read his postscript out loud to her brother.

'So it looks as if your wedding is going to have to wait a while longer,' Nicholas commented.

'Not if I can help it,' Alice said defiantly. 'This puts a different perspective on things. Mother and Father will have to withdraw their condition that we wait. It will disappoint Mother's desire for a big wedding, but she'll just have to get used to it.'

'Why can't we all go to South Africa?' said Nicholas. 'Our parents might be more agreeable now that Steven says things are easier there.'

Alice gave a little laugh. 'They just might, we'll see.'

24

'Cecilia, you are quiet.' She knew from the way her husband commented on it that he required a reason why she had barely spoken during their lunch in York.

She tightened her lips, but knew she might as well tell him now otherwise he would keep on asking until he had forced it out of her. He would say 'a trouble shared is a trouble halved,' which would annoy her; and what she had overheard in York had greatly distressed her.

He leaned towards her on the back seat of the taxi and patted her hand. 'Come on, tell me what upset you.'

'I suppose it could be nothing or something, but it is the repercussions there might be for us that worry me.' She paused as if to gather her thoughts.

'For us? From what?' he prompted.

'Something I overheard.'

'Ah, you shouldn't listen to gossip.'

'But this had fact behind it, and there could be poison too if it is spread around. I have no doubt that it will if my judgement of the two ladies whose conversation I overheard this morning is correct.'

'Real gossips, eh? Ready with tittle-tattle. Did you know them?'

'No, but there was some truth in what they were saying.'

'So you knew what or who they were discussing?'

'Yes. Mrs Cheevey and Mr Smyth.'

'Ah, I see.' He nodded his head slowly.

'They had their facts right and were condemning our neighbours for "living in sin" as they put it. They knew little about John except that he is a solicitor, but were of the opinion that it would damage his business. They were quite ferocious in their attitude towards Emma, declaring that she certainly would be snubbed by many of their friends. It was this statement that particularly upset me. Our daughter is hoping to marry one of Emma's sons. When that becomes known, are we to be shunned too because of our association with her?'

'If people treat us so badly then they cannot consider themselves friends.'

'But there are strong views where divorce is concerned. More often than not it is the woman who suffers most. It is she at whom the finger of blame is pointed. Society is very unforgiving when conventions are flouted.'

'We have never witnessed anything we can actually criticise Emma for; she has always been charming, and I can honestly say that I will always regard her and John as friends. Yes, divorce is unpleasant, but we have got to place our friendship to the fore because of Alice. Anything we can do to prevent Emma and John's situation from harming the Cheevey family and ours must be done.'

'I am pleased to know that is what you think because there was something else. One of them knew of Alice's association with Steven, or as she put it, "The Wares' daughter surely wouldn't think of marrying the son of a divorcee?" That made me think gossip will certainly flow when the marriage is announced and I should hate the young ones to be damaged by it.'

'Surely sensible people would not condemn our daughter's marriage because of Emma's way of life?' Raymond pointed out.

'People's tongues can be hurtful, especially when gossip is exaggerated and gets out of hand.

'What I overheard led me to give serious thought to the wedding. If we were to attend, even long-standing friends could point the finger and shun us for condoning it. That would upset Alice and Steven.'

'But...'

'Let me finish. I had always visualised a splendid wedding for our daughter, but I don't want it to be spoiled by people's prejudice. I suggest we talk to Alice, put all these facts to her, and tell her we will allow her to get married in South Africa, but that we ourselves will not be there except in spirit. That way, no one can say we are condoning the wedding and there will be no complications for Alice and Steven. Nicholas can be Alice's escort to South Africa, and he can give her away. I don't think the gossips will bother about that.'

Raymond did not answer his wife immediately. It was rare for him to look so solemn, but Cecilia recognised he was deep in thought and maintained her silence too. She waited. After a few minutes he gave a little cough.

'I go along with what you are suggesting. I think you have taken a very wise course, which will counteract whatever the gossips stir up, especially if we stand firm on this change of plan.'

'We had better contact Emma before we reveal our decision to Alice and Nicholas,' said Cecilia. 'If Emma has any objections to the wedding taking place in South Africa, we will have to think again.'

Lady Cecilia had to wait two days before she could seize the opportunity of Alice and Nicholas being invited to an evening birthday party with an overnight stay at Westwold House, set in the splendour of the Yorkshire Wolds. She wrote to Emma, inviting her and John to visit that same evening when Alice and Nicholas would be absent from Wooton Hall, an invitation that Emma was pleased to accept.

When their guests' arrival was announced, Lady Cecilia and Sir Raymond hurried into the hall to greet them. Soon they were settled comfortably in the drawing room with pre-dinner drinks and pleasant conversation passing between them.

Judging the moment to be appropriate, Lady Cecilia said, 'I am going to come straight to the point of inviting you here this evening.' She left a little pause, then seeing she had their rapt attention went on, 'We are going to approve of Alice and Steven marrying in South Africa, but only if you agree with the plan.'

There was a moment of complete silence as the implications of this hit home with Emma, but her response expressed only delight. 'I'm so very, very pleased,' she said. She glanced at John and noticed his smile, which she could only interpret as one of approval. 'You can take it that we both entirely support your decision, as I am sure Robert will too,' Emma confirmed. 'I will send word to him once Alice and Steven are told.'

'I am joyful for them. They will make a handsome couple and I'm sure they will be very happy together,' John supported her.

'I think this deserves another drink to celebrate and to toast the health of the two young people,' said Raymond, rising from his chair.

By the end of the evening an understanding had been reached that would cement their friendship and the two women were in complete agreement regarding the things that had to done, even though the wedding would take place thousands of miles away.

Once Alice and Nicholas had returned from Westwold House the following day and regaled their parents with the local news they had picked up at the party, their father said, 'We are pleased you had an enjoyable time and are glad to hear that our friends are all well. Now, we have some important news for you.' He looked at Cecilia in a way that told her she should have the privilege of disclosing it.

'To come straight to the point, Alice, we have decided that you can marry Steven in South Africa.'

She could hardly believe what she was hearing. Was her mother's statement really true, or were these words the result of her own wishful thinking?

Seeing her dumbstruck, Lady Cecilia added softly, 'It's true, darling,' and added for confirmation, 'you can travel out and marry him soon.'

Excitement made Alice breathless. She leaped

from her chair and hugged her mother. 'Oh, thank you, thank you!' She turned to her father then and kissed him on the cheek, again crying out her thanks.

Overwhelmed by the unexpected news, Nicholas embraced his sister.

They both turned to their parents, looking for an explanation for this momentous change of heart.

'Sit down,' said their father.

He told them what Cecilia had overheard in York and how, after due consideration, this had led them to change their minds about the wedding.

'The one drawback is,' said Lady Cecilia, 'that we shall not be attending the wedding.'

'But, Mother, you have to!' cried Alice.

'Nicholas can go. He will be your escort to South Africa and give you away.'

With damp eyes, Lady Cecilia explained, 'Vicious tongues will still brand you, and us, as being tainted by Emma's conduct – a married woman living with an unmarried man, albeit a widower. We don't want to cancel the wedding and destroy your happiness, so if we don't attend the ceremony it will look to those mischief-makers as if we disapprove of the marriage and they will have no grounds for further malice.'

'I can see by your expressions that you think we should ignore their attitude,' said Sir Raymond, 'but it is not so easy as that. Such things are not easily forgotten, and if friends start to cut us out of their lives it could lead to much unpleasantness and unease that will be hard to set aside. If we don't attend the wedding, people can hardly point the finger.'

'But what about Steven's mother?' asked Nicholas.

'She accepted our explanation as to why we are doing this. Blaming herself, she felt both sad and grateful, but is sure this decision is the right one. It has all worked out well in the end.'

'There will be a lot to do,' Lady Cecilia warned, 'even though there will be no arrangements to make here regarding the service. But there will be your passages to South Africa to book, your dress, Alice, your trousseau and your wardrobe for Africa. You must write to Steven straight away.'

My dearest one,

I write with joyful news. My parents have given me permission to marry you in South Africa!

WONDERFUL!

By the time you get this letter, arrangements will hopefully have expedited that wonderful day. I hope you will accept this news without asking for details of how and why it has happened. Sadly, as much as they want to, my parents will not be attending. The reasons are good ones. They have nothing to do with you, but to spare us any embarrassment, because of certain social pressures, they have decided a wedding in South Africa will be best for all of us. Your mother approves of it, as no doubt she will tell you.

Let us now be happy in our good fortune.

Take care, my love.

Oh, I nearly forgot. Nicholas will be my escort to South Africa and will give me away when we marry.

Your ever-devoted,

Alice.

P.S. Will Matthew be your best man?

25

When Alice woke the next morning there was joy in her heart because of the unexpected change of attitude towards what she saw as the biggest event in her life. She could only be happier on the day that she would say 'I will' to Steven. As she hugged herself with delight, thoughts of Matthew crept into her mind. Should she write to him, expressing her pleasure that she would soon be his sister-in-law? She lay for a few minutes considering this question and finally decided that she would do it immediately she was ready for the day.

Her lady's maid knew the symptoms of high excitement and lost no time in assisting Alice to dress. Once she had had her breakfast she excused herself and returned to her room, opened her secretaire, took up her pen, and wrote:

Dear Matthew,
    You will no doubt have heard the news from your mother that Steven and I are to marry. The wedding is to take place in South Africa, for a variety of reasons with which I will not bore you here. Suffice to say that I am tremendously happy and I hope you will be delighted for me, give your blessing to our marriage, and remain my dearest friend.
    Alice

She re-read the words, decided she had said all

she needed to, and sealed the letter for posting.

Four days later she received a reply.

Dear Alice,

Of course I am happy for you. I always will be. I once harboured hopes of winning you myself but, when Steven arrived, I realised I didn't stand a chance. You and he will make the ideal couple. Marrying a man of superior Army rank and heir to the Heatherfold Estate gives you much to be thankful for. I look forward to being your brother-in-law. Please let me know when you will be at home so that we can start cementing that relationship.

I look forward to seeing you again.

Respectfully,

Matthew

As she put the letter back in the envelope and deposited it in the drawer of her dressing table, Alice was thankful that nothing too serious had passed between them. She felt a strange sort of freedom in the thought that her wedding would soon take place on a different continent.

Two days later, when Sir Raymond had left his wife and daughter to finish their breakfast while he and Nicholas headed for the York cattle market, Lady Cecilia produced a sheet of paper and smoothed it out beside her empty plate.

'Alice, I have made a list of things we should start seeing to. We want to avoid any late decisions. Inevitably there will be last minute arrangements but we want to make those as few as possible. Hopefully your father and Nicholas will find time today to get information on sailings for South Africa. Top of my list is for you to make a decision about your lady's maid. Are you going to ask Stella if she would like to accompany you?'

'I would very much like to have her with me. And that way I would feel I had a link with you and home.'

'Good, I'm pleased you think like that. You will be moving into a strange new world and to have someone dependable there with you should help you settle more easily. And remember, Stella could be a valuable support when Steven is away on Army matters as he is bound to be. So if you are sure, let us ask her.'

Stella gaped and gulped when the question was put to her. She had known Alice was going to marry in South Africa and had thought that would be an end to her service with the Ware family.

'Oh, M'Lady, Miss.' She looked from one to the other. Her throat tightened and her eyes dampened. 'I thought I wouldn't be wanted any more. I didn't know what I would do. I have no one of my own, You have been my family ever since you took me in and trained me to be Miss Alice's lady's maid.'

'So you would like to come with me?' said Alice.

'Yes, please, Miss.'

'Then you shall.'

'Oh, thank you, thank you.' Stella's eyes were bright as she said, 'When do you want me to pack, Miss?'

Mother and daughter smiled.

'Slow down, Stella, we aren't going tomorrow.

There is a lot to do before we sail.'

'Did you have a good day?' Lady Cecilia asked Sir Raymond when he and Nicholas returned from York.

'Interesting, but we didn't buy anything. There was nothing in the class of cattle we wanted,' he told her. 'We did however find time to check on sailings to South Africa. We can get passages four weeks tomorrow from Southampton, sailing in *Orion's Star*.'

'I've read about that ship,' said Alice, excitement sparkling in her eyes. 'There was publicity because she's new to the Star Line.'

'The latest in luxury,' put in Nicholas, 'and the newest engines so she should do the voyage in seven or eight days.'

'Wonderful,' said Alice.

'Did you make a booking?' asked Lady Cecilia.

'I've put our names down with the shipping agent. Told him that we require two separate cabins, first class, with every convenience.'

'Good,' Lady Cecilia approved, 'but you will need another cabin too. Alice was keen for Stella still to fill the role of her lady's maid. Stella has accepted.'

'Good, I'm delighted about that,' said Sir Raymond. 'So now you have a deadline to work to. You should be ready to leave Wooton Hall and the place of your birth within the month.'

'Oh, Father, don't sound so mournful. You'll have Mother and me weeping. We aren't going to the moon.'

He gave a weak smile. 'I know, love, but I don't

like losing my little girl. There's a big world out there.'

'She'll cope with it,' said Nicholas reassuringly.

The next day Alice had had her morning cup of hot chocolate served on the terrace and had settled to enjoy it when the sound of hooves made her turn to identify the rider. Matthew gave her a wave and turned his horse in her direction. By the time he reached her, Alice had called for a maid to bring another cup of chocolate for their visitor.

'Thank you,' he said, swinging out of the saddle. 'A lovely thought from a lovely girl.' He came quickly on to the veranda and sat in the chair next to Alice's. 'More leave?' she queried.

'Yes,' he replied, 'Special. Allowed home to await a new posting.'

'So you don't know how long you'll be here?'

'No. I don't mind. It will give me more chances to see you,' he added, with a twinkle in his eye. 'When I go back I think I'll be moving on.'

'Where to?'

'I don't know yet. Now tell me about you. You are looking very pleased with yourself.'

She laughed. 'Is it as obvious as that?'

'I would say so. What is it that has made your eyes so dazzling? I would venture to guess, you have received good news.'

'You are right. Father was in York two days ago and came back with the news that Nicholas and I can sail in a month's time.'

'That sounds splendid. I'm sure you will soon be settled into the life of an Army officer's wife in Africa. It will be very different from home. But enough of Africa – what do I know of it yet? Only talk I overhear from fellow officers. So let us forget about it and walk in the garden instead.'

They strolled, they chatted; Africa seemed far away in this English country garden.

Lady Cecilia came out to speak with Matthew, resulting in her inviting him to stay for lunch, which he politely accepted.

As he was leaving in the mid-afternoon, Alice said, 'I have so enjoyed your company. Please come again before I sail.'

'And I must know the name of the ship that will take you away.'

'Unless there are any setbacks, it will be *Orion's Star*, a new ship of the Star Line's. It will be her maiden voyage.'

'No more than you deserve. It sounds like a fitting vessel for the wonderful person I shall be delighted to have as my sister-in-law.'

Alice kissed him on the cheek. 'You are so kind.' She watched Matthew ride away. As she walked slowly back into the house thoughts of Africa filled her mind.

Its hold began to exert itself more strongly the next day when she picked up a letter from the hall table addressed to her in Steven's recognisable hand. Her heart raced. She ran up stairs to the privacy of her room, where she tore open the envelope to read the first letter from him since she had informed him of her parents' change of mind.

My darling Alice,
What wonderful news! Unexpected, and out of the

blue. The world became brighter at once, shimmering with the joy of your words. Now time cannot pass quickly enough to bring you into my arms.

The whys and wherefores of the change of heart don't matter now; I will hear them all in good time.

I am sorry that our parents will be not be attending but I respect their reasons.

Let me know as soon as you learn your sailing time so that I can make arrangements here, though I have already informed the padre that he will have a wedding ceremony to perform at some time in the future.

I am thrilled and overjoyed. I need you in my arms, knowing that you can never escape them.

My love is ever yours,
Steven

26

'Alice, we should consider your wedding dress,' said her mother as they settled down with their afternoon cup of tea. 'When we talk about the style, we should bear in mind that the dress will have to be packed to travel to Africa. It should naturally suit you. Have you given it any thought?'

'A little, but there are so many other things to think about.'

Cecilia smiled. 'That's a wedding, my darling.'

'As you say, we must consider packing so I think it should be simple with few flounces,' Alice suggested.

'Let's bear that in mind. We'll go into York

tomorrow and visit Leak and Thorpe's wedding department. We were more than satisfied when we fitted you out there on your return from France.'

They left soon after breakfast the next day. As they made their first enquiry of the shop assistant, Alice was overcome by the feeling that she was stepping into a new world.

'If you'll allow me, Ma'am, I'll bring the manageress who deals exclusively with wedding dresses. May I give her your name?' said the assistant.

'Of course. I'm Lady Ware of Wooton Hall and this is my daughter Alice.'

'Thank you, Ma'am.'

In a few minutes the assistant returned with an attractive young woman, immaculately attired in a black dress, its only adornments being a lace collar and matching cuffs. Her smile and pleasant greeting impressed them immediately. 'Lady Ware, Miss Ware, I am Flora. How may I be of help?'

'My daughter is getting married to an Army officer in about two to three months' time, in South Africa.'

'Ah, so we should consider a cool material. Before we go into that, may I ask if you are considering a full trousseau?'

'Two dozen sets of new underclothes and two dresses for the voyage, I think. Any other clothing my daughter can buy in South Africa. I see no call for shipping it all from here.'

'Quite right, Ma'am. So let us see if we can decide on a wedding dress. Do you want a train?'

'Ever since I was a little girl I have always imagined myself in a long flowing train, but I realise that won't be practical to ship to South Africa.'

'It can be done, but a long train might not be realistic where you are going, particularly if your wedding won't be held in one of the main towns.'

'That will depend where my fiancé is stationed at the time, and that I won't know until I am there.'

'May I suggest that if you are keen to have a train, we consider a short, detachable one?'

'Can that be done?'

'Oh, yes. Some brides prefer them; it makes it easier to adapt the dress to other uses – an evening gown for example. You get good value for the money you've spent on the dress that way. Let me show you.' Flora signalled to the assistant, who had been standing by, and instructed her as to the sample she would like bringing.

Lady Cecilia was doubtful about the detachable train until she appraised its security and practical application. Not only was the train removable but the lace chemisette and matching sleeves could also be removed, leaving an attractive dress for evening wear.

'I like that,' said Alice, 'and the feel of that material is beautiful ... so soft.'

'Silk satin, Miss.'

'Is that your choice of material, Alice?' asked her mother.

'Yes.' There was no hesitation in her voice.

'What about the design?' Cecilia queried.

'I like that too, Mother.'

Flora stepped in. 'I have another dress I can show you, and several photographs. There may be something among them that you prefer.'

Nearly an hour later, Alice said, 'Thank you for showing all those to me but I keep coming back to the first one.'

Flora smiled. 'I thought from the start you had a particular liking for that one. I made no comment because the final choice had to be yours without any pressure from me. I believe you have made a good choice. When that design is adapted to that material and fits you perfectly, everyone who sees it on you will be charmed.'

'I am pleased to have it settled,' said Cecilia, 'but now comes the cost.'

'Ma'am, if I have measurements taken now, I will be able to give you a rough estimate. It may differ from the final cost if we run into a snag but it will only be a slight adjustment. Also the other way, if everything goes smoothly, we might be able to make a reduction of my estimate.'

'That sounds fair enough to me,' said Lady Cecilia.

'I'll get one of our dressmakers to take the necessary measurements. May I offer you coffee while that is being done?'

'That would be kind.'

Flora had a word with her assistant and the room soon buzzed with people, taking measurements, bringing coffee, deciding on Alice's trousseau, and picking out the dresses she would need for the voyage.

Once she had the measurements, Flora worked quickly on the cost of the wedding dress and was delighted that the price came as a pleasant surprise to her customer. First fitting dates were arranged and both Lady Cecilia and Alice left with a feeling of achievement.

'After that I'm ready for lunch,' said Alice's mother.

They relaxed over an enjoyable meal and then returned to Wooton Hall to report to Sir Raymond and Nicholas how they had fared and what they had accomplished. They knew that between now and the day they left for Southampton, life would be one long whirl of planning, packing and personal goodbyes, but amongst it all Alice was determined to find time to store up memories that would sustain her in a strange land.

One day, with a troublesome piece of packing conquered, she said to herself, 'No more planning today. I'm going to escape and ride.'

She galloped away from Wooton Hall and was driven to see Deepdale once more, so that she could hold it in her mind in her absence. She found the place that she recalled as giving the perfect viewpoint. She sat there quietly on her horse, taking it all in. It was little different from that day when she had just returned from France, except that the small part of the house that was visible through the trees showed some of the repairs that had been carried out. Those improvements did not mar her recollection of the day she and Nicholas had explored further; the cobwebs clinging to the dusty window-panes, the ballroom she had longed to dance in, but most of all, the total peace she had felt among the stones that had stood through time holding stories of their own. The longer she sat there, the deeper immersed she became in the same atmosphere she had experienced then. She gave a little shiver and automatically looked around, expecting to see someone beside her but there was no one. Silence bore down on her but did not worry her. She felt contentment in this spot. Was the house or something else trying to tell her: This is really where you belong? She shuddered. The moment was gone. 'Don't be stupid,' she muttered to herself.

'Did you say something?'

The voice startled her. Her heart beat faster. She looked round and relief flooded over her. 'Oh, it's you,' she gasped. 'I was so lost in my thoughts, I didn't hear you coming.'

'I'm sorry I disturbed you,' said Matthew. 'You did seem far away.'

'Remembering,' she said, with no further explanation.

'To recall the scene in Africa, no doubt?'

She nodded. 'I didn't expect to see you here.'

'I was given three days' leave. Whenever that happens, I grab time to visit Deepdale. Should we ride, for old times' sake?'

'Why not?' she agreed, thankful for the company that had broken the spell Deepdale had been casting over her.

They rode to Wooton together, but stopped short of the house when Matthew declined her invitation to visit.

'I told Mother I wouldn't be long so I had better get back. It has been enjoyable seeing you. I hope I'll be here again before you go.'

'I hope so too.' Alice put her fingers to her mouth, turned them towards him and blew the kiss to him. He caught it and put it to his lips, then exchanged another with her.

As she rode the short distance to the stables she realised those final exchanges with Matthew were imprinting themselves on her mind also. She pulled herself together and tried to dismiss them, but she knew they were indelible.

27

Alice woke feeling disorientated. She did not know where she was at first then her mind began to clear. She was in a hotel room in Southampton. 'You are on your way to South Africa,' she muttered to herself, the words bringing her abruptly into the new day.

She was about to jump out of bed when there was a knock on the door. There was a pause, and then it was pushed open slowly. Stella peeped in; seeing her mistress awake, she stepped into the room.

'Good morning, Miss, I trust you slept well.'

'I did, thank you.'

Alice left her bed and preparations for the day began. Every moment ahead of them was filled with excitement. Alice was pleased that Stella was young, a little over two years older than herself, for it meant she had someone closer to her own way of thinking, except for the social canyons that Stella could not cross.

Lady Cecilia, Sir Raymond and Nicholas were already in the dining room when Alice appeared.

Most of the tables were occupied and, from the buzz of excitement in the air, it was obvious that a number of the diners were passengers on the same ship.

On finishing their breakfast the Ware family made their final preparations to leave the hotel. At mid-morning they were advised that a guide would escort them to the embarkation officer, who would take responsibility for checking the passengers in. Once he had done that, he signalled to two junior officers who, with two ratings taking charge of their hand luggage, escorted the brother and sister to their cabins.

Alice was pleased that this excitement enabled her briefly to forget the separation looming nearer and nearer.

Nicholas and his sister were charmed by their luxurious cabins; the walls were of light oak inlaid with mahogany depictions of African animals. Each cabin had its adjoining bathroom, one of the latest developments to attract more passengers to choose a luxury voyage.

Alice ran down the gangway and flung her arms round her father, hugging him tight. 'Thank you, thank you!' she called excitedly. 'Thank you for booking us such lovely accommodation.'

'Enjoy every minute of it,' he said, happy he had pleased her. 'If you've seen all you want to see, I think you should go back and enjoy what's going on out on deck.'

As Alice made her way to the deck, she met Stella rushing to find her. 'Oh, Miss!' she called. 'It's so wonderful ... a cabin all to myself! Not as nice as yours, though. Oh, I hope you don't mind,

I peeped in when I was coming to find you.'

'Of course I don't,' replied Alice. 'You had to see it sometime. Do you like yours?'

'Oh, I do. I do. Far better than I expected.'

'Thank my father. He made the booking.'

'I will, Miss, I will!'

'Go and see us set sail.'

Stella went off, humming happily to herself.

A flurry of activity swept through the ship when it was announced that people who were there to see their friends off would be allowed on board on display of special permits.

Alice made her way outside and found her mother and father with Nicholas at the rail close to the gangways on the port side. They were all swept up in an atmosphere that is only experienced when a passenger ship is due to set sail.

Those people who did not have the privilege of being allowed aboard crowded the jetty to see the new ship sail on its first commercial voyage. Comradeship swept through the crowd that was filling almost every inch of the quay. People were calling out, 'Bon voyage!' to passengers massing along the ship's rails, even when they were strangers. Swept into the fun, those on board threw paper streamers at those on the quay leaving a colourful waving trellised effect the full length of the ship.

Though they were all approaching a watershed in their lives, the Ware family tried to keep a brave face, but when Cecilia, needing some comfort, slipped her hand into her husband's, they both allowed a few tears to trickle down their cheeks. They brushed them away and sought consolation in trying to give last-minute instructions to Nicholas or some instantly forgotten advice to Alice.

That was interrupted by a shout from Nicholas. 'There are Mrs Cheevey and John!'

Surprised by this unexpected appearance, everyone turned to look in the direction he was pointing. They saw Emma and John hurrying up the gangway.

'Good gracious,' said Cecilia. 'I didn't expect them to be here. I thought they had said their goodbyes to Alice on her last visit to Deepdale, but it's very good of them to come.'

The Wares moved through the press of people to get nearer the gangway.

Cecilia grabbed Emma, who nearly tumbled as she stepped on deck.

'Thank you!' she panted. 'Have you seen Matthew?'

'Matthew?' Cecilia looked mystified.

'Oh, no, of course, you wouldn't know. We only got the telegram last night, telling us he was sailing on this ship today. I hoped we would manage to get here before he left.'

'You've only just made it,' said Raymond. 'It will soon be sailing time.'

'I'll see if I can find him,' said John. 'You stay here, Emma, then I'll know where to find you.'

'He's coming,' called Alice, confused by another unexpected arrival.

Matthew weaved his way over to them, managing to say 'Hello' to Alice as he passed her. The smiling wink he gave her unsettled her heart momentarily. He embraced his mother and then explained, 'A last-minute posting for three of us, sort of advance party to find out the situation at the front in order to fill in the others when the body of the regiment arrives.' The next quarter of an hour was hectic as everyone tried to say their final words without missing anyone or forgetting what they'd wanted to say.

'A surprise especially for you,' Matthew said to Alice the moment he was able to get her to himself.

'Well, thank you, good sir.'

'And another thing to remember me by.'

'Will you stop your flirting! And no more of it on the voyage,' she said sternly.

'Wouldn't you want me to?' he teased.

She did not answer his question directly, but said quietly, 'Remember why I am going to South Africa.'

There was no time for more. The call for all those not sailing to depart came loud and clear throughout the ship. The Wares made their last goodbyes, holding back tears and making no attempt to offer further advice. Emma and John were bidding Matthew farewell and good luck in his new posting. He held his mother tight and whispered, 'Be happy.' He watched her and John go down the gangway to the quay to join the throng awaiting the sailing.

Orders flew along the ship; ropes were cast off, a brass band struck up. Slowly, so slowly, *Orion's Star* slid away from the quayside. Desultory cheers and shouts faded into singing that gathered momentum as the space between the ship and the land widened and widened.

I loved you as I never loved before

246

Since first I met you on the village green
Come to me or my dream of love is o'er

Alice remembered her father singing those words once and thought how suitable they were for her and Steven.

Matthew heard the tender melody above the sound of the water against the ship's hull, and wondered.

The singing grew louder until it seemed the ship was attempting to leave those on shore with a memory that would stay with them for a long time. Then, as *Orion's Star* cut through the water with more speed, the singing faded until all was silence.

With the wind against their faces, Alice and Nicholas settled at the ship's rail, watching England slowly disappear. Now they were on the water they were thankful that they had each other's company.

'It's a coincidence having Matthew on board, but a pleasant one,' Nicholas remarked. 'No doubt he'll introduce us to his two fellow officers, so I reckon our time on ship won't be dull.'

'I suppose not,' agreed Alice with a little smile. 'Did he reveal why they are travelling on this ship rather than the troopship I heard about?'

'Not really. Said they are on a special assignment but he could not tell me more,' said her brother.

Alice nodded. Matthew had told her that too. 'Maybe we'll never know.' Spotting Stella on a lower deck, part of which had been reserved for maids travelling with their employers, she called one of the stewards. 'Would you ask my maid to meet me in my cabin in five minutes?' She pointed Stella out.

'Certainly, Miss.' The steward hurried away and left Alice arranging to meet Nicholas for lunch.

Stella was waiting when Alice reached her cabin. Once inside she produced a key. 'You'll need that to get in, Stella. Just do your duties as you would at home. Keep everything tidy, care for my clothes ... all the usual things. You know them as well as I do. You'll have no cleaning of the cabin; that will be done by one of the ship's crew. You'll be told of the mealtimes for servants. Any spare time will be yours to spend as you please.'

'Yes, Miss. Thank you, Miss. I will be available at any time, Miss.'

'Good, then we have an understanding. Enjoy your voyage.'

'I hope you will too, Miss.'

'I'm sure I shall,' said Alice, thinking of the attention the three Army officers would pay her.

When she and Nicholas entered the huge lounge that evening for pre-dinner drinks, Matthew was on his feet immediately. He spoke briefly to his fellow officers and moved quickly towards Alice and Nicholas.

'I hope you won't think me presumptuous but I have booked a table for five for this evening. I thought it a good idea for you to become acquainted with my fellow officers at the start of the voyage.'

'That is kind and thoughtful of you,' said Alice.

'It will be a pleasure to meet them.'

Nicholas agreed. 'Resplendent in your uniforms, you will certainly attract attention and will not lack for company, so I'm rather flattered that you singled us out.'

'I know none of the other passengers so let me introduce you to two gentlemen I do know.'

As they approached, the two officers sprang to their feet.

'May I present Miss Alice Ware and her brother Mr Nicholas Ware?' Matthew then presented his fellow officers. 'Lieutenant Charles Fitzallan and Lieutenant Otto Sylvester.' They clicked their heels and gave a bow to Alice and shook hands with Nicholas.

Introductions made, Nicholas indicated the nearly empty glasses and asked, 'Same again?'

'That is very civil of you,' said Charles, and Otto nodded his agreement. Knowing what he and his sister would choose, Nicholas signalled to a waiter and gave the order.

They settled down in good companionship, leaving behind the sadness of their partings on Southampton's quay. Conversation flowed easily, the meal was enjoyed and they exchanged conversation with several of the other passengers. Eventually they retired, looking forward to another day that they vowed to make as pleasurable as this one.

But the pleasure was marred when they awoke to find the ship dealing with a wayward sea that seemed determined to make most of the passengers suffer.

Alice moaned and wished herself safe on Wooton's firm ground. 'If only I could escape this ship and walk to South Africa!' she muttered miserably. 'Why did I choose an Army officer serving overseas? There was talk last night that one day people might fly, but would that be any better?' Swaying in unison with the ship, she slipped into a restless sleep. When she awoke she sensed something was different. The ship was steadier! She let out a groan that had thanks somewhere in it. At that moment her maid came in.

'Good morning, Miss,' Stella said, bright and breezy.

'Good morning,' slurred Alice.

'You don't look quite yourself, Miss.'

Alice glanced at her, noticed Stella's glowing complexion and said, 'You have no right to look as you do. That was a most unpleasant night.'

'Sorry, Miss. It didn't affect me. In fact, I rather liked it.'

'You couldn't!'

'You'll be better after you've had something to eat. There's porridge on the menu, I'll get you some. When you've had that, I'll help you get dressed and take you outside for a breath of good sea air.'

Alice, with little to say in reply, succumbed to the treatment. When she and Stella stepped on deck they were both pleased to find that the wind of the night had become a gentle breeze. Though the sea was running fast, the ship seemed to have settled on to its course.

When they returned to Alice's cabin, Stella made her comfortable on the bed. 'I will stay with you, Miss, just in case, but I think you will be all right after another sleep.'

'How do you know all this?' Alice asked.

'When I saw you to bed last night, you weren't looking too good. The ship was rolling a bit. I asked one of the crew what the best thing to do for seasickness was? He gave me some advice from personal experience: food and fresh air.'

'You did well, Stella. Thank you.'

The comfort of having her maid nearby eased Alice's mind so that soon she fell asleep.

Three hours later Alice awoke but Stella did nothing until she saw her mistress was fully awake.

'You have slept well, Miss. How are you feeling now?'

'Much, much better. Thank you. And thank you also for staying with me.'

'Part of my job, Miss. Now if you will just stay there, I will fetch you a cup of tea.'

When Stella returned she was pleased to see Alice looking much brighter. 'I informed Mr Nicholas that you were awake, feeling much better and that he could visit you. He said he would be along in a few minutes.'

'Very good, I'll get up to receive him.'

Nicholas arrived when Alice was having her second cup. 'Ah, it is good to see you up. Sorry about the rough sea.'

'Did it affect you?' Alice asked.

'No,' he replied proudly. 'Not at all.'

'Trust you not to suffer,' she muttered grumpily.

'I reckon now you've got it out of the way, it won't recur and you'll have a splendid voyage.'

'I hope so.'

Their chat was interrupted by a knock on the

door. Nicholas answered it and called over his shoulder, 'Matthew's here to see how you are.'

'Don't leave him standing there, let him in,' called Alice.

Matthew's expression showed concern when he entered but it disappeared when he saw Alice was not confined to bed.

'Good to see you looking perky,' he said. 'Was it just seasickness?'

'Yes. A bad case though,' she replied. 'I wished I could die.'

'Goes with the malady. Good job you didn't, though.' He allowed his eyes to meet hers as he continued, 'I don't know what my brother's reaction would have been if you had, except he would have blamed us and not the sea.'

'Well, here I am, so he can't do that. But you'd better start taking me into your care.'

The men exchanged a wink and said in mock seriousness, 'We'll be sure to keep our eyes on you.'

She returned in the same teasing manner, 'Provided you don't cramp my style with those handsome Army officers you introduced me to, Matthew.'

'Would I do that?' he chided. 'But I do have my brother's interests to look after.'

The mood for the voyage had been set: enjoyable, easygoing, flirtatious. Alice had been moving towards the door while he had been speaking. She opened it for him and, as he made his farewell, managed to whisper, 'Would those interests get in the way of our fun?'

Fully recovered, Alice mixed freely with other passengers but always looked forward to spending time with the Army officers; they were young, close to her own age, and determined to make this unexpected luxury voyage memorable. And after all, she was soon to be married. She might as well enjoy their company while she had the chance, and they might as well enjoy the luxury of a trip on a liner when they could just as easily have been assigned to a troopship.

Alice did not lack attention from them and enjoyed their boisterous attitude but, amongst that, she noted Matthew's attention was often fixed on her.

One evening after an enjoyable meal, specially arranged through the head waiter to celebrate Otto's birthday, the party continued in the smaller lounge. Passengers kept looking in personally to wish Otto good tidings for his birthday. Gauging a moment when the lounge was particularly full and Nicholas engaged in conversation, Matthew issued an invitation. 'Alice, I've taken a look outside, it's a beautiful night, walk with me.'

'I would like that but…'

'There's no good reason for any but,' he cut in gently. 'Just say yes.'

'All right. I'll get my wrap.'

'I'll see you at the bottom of the main staircase on deck three.'

There was no need for any further words, they felt instinctively drawn together.

Matthew made a quick visit to his cabin but lost no time in reaching the designated meeting place. A few minutes later, hearing footsteps, he turned to see Alice coming down the stairs. She saw admiration in his eyes. 'I noted your dress earlier this evening; it drew my attention immediately. That flame red colour ... well, it is striking and just right for you.' He had taken hold of her arm and was leading her to the door. 'Use that wrap. It isn't as cold as it has been but I'm told some nights the temperature can drop suddenly.'

He opened the door and held it for her while she stepped outside. As she felt the change in the air she drew her wrap more closely to her and allowed him to help her.

They moved to the rail and stood in silence, intent on the moonlight and the thread of white reflected on the crests of the undulating waves.

'Beautiful,' she said, scarcely above a whisper. 'Beautiful.'

How long they stood there neither of them could tell, lost as they were under the enchantment of the stars glittering against the dark canopy that accentuated their existence for all the world to see. Even the slow movement of Matthew's arm slipping around Alice's shoulders did nothing to disturb the wonder of the night for her. She did not move; she did nothing to approve of what he had done nor was there any complaint from her, she was still lost in the wondrous display that surrounded them.

'Beautiful,' she whispered once more.

'And you add more loveliness to it. You are a rare jewel among all those distant diamonds. These moments spent with you will live with me for ever.' He turned her gently to face him, searched her eyes and, finding what he wished for, kissed her.

As gentle as they were, his lips were charged with unmistakable passion. They lingered, their kiss sending signals that would not be denied. Fingers entwined, hers issuing an invitation, his acceptance, they walked slowly across the deck – with one last look back to drink in again the magic of the night that had drawn them together.

'Matthew! Matthew!' The words were quietly spoken but there was an urgency to them that brought him sharply awake. 'The time ... Stella will be coming!' Now he was truly awake. No chance to study one other. In a matter of moments he was dressed. He leaned over Alice, kissed her and was gone.

'Did you meet anyone?' Alice queried later with a worried frown, when she sat down beside Matthew at breakfast.

'No one,' he replied.

The relief that swept over her was palpable. They both gathered themselves together. Then he made a comment that set her mind awhirl. 'You were wonderful.'

Though each could sense the other would have liked, and wanted, a repetition of their night together, circumstances conspired against them and they were unable to engineer an opportunity.

Normality had to be resumed, but neither of them could forget what had happened between them.

28

Alice sank on to the only chair in a corner of the deck. No one could join her there; there was no room. Her mind was in a whirl and she needed time to think. Had she regrets about what had happened with Matthew? She tried to dismiss the thought, but remained indecisive – yes and no.

I took the lead by taking him to my cabin. I could have stopped it there and then but I didn't want to. Perhaps it was the wine I had at dinner, but it had not blurred my judgement. I knew what was happening and I went along that path willingly. Matthew said I was wonderful and that thrilled me and made me wish to be with him again, but ... and it is a big BUT ... I am on my way to marry his brother!

I feel torn apart by remorse for what I have done. I still love Steven but I cannot take back the last twelve hours. How can I drive away a memory I helped to create? I can't; I will be marked by it for the rest of my life.

Twenty-four hours later, the words 'Table Mountain' swept through the ship, sending excitement coursing through the passengers. They hurried to see the symbol of homecoming to many, and adventure in a new land to others.

Alice threw a coat around her shoulders and hurried on deck where she was joined by Nicholas

256

and Matthew.

'Thank goodness the sun is shining for us,' commented her brother. 'One passenger has been singing the praises of the approach to Cape Town.'

The ship was steaming towards a smudge of land near the horizon. They watched it unfold into something more substantial and then gradually make its impact on all aboard, almost as if it was challenging and daring them not to be impressed, even overwhelmed, by the delights it was offering.

'It looks all right from here but it might be a different story when we get ashore!' they overheard a nearby passenger say to his companion. Nicholas raised an eyebrow at this comment and, with a touch of disdain, said quietly to Matthew, 'Can't he enjoy what he has now?'

Alice caught the words which she applied to her own predicament. Which do I choose? she wondered. She watched the mountain seemingly rising higher and higher from the sea. 'The solution lies in this land of mine,' it seemed to say. The sight sent a little shiver through her in spite of the warming sun. She immediately tightened her lips and chided herself for getting into this predicament.

'You are quiet,' commented her brother.

'I'm taking it all in.'

'You'll soon be seeing Steven again.'

'I know, but I've no idea if he received our arrival details – there was no letter from him before I left.'

'No doubt he'll be at the quay to meet you.'

'I expect so.'

They watched the scenery with admiration and then allowed the activity at the dockside while they tied up to occupy their attention.

Their eyes searched the crowds on the quayside.

'Can you see him?' asked Alice.

'I didn't expect so many people to be here,' commented Nicholas.

'Steven should be easy to pick out,' said Matthew, 'he'll be in uniform.'

But they did not see him.

Alice experienced a sinking feeling and was hurt that her fiancé was not here to welcome her. I have come all this way to marry him, at least he could have been here, she thought to herself. She felt bereft and lonely, even though she had companions. But, in a strange way, she also felt his absence negated a little of her guilt.

'This might be news!' said Matthew as an Army car sped on to the quay.

As soon as it stopped near the gangway, a young lieutenant sprang out of the front passenger seat and made for the ship. He was stopped by one of the crew. They saw words exchanged, papers shown and permission granted for the officer to board ship. He disappeared from view but within a very short time appeared on their deck together with one of the ship's officers. They stopped, exchanged a brief word, and then the Army officer approached them. He saluted smartly and asked, 'Miss Alice Ware?'

'Yes,' she said.

'Welcome to South Africa, Miss. I am Lieutenant Pat O'Shea. I am stationed here in Cape Town. Major Cheevey is sorry not to be here himself.

Duty called and I was delegated to see you and your fellow passengers safely to Pretoria. Everything is in hand for your journey.' He tapped his breast pocket. 'Necessary tickets and passes are in here. Your luggage is already being dealt with.'

'Does that include me, Lieutenant Cheevey, and the two other officers who were posted to South Africa with me?' asked Matthew.

'I am pleased to meet the three of you. I was also asked to oversee your transportation to Pretoria. Everything has been arranged. You will be in the adjoining coach to that occupied by Miss Ware, her brother and her lady's maid.'

He called them all together and informed them, 'I must ask you to stay in your carriage whenever we stop unless I authorise you to leave it. Though we are on top in this war and the main conflict lies to the south, there is still danger from Boer marauding parties eager to disrupt any transport. We have special guards on the train so there should be nothing to worry about.

'Also you will notice at intervals along our route there are block-houses with machine guns and searchlights mounted on platforms on the upper storey. These accommodate six or eight soldiers who guard the track, and so far they are proving successful. No railway bridge has been attacked since they were installed. My squad and I will be in the next carriage to the rear, if you need to call us. Beyond that there are three carriages with troops we are dropping off at various locations. That will cause some delay but, all being well, we should reach Pretoria in a week. Only one thing: we are due to leave here in one hour. Please be on board by then.'

Alice boarded the train and quickly cast an eye over her accommodation. She had to soothe Stella's concern that she was travelling in the same coach as her mistress although in a separate compartment. 'It's not right, Miss,' she protested. 'I shouldn't be intruding...'

'Stella, it is perfectly all right,' Alice insisted.

'It wouldn't have happened in England.'

'You are right, it wouldn't, but we are not in England, there is a war on here so we can't expect the standards to be the same as at home. I think you might find protocol nearer to what you are used to when we reach Pretoria.'

Reassured, Stella settled down to arranging their accommodation to suit their needs for the journey. Nicholas checked that his sister's compartment was to her liking. Half an hour later Matthew also checked on her, but there was no mention by either of them of a certain night aboard *Orion's Star*.

That was one topic that could not be wiped from her mind by the changing landscape of veldt and bush, or the spectacle of a silver dawn, or the blazing red of a setting sun painting the vastness of the land, nor even the electric storm that shattered the calm one day. It would take more than rain to wash away thoughts of the past.

Lieutenant Pat O'Shea was ever attentive to their well-being and needs. When they were nearing Pretoria he met Alice and Nicholas and informed them that rooms were booked for them at the town's best hotel. 'Major Cheevey left full instructions about it. Naturally he will be in touch with you as soon as he returns from his mission. When I have seen you to your hotel, I will try to get news of him and will report to you.'

'Thank you, Lieutenant, you have been most helpful on this journey,' said Alice. 'I will make sure Major Cheevey knows.'

'Thank you, Miss. Please remain in your compartment after the train has stopped in the station. I will be in contact with your brother and we will join you for onward transportation to your hotel.' As he went he said, 'I will be back with you in about ten minutes.'

When he'd left the compartment Stella looked in. 'Our hand luggage is ready, Miss.'

'Good, come in and sit with me until we leave the train.' Seeing her maid hesitate, Alice added firmly. 'Sit down, Stella. You are still my maid, so do as you are told.'

Looking sheepish, she said quietly, 'Yes, Miss.'

'Shortly Lieutenant O'Shea will be back and we will be stepping into what is for us a new and strange world. We have had glimpses of it, but now our lives here begin and you and I will be tested. I want you to know that you can come to me if ever you have a problem.'

'Thank you, Miss. I have been wondering how I will manage among such a mixture of people.'

'Just be yourself and you'll get by and soon adapt to new ways. And I would like to think that in this new world I will always have your loyalty.'

'Oh, you will, Miss, no matter what happens.'

Nicholas appeared and said brightly, 'Well, here we are, thousands of miles from home. Whoever would have thought it six months ago? My hand luggage has been taken, the porter will be here for yours in a few moments. Lieutenant O'Shea is with him.'

The words had hardly passed Nicholas's lips when the lieutenant appeared with a native porter who handled the luggage quickly, having been instructed where the Army car would be.

They had reached it when the three officers who had been with them since leaving England came to make their goodbyes. In all the mêlée, Matthew managed to say to Alice, 'I'm off to Army quarters. Apparently we three will be based in Pretoria for a while. I've learned where you are staying, I'll call on you this evening.'

Alice felt an intense desire to speak with him in private but that was impossible; she would have to wait until this evening and hope that they could snatch a few moments together alone. During her last hours on the train she had come to a decision about the night they had shared on board ship.

She and Nicholas had finished dinner and were settled in the lounge when they were invited to join an English man and his brother who were on their way to Rhodesia. Nicholas had become friendly with them on the voyage from England. Alice made her excuses, 'That is very kind of you, Nicholas has always enjoyed talking with you and he will no doubt do so this evening, but I must refuse your kind offer. I have arranged to see Lieutenant Cheevey. As you know he is a neighbour of ours in Yorkshire.'

'Then it is right for you to keep the appointment,' said one of the men. 'It will be our loss. Tomorrow we set out for Rhodesia where we have an investment proposition that could interest your brother.'

Seeing Matthew arriving, Alice rose from her chair, flashing her brother a warning glance. He should be wary of making any investment unless he was convinced everything was above board. She wished the men a safe journey and went to greet Matthew.

'Shall we sit in that corner?' Alice asked, indicating a small table set in front of two comfortable chairs facing into the room.

'Ideal,' he approved. He signalled to one of the waiters, who gave them a broad smile when he took their orders. They exchanged a few trivialities until the waiter had brought their drinks and they were out of earshot of anyone.

'Matthew, I am so glad we were able to meet,' Alice began. 'I have something I must say so I will come straight to the point. I have made a decision, and it is only right you should know what it is.'

He looked into her determined eyes. 'I can guess the subject. It raises certain questions. They have troubled me, and I assume they have worried you too.'

'You judge correctly. I have turned what we did over and over in my mind. Ever since I stepped ashore and Steven was not there while you were, memories of our night together have haunted me.' Alice paused as if plucking up the courage to go on. She straightened her back and looked Matthew resolutely in the eyes. Her next words came as a huge shock. 'I am going to confess to Steven.'

Matthew stared at her in disbelief. 'You can't.'

'I can and I will,' she said with fierce determination, yet keeping her voice down so that others in the room could not hear.

He was aghast. 'But why? Only you and I know. No one else need ever learn. And definitely not Steven.'

'But *I* will always know.' She looked pleadingly at him.

'My lips will remain sealed.'

'I know that, Matthew, and I trust you implicitly. After all, you have as much to lose as I. But I will always have what we did on my conscience. The only way to be rid of that is to confess all and throw myself on the mercy of your brother.' Her expression begged for understanding.

'Do you expect him to forgive you?'

'That is up to Steven.'

'You're expecting too much of him.'

'Perhaps, but at least I will have confessed.'

'Do you think that will be an end to it? That he will forget it as if nothing had happened. Have you thought of the scandal that will follow? Confessing to my brother will be disastrous. He won't give you or me any consideration, will do nothing to prevent us being cast out by society. You don't know him as I do. Steven won't care how much our names are blackened, he'll make sure none of the scandal rubs off on him. He will still play the wronged man, jilted by his intended, and he will enjoy the attention he receives.'

Alice held up her hand. 'Stop! There is no "us". Matthew, I love Steven and I still hope to marry him. I know you are trying to make a case for saying nothing, but it is I who stand on the verge of marriage. If I don't do anything about this, it will haunt me for the rest of my life. I'm sorry, but our night together on the ship was a mistake; that's the way it is. If it makes things any easier on you, I will accept all the blame. I will say I was the seducer.'

'No!' Matthew rapped out sharply. 'I was as much to blame as you in that respect. If you are bent on confessing to Steven then so be it, but don't expect me to be standing by your side when you do.'

29

One, two, three days, and still there was no news of Steven's unit. Tension began to mount. The coming meeting began to prey on Alice's mind, eating into her resolve and making her wonder if she had made the right decision. Such thoughts disturbed her sleep and she knew they were taking a toll on her when Nicholas sat down at breakfast one day and said, 'Are you all right, Alice? You're looking pale.'

'I'm not sleeping too well,' she replied, and went on quickly to prevent any searching questions, 'anxiety I expect. Wishing Steven were safely with us.'

'He'll be all right. The news from the front is good. Steven can take care of himself.'

Alice smiled. 'You're a comfort, Nicholas, I am

glad you are here with me. It would have been a lonely wait without you. Even though the Army wives are very considerate, they are not my own flesh and blood.'

'I bumped into Matthew in town yesterday. He sent his good wishes. I invited him to dine with us tomorrow evening but he had to decline. Some important meeting with higher authority, to do with his deployment in areas where hostilities have ceased or are on the verge of ceasing. It's something he had special training in, along with Otto and Charles, while he was in England apparently.'

Alice forced herself to show interest but her one desire at the moment was to have the meeting with Steven over and done with. Her future would be determined by whatever course that took.

Three days later news of an important victory swept through Pretoria. A large force of Boers had been scattered and many prisoners taken, meaning that there would be no further threat from that area; a great stride towards a final peace settlement had been taken. The regiment on standby in Pretoria had already begun to move out to relieve the one still in the field, news which sent waves of relief through Alice. It meant Steven would soon be back.

The relieving force was given a magnificent send-off. Even as the last man marched out of the town, plans to welcome the heroes from the front were being prepared. People remained on edge until four days later when word passed from person to person reporting a significant dust-cloud. Their troops returning from the front.

Excitement swept through the town and before long crowds were singing and dancing in the streets. The joyous exhibition turned into cheering laced with shouts of welcome and praise. The weary troops responded by assuming marching order. They were brought to a halt in the town centre where, after presenting arms, they were ordered to stand easy and then to fall out. Joy and relief flooded Pretoria as wives took husbands in their arms, soldiers sought the girl they had left behind, while girls looked for the man they had last seen marching off to war. Others among the crowd searched and did not find the man they sought, queried and questioned, hoping they would not receive the answer they dreaded.

When she saw tears, brought on by bad news, begin to flow amongst the previously joyful, Alice was more than pleased that she had already seen Steven, marching strongly, his face breaking into a broad smile of utter relief and pleasure on seeing her. Maybe their meeting would not be as catastrophic as she had imagined. The thought came again: should she say nothing? But, even as she entertained that option, she dismissed it. The only way ahead for her was to beg Steven's forgiveness.

On the order to fall out Steven started towards her, his step quick, his eagerness obvious. Her heart lurched and she felt love overpower her.

Tears of joy and regret mingled as Alice held out her arms to him. They closed around him as his seized her. Her face tilted up. Steven's eyes devoured her, taking in everything he had missed about her.

He bent towards her. His lips touched hers lightly, lingered, and then passion flared between them. He felt the love he had yearned to feel. Now they were together again and nothing would ever part them. The future burned brightly with the dreams that had kept him focused while he sweated under the African sun, or shivered in the cold that swept across the veldt with the coming of night. It was almost within his grasp.

Alice was lost in his embrace, sure of her love for him. She clung tightly to him, as if she never wanted to let him go. 'Oh, I do love you so,' she murmured. She raised herself on her toes and kissed him passionately, hoping it would purge her of all she now regretted. With that came the firm resolve to meet the consequences of her actions head on.

'When will you be free?' she asked Steven.

'We'll soon be called to order then we'll march to the barracks, get settled in and be free until lights out, which means back in our billets by eleven. Once I have seen my men re-established, I will come to your hotel.'

'How long will that be?' she said with nervous eagerness.

'No more than two hours from now, but hopefully well before that.'

Alice nodded and was about to say something more when they heard the raucous voices of the sergeants calling for the men to fall in.

'I was sorry I was not here when you arrived from England. Have you been all right and well looked after?' Steven enquired.

'Yes, I had Nicholas...'

'You said in a letter that he was coming with you, to give you away. I haven't seen him, where is he?'

'I think he's keeping out of the way while you and I...'

'Ah, here he is.'

The two men barely had time to exchange greetings before Steven had to excuse himself.

'Come with Alice this evening,' he called out as he started away.

'No, thank you,' returned Nicholas. 'You will both have a lot to talk about and planning to do. Better for you to be on your own.'

'All right, if that's what you prefer. We can get together another night – a celebration of our engagement.' Steven kissed Alice one final time and was away before any more could be said.

'Everything all right?' asked Nicholas, his eyes on his sister.

Alice looked wistful. 'Yes,' she replied. 'The waiting was longer than I had expected and all this has been rather overwhelming.'

'I'll wait with you in the lounge this evening until Steven arrives.'

'That's kind. Thank you.'

'No regrets?' he queried.

She shook her head. 'No.'

'Then be happy and look happy.'

As she waited in the lounge that evening, Alice found it difficult to keep calm but hoped her chatter was preventing Nicholas from noticing her unease.

After five minutes her heart missed a beat as she

noticed Matthew walk in, accompanied by Otto and Charles. Seeing Alice and Nicholas, they came over and paid their respects. Alice was on tenterhooks until Steven appeared.

He made his greetings to the others quickly and said to her, 'Shall we go?'

After helping her to her feet and draping her wrap around her shoulders, he escorted her to the door.

'Where to?' asked Alice.

'A small restaurant a little further down the road. There's a private room for hire. Your hotel will be exceptionally busy this evening so I decided, with so much to talk about, we would have more privacy elsewhere.'

'A good idea,' Alice said trying to put some enthusiasm into her comment. He had given her the opportunity she needed, but still she dreaded his reaction when she made her confession.

The proprietor saw them settled in a small side room. Wine and food were ordered and he discreetly withdrew.

Steven raised his glass. 'To you, my dear Alice. May our life together be full of happiness.'

Emotion welled in her. For one moment she told herself to say nothing, but her guilty conscience won. She hesitated, dragged her eyes away from Steven to look unseeingly at her glass.

'Your wine,' he prompted, puzzled by Alice's reaction to his toast.

Gripping her hands tightly together on her lap, she looked up to meet his questioning eyes. They filled with concern when he saw silent tears begin to flow down her cheeks.

'What is it, Alice?' he enquired anxiously.

She looked down sadly and summoned what little courage remained to her. 'I cannot marry you, Steven,' she whispered.

Remembering her kisses of a few hours previously, her words made no sense to him. Then shock and disbelief coursed through him. All he had dreamed of since Alice had said yes to his proposal seemed like a mockery now. The thoughts that had kept him going through the heat of the day, the cold of the night, the skirmishes; the battles where life had balanced on a knife edge, were as nothing now that his world had been shattered by five words.

'But why? What has happened? You haven't come all this way to say no? You were so...'

'Stop, Steven!' Her voice was harsh, strained from holding back her sobs of remorse. 'I slept with your brother on the ship,' she confessed.

He stared at her. Although the words rang out like a thunderclap, he still could not believe them. This was Alice speaking so it couldn't be true. But if there was no truth in it, why had she said it? Matthew! He must be at the root of all this.

'Can you repeat that?' he said slowly.

'It's true.' She had to state the truth, dismiss his doubt, or else the confession would be worthless. 'I slept with your brother. It was a mistake I will regret for the rest of my life.' She deliberately emphasised each word.

Steven's face darkened with anger. Now his eyes bored into her. 'No!' he yelled. 'You couldn't have! I know you couldn't do that! He must have raped you...'

Tears were streaming down Alice's face. She was aghast at what he was saying. She had to put an end to a charge which, if pursued, could completely ruin Matthew's life.

'No, he did not force me. At the time I went willingly.'

Her words appalled him.

'Why? You knew I was waiting to marry you when the fighting was over. It was the thought of you that kept me going through those dark days.'

'All I can say is, it was a magical night. We were alone together, and … I gave myself to him.' Alice put her head in her hands then and sobbed.

Her explanation did nothing to assuage Steven's rising anger. He jumped to his feet and stepped towards her, one fist clenched, his eyes fixed and staring. She looked up fearfully and awaited punishment, but it did not come from his fist.

He said viciously, 'You will wait here. I shall soon be back.' These were orders she knew she dared not disobey. 'We will have our meal together as if nothing had happened and while we do I will tell you what is going to happen. I will have a word with the proprietor now and ask him to delay things for a short while.' Steven gave her one last look of contempt and hurried away.

She sank back in the chair, spent. What about the other lives that would be affected when it became known, as surely it must, why she was returning to England unmarried?

Unless Steven had a solution to that? Could he possibly hold the key to settling this dreadful situation?

At that very moment Steven was not giving any thought to such considerations. He was hurrying the short distance back to the hotel. He did not slacken his stride as he burst through the front door and crossed the vestibule without a glance at the clerk on duty.

'Sir!' the clerk called after him, but it did not deter Steven. He flung open the dining-room door and walked straight in. Without altering his step he took in the room in one quick glance, locating the table around which the four people he'd expected to see were seated. The crash of the door caused them and the other diners to stare at the cause of the sudden intrusion.

With eyes set on his brother, Steven walked to his table. Giving Matthew no time to react, his brother grabbed him by the jacket collar with his left hand and heaved him to his feet. In one swift movement his right fist came up and struck Matthew hard on the cheek. At the same moment Steven released his grip and Matthew flew backwards, hurtling into a neighbouring table and sending its contents crashing to the floor. Its occupants sprang to their feet to try and avoid the food and wine that flew in every direction. Shouts of anger were hurled at the perpetrator of the chaos. Otto and Charles sprang to the aid of their fellow officer, while Nicholas automatically stepped in front of Steven to prevent any further attack.

Steven stepped past him to head for the door, pausing briefly to glare down at his brother and hiss with venom in his voice, 'You deserve horse-whipping.' He strode quickly for the door, stating as he passed the reception desk, 'I'll pay for any damage. They'll tell you who I am,' he added, indicating the people he had just left. Within a very few minutes he was sitting opposite Alice at their table.

She quaked at the anger in his expression. 'What have you done?' she asked, concerned by the blood she saw on the knuckles of his clenched fist.

He held it up. 'That's my brother's blood. As if you hadn't guessed.'

Disgust rose in her. 'Did hitting Matthew give you any satisfaction? Did it solve anything?' Steven hesitated over his reply. 'Well, did it?' she demanded.

'I suppose not. But I'll tell you this, young lady, you've caused me to do something I have never done before. I hit my own brother in anger! Oh, as children we fought, but if we were angry it was only of the moment; there was no malice in it, not like this time. As from now, Matthew is no longer anything to do with me.' His eyes narrowed as he told her, 'This was all your fault. You offered him something he could not resist. You couldn't even wait until we were married! You are a thoughtless hussy who has made a mockery of our betrothal.'

With these harsh words, her tears started up again. 'Oh, Steven, it's you I love. What can I do to put things right?'

'Nothing. You must face the consequences of your own actions. I will speak to Nicholas. You will keep to yourself until I can find a ship to take you back to England. I will see you safely on board. I will watch the ship sail, taking you out of my life for ever. What you do then and what you tell family and friends is entirely up to you ... that is, if you tell them the truth or not. But remember: any time I choose to, I can let it be known exactly what happened and with whom. Your reputation will then be ruined. Think about that – think about what you have done!'

30

Alice sat there not knowing what to do, frozen by Steven's harshness to her. He was throwing her to the wolves. How could she face her family and his? They would want to know everything that had happened. She had gone to Africa to marry him. She would have to offer an explanation as to why she had returned so abruptly.

Who could she turn to? There was Nicholas, her dear brother, but could she tell even him the truth? She would have to, she decided.

At that moment the door swung open and Nicholas strode in, his expression thunderous.

'What on earth was that all about?' he demanded, eyes fixed on Steven.

He met the challenge with, 'You'll have to ask your sister! But I'll tell you this: I am sending her back to England on the first ship on which I can book a passage. No doubt you will wish to accompany her as you will have no cause to remain in Africa, so I'll book one for you too.'

Nicholas looked completely mystified. He glanced at Alice, who lowered her eyes, not wishing to talk.

'The meal's paid for. You might as well enjoy it, if you have the stomach to eat,' rapped Steven, well aware of how his dismissal of her was piercing Alice's heart. He strode from the room.

Alice sat there, stunned. When her brother had walked in she had hoped that his intervention might help her in some way. The door slammed behind Steven, leaving a charged silence in the room. Tears streamed down Alice's face, which was the picture of abject misery.

'But I love him,' she whispered to herself. Nicholas's heart lurched with pity for her in her distress. He pulled out a chair and sat down in front of her, taking her hands in his.

'Tell me,' he said quietly.

She hesitated.

'Come on,' he said, watching her closely.

Alice bit her lip and cried out, 'Oh, Nicholas, I've been such a fool and lost the man I love, the man I came here to marry.'

'Tell me everything.'

'How can I when it's so terrible that you'll walk away from me and shun me for the rest of my life?'

'Try me. I don't like seeing my sister in this state. It sounds as though your life has broken down. Alice, you are so dear to me, I want to help.'

With repeated gentle persuasion he gradually extracted the story. Silence filled the room when she had finished telling it. Nicholas's expression betrayed the shock he still felt.

'But with Matthew? What on earth were you thinking of? He was betraying his own brother and you your future husband.' The sharpness of his words hit home. 'This foolish action will have serious repercussions. I can sympathise with Steven's attitude, but that doesn't help you, I know. What are people going to think? Oh, Alice, why were you so stupid?'

All she could say was, 'Nicholas, what am I to do? I can't go home. I just couldn't face Mother and Father, and definitely not Steven's parents.'

'You may have to, but don't consider that yet. We'll check other possibilities first. I think we should begin by talking to Steven.'

'I am certain that will do no good; he won't even listen. With me safely out of the way, he can pass it off as a change of heart on my part. No real blame can then be attached to either of us. It is the simplest way. Both he and Matthew will want the whole incident at the hotel hushed up too, and that can easily be done. They'll say it was a drunken brawl after the victory celebrations.'

Alice wrung her hands. 'My real concern is what will happen at home. What explanation can I present to Mother and Father without shocking them? And what about Steven's parents? I'd need to tell them all the same thing as they're bound to talk to each other.'

'That is going to need further consideration but we need to do it quickly because we don't know when Steven will find passages for us. But you're all in, Alice. Let us both get some sleep and see what tomorrow brings,' Nicholas advised.

The following morning, when Nicholas left the hotel his enquiries led him to the parade ground where Steven was visible, issuing orders to some of the returning troops.

Seeing him, Steven handed over to his sergeant. He greeted Nicholas with cold civility and added, 'I expect Alice has explained what happened so if you've come to try to smooth things over you are wasting your time.'

'Even if I tell you that she still loves you?'

'Yes, of course! What she did can never be forgotten. How could it be otherwise?'

'Alice has admitted what she did was wrong and knows it was a mistake. She lays no blame on your brother. He did not seduce her. They were overcome by the moment.'

'I believe that, but it does not excuse her betrayal of our betrothal. That is the end of the matter as far as I am concerned, except for making sure she is soon on a ship leaving for England. I am glad you are here; it will save me having to find you to tell you that I have made enquiries early this morning and learned the *Capricorn* will be docking in Cape Town in four days' time. It will be an immediate turnaround to return to England. That means three days in port. I will let you have all details in writing and the necessary authority for your journey – train from Pretoria to the Cape.

'It's no use Alice expecting a reconciliation, so please do not contact me again or let her try to do so. Warn her lady's maid of that as well. I want no further trouble between us. The episode, as I will call it, is over and done with. No more will be said, except for one thing: I am sorry this has come between you and me; I think as brothers-in-law we could have been good friends.'

Nicholas could see that put an end to the matter. He hesitated then held out his hand. Steven shook it, turned and walked away. Nicholas walked back to the hotel.

Alice, who had guessed her brother had been attempting to forge a reconciliation, could not disguise her anxiety when he walked into her room. Her heart sank when he gave a little shake of his head.

'I'm sorry,' he said. 'I tried but my attempt was in vain. There was no scene but he was adamant that he would not reverse his decision. In fact, he has acted very quickly. Our passages are already booked on the *Capricorn*, docking in four days' time. It is to be a quick departure so we must be there almost as soon as she arrives. The railway tickets have been organised. I'm afraid this is the end of the matter; we can't do anything else but comply. It looks as if Steven is anxious to see us out of the way, out of his life. I'm sorry, Alice, but we are facing a brick wall so far as resolving this goes. You must put on a brave face and make your own future.'

A week later Alice stood at the rail of the ship that would take her back to England. A railway porter at Pretoria had seen them to their accommodation on the train. The fuss he made over seeing to their luggage had led Alice to speculate that he had been given this assignment by Steven, to ensure that she and her brother had definitely left Pretoria. It had made her wonder if there would be another check at the docks. Melancholy settled over her as the train chugged and puffed its way out of Pretoria, on what proved to be an uneventful journey.

Now, from the deck, Alice watched the last of their contact with a land that had offered so much to her. She stood alone because Nicholas had recognised that she wished to be by herself.

The dock bustled with activity. Last-minute supplies were being taken on board. Late-arriving passengers were hustled quickly up the appropriate gangway. People milled around to communicate with friends who were sailing, shouting good wishes, instructions for their arrival at their destination, and as always there were those who loved to share the special atmosphere of arrivals and departures associated with ships.

Alice watched with unseeing eyes but with hope of salvation just lingering. That will never happen ... I can't expect it to, she told herself. A tear trickled down her cheek and she chided herself for being such a fool, for nursing even that slimmest of hopes. Minutes ticked by. Why am I standing here? she asked herself. She didn't answer her own question but neither did she move away. A rising tension compelled her to stay and watch as final checks were made; orders were shouted, gangways were dragged away. Ropes were taken off the dockside capstans. In a few moments the ship would begin to move, severing all contact with South Africa's solid ground.

A movement on the periphery of a cluster of people on the quay caught her eye. Someone had pushed a way through to get closer to the ever-widening space between the ship and the dock. Could it be him? No, he wouldn't come all the way from Pretoria just to... She shook her head. She must stop seeing what she'd wished to see. Then their eyes met; she knew then she was not seeing a ghost, and that Steven had seen her too. Her thoughts ran wild. She pulled them up. Why is he here, if not to make peace? Oh, if only he had been here a few minutes earlier! She started to raise her arm, but stopped herself. He had not made any move towards her, any gesture of forgiveness. The cold light in his eyes was still there – unemotional and unforgiving. She cursed herself for being so foolish as to suppose he had come to her in love when all he had done now was to check that a source of embarrassment was out of his life.

She turned away from the rail and, without a further glance towards the quay, went to join her brother.

They had her future to arrange before they docked in Southampton.

31

When Alice laid her fingers on Nicholas's hand, she felt the tension within him. Knowing she was the cause of his distress brought silent tears trickling down her cheeks.

'I'm sorry for hurting you and for all the trouble I've brought you,' she said.

He gave a little shrug.

'We've got big decisions to make. You have to think carefully about what you want to do next.

281

You can't put things right but you mustn't destroy other lives by your choices.'

Alice stared at him gravely before she spoke.

'Before we start considering a plan of action, I wish to say there should be no attempt to try and justify what I did, nor should blame be laid on Matthew or Steven. I have done with them both now and they need only be mentioned in passing when other people are told of my mistake.'

'That is exactly how we shall have to pass it off,' said Nicholas sharply. 'A mistake by you. You arrived in Africa, found it was not as you had hoped and decided it would be best to burn your boats and return. However, I don't think that will be good enough for Mother and Father. They know when either of us is holding something back.'

Alice nodded. 'That has been bothering me. Then do we explain to them what I did?'

'It seems to me that that is the first thing we have to decide, and it is not going to be easy. I think we should look at all the implications. And remember, we will have to do the same for Steven's mother and father also.'

Alice screwed up her face. 'I'd rather not tell any of them, but...'

'Don't start putting in buts – they can cause all sorts of problems,' cut in Nicholas. 'So let's start by considering the situation if we don't tell them.'

'You're forgetting that Steven can decide to do so at any time,' she said in a quiet voice.

Nicholas looked doubtful. 'But surely, as a gentleman...'

Alice sighed. 'We are going round in circles and getting nowhere. We have some days left before we reach England. Let's not make a decision in haste.'

Two days out of Southampton, Nicholas brought up the subject again. Alice seemed pleased that he had.

'I should tell you that something happened the night before last,' she began. 'I spent most of yesterday thinking about it.'

He looked questioningly at her. 'Go on, I'm eager to hear if you have reached a solution.'

The words flowed out uninterrupted then. 'I woke up and couldn't get to sleep again. I had been running over in my mind everything that had happened since my return from France, how I had enjoyed being at home. Then I began to think about Wooton, the love I have for it and that part of Yorkshire.'

'So where exactly is this getting us?' Nicholas asked, looking doubtful.

'Hear me out,' she countered.

'That led me to Deepdale and the day you and I rode there, thinking it was still an abandoned ruin. What do you recall about that?'

'You had some strange feelings about the place you interpreted as being caused by its history as a monastery or convent or something like that.'

'And you mocked me, saying it was the result of a convent education and my own over-active imagination.'

'Yes, well, what else do you expect?'

'Respect for my feelings, which must have been genuine enough or why should they recur here, on a ship in the Atlantic, with absolutely no connection to the old ruins in Deepdale?'

'So what is this telling you?' said Nicholas, with a slightly exasperated tone to his voice.

'Don't you see? I'm being told to seek solace in a convent.'

'A convent?' Nicholas shook his head in dismay. 'What exactly is that going to solve?'

'It will give us time to decide what to do next. It will be a perfect place for me to disappear. No one would think of looking for me there. Only you will know where I am. The nuns are sworn to keep secrets, but it won't be necessary for them to be told why I have gone there.'

'So you are prepared to lock yourself away for ever just to keep your one indiscretion a secret?' He frowned his disapproval.

'It's only irrevocable if I've decided to join the Order. Besides, I might find the life of a nun *is* for me.'

'You're only using it to run away from your problem. From a real future, for that matter. I can't say I approve.'

'It would give me time to consider that future, free from distractions such as our parents' questions.'

'Won't you have to take vows, make a commitment to become a nun?'

'Before that happens, a novice is always given time to consider. And it also gives the abbess time to decide if I would be an asset to the community and possess the devotion required to live as a nun.'

Nicholas gave a perplexed shake of his head.

'You will have your part to play in helping me make my decision though, Nicholas.'

'Me!' His face clouded. There was anger in his

eyes. 'What more do you want of me? If I agree to take you to this convent, wherever it may be, what then?'

'You must plead ignorance of my whereabouts.'

'What?' His voice rose in indignation. 'I have to keep this a secret, even from Mother and Father?'

'Yes! Well, for the time being, until I know what I wish my life to be.' Alice saw doubt in his eyes. 'Please, Nicholas, do as I ask.'

'And what do I tell our parents when they ask where you are?'

'Just that you know I am safe and will be getting in touch when I choose to. That will depend on the information you will send me about their attitudes and those of Steven's parents. When you think they are prepared to accept me back into everyday society, I will resign from the convent community.'

'And return to your family?'

'Yes.'

'You make it sound so simple. It's much harder from where I am standing.'

She leaned forward and grabbed his hands. 'It can be fairly straightforward, with your help and support.'

'You are not prepared to talk to Mother and Father yourself?'

'Not until the time is right.'

Still Nicholas hesitated to be part of this.

'Come on,' she pleaded, 'It's the only opportunity we have. It gives a perfectly good excuse for my returning from South Africa, where supposedly I found my true vocation: the religious life.'

'I agree there are possibilities in this,' said

Nicholas, still annoyed by her thoughtlessness towards him in the matter.

'Then please let us try it.'

'Don't you think Mother and Father will see through your deceit?'

'I'm not going to face them. I shall go straight to a convent when we leave the ship.'

There was still doubt in Nicholas's mind, even though he saw a glimmer of sense in her idea. 'We have two more days before we dock. Let us use that time to think the idea through thoroughly.'

Alice knew she had almost won him over. She jumped up and flung her arms round his neck. 'You're an angel,' she gasped. 'I don't deserve you.'

'And you are a persuasive devil,' her brother countered. 'See that nothing goes wrong with this scheme or that's when you lose me for good!'

32

Alice felt uneasy watching the approach of land as the *Capricorn* sailed up the Solent. Where was life taking her? Even with Nicholas beside her, and plans for the immediate future made, she knew she was stepping into uncertainty. She felt doubtful of her ability to manage by herself, and had to counteract that with the reminder that it was her own fault that she was in this situation. As the ship brought her back to England's shore, she decided she would put Africa behind her forever.

Nicholas was happy to find her in a determined

mood and hoped it would continue. He was going to leave any suggestions and decisions to Alice. She must be mistress of her own future.

'I have decided what to do,' Alice told him later that night when they had disembarked and found a hotel. 'There is a convent on the west coast of Scotland, established years ago by four nuns from the school I attended in Yorkshire. They were given their independence two years ago after the number of sisters had trebled. I understand the site is remote and not to every applicant's liking. If anyone wants to find me it is highly unlikely they will look there.'

'And I am still to be the only one who knows where you are?' asked Nicholas.

'Yes.'

'Are you really sure you are doing the right thing?'

'I don't know, I will have to see how things work out. I have chosen this place because it is in a very remote area about ten miles from Fort William. I know they are a kindly and welcoming order, I should be safe with them.'

'Are you sure the community does not attempt to compel women to join them?'

'Yes, certain.'

Nicholas did not speak for a moment.

'Well?' she asked.

'I don't want to lose my sister,' he said in a sad tone.

'You won't be losing me whichever path I take. I promise you that.'

'Even if you decide to join the Order permanently?'

'Not even then. Remember, that is only a possibility. I am going there primarily to contemplate what has happened to me, and hopefully purge myself of the wrong I did.'

He nodded, hesitated for a moment then said, 'Very well. Let us proceed. Steven will write to his mother, no doubt, though he may hold back for a while. He won't be relishing the thought of informing her that there will be no wedding, but I don't believe he will deliberately blacken your name. Nor will Matthew want to disclose his part in all this. I think it might be wise to write to Steven, informing him that we are back in England. After all, he did make sure we had sailed. I will tell him not to disclose to his mother any more than that you left because you didn't like the life you were expected to live in South Africa. We'll keep it simple.'

'Please don't give him a hint of what I intend to do,' pleaded Alice.

'Your secret will be safe with me. Our parents are bound to ask more, so for them you have disappeared while trying to come to terms with what has happened and will be in touch with them as soon as you have settled in England.'

'I had better tell Stella I don't need her services any longer.'

'Do it now then. The sooner we get you to Scotland, the better. I will organise your travel.'

Alarm flashed into her eyes. 'Our travel. You're surely coming with me, Nicholas?'

'You know I don't approve of what you did, nor of how you are handling your life now, but I will not desert you. I will take you there, if you desire.'

288

Relief surged through Alice. She laid her hand on his. 'Thank you,' she said in all sincerity. 'I couldn't do this without you. You deserve every happiness, and the girl who wins your heart will be the luckiest one in the world.'

Embarrassed, he stood up. 'Come on. This is about you, not me.'

Alice found her personal maid. 'Stella I want a word with you.'

'Yes, Miss?'

'I'm afraid I no longer require your services.'

'Oh, Miss. What have I done wrong?' Tears came to the girl's eyes.

'Nothing, Stella. You have been and are a special servant, but I will have no further need of a lady's maid.'

'Not ever, Miss?'

Alice was touched by the forlorn note of hope in Stella's question.

'Who knows, Stella?'

'You'll send for me if you do want someone? Oh, please say yes, Miss.'

'If it arises I will find you, but don't rely on that. I don't know how things will turn out for me in the future. However, there is one thing I will ask of you: do not speak to anyone of anything you may have heard in Africa. If you are questioned by any-one, you must answer, "I do not know." You can say that I left South Africa because I did not like the life there.'

'Yes, Miss. I won't speak of it at all.'

'Good. I depend on you to keep to that. I will give you a good reference, and the address of an employment bureau. I will pay you an extra six months' wages.'

'Oh, Miss! Thank you.'

'You will leave us in York. I expect that is where you will want to be. My brother and I will be travelling further north.'

Stella nodded mournfully. 'Yes, Miss.'

Amidst the hustle and bustle of Edinburgh's Waverley station, a porter took charge of their luggage and led them to a first class compartment on the train that would take them to Callandar; from there their route continued through breathtaking scenery that commanded their attention and enabled them to blank from their minds the purpose of their onward journey.

The backdrop of rounded hills and soaring mountains, against sea and loch, stirred Alice to make comparisons to the land she had briefly seen in South Africa. She felt more comfortable with what she was experiencing now, away from the searing heat. This was her land. She had missed it during her travels so perhaps what had happened had some element of recompense. It had brought her home at least.

As the train rumbled on she reflected on her transgression in Africa. Would she ever escape the consequences and be able to face her mother and father again? Would St Mary's Convent in a remote part of Scotland help her to resolve the conflict in her mind?

In Oban Nicholas hired an automobile. It was fortunate indeed he had learned to drive one on the estate and occasionally used it when bad weather precluded taking a horse out.

'These are drovers' roads we're on, rough but they could be worse,' he explained. 'From what I have heard about this convent's location, it will not be easy to find. You'll need to keep a close eye on the map.

'We are making good time,' he observed later. 'I had thought of stopping overnight in Fort William, but I'm all in favour of reaching our destination as quickly as we can.'

'I'm in your hands,' replied Alice. 'If that is what you prefer, then let us do it. We need to take a road to the left about four miles north of Fort William. It soon becomes a track apparently, but is usable with care.'

'Sounds as though we are going into the back of beyond, but we shall see.'

What was termed a track was unsurfaced with two well-rutted depressions in it where the wheels of their vehicle found some purchase. And all the while the mountains around Ben Nevis seemed determined to make their presence felt, even though the two travellers knew they were slowly increasing the distance travelled away from them. The remoteness of their immediate surroundings was strongly impressed on their minds.

'Are you really sure you want to go through with this?' asked Nicholas. 'The convent is very isolated. Won't you feel trapped after I leave?'

'I don't think so. I might have experienced that if the convent had been more in the shadow of Ben Nevis, but ahead of us the country is opening up.'

As they were traversing the next mile, the track began to climb a gentle incline. The scenery revealed on every side brought expressions of delight and admiration from both of them. On a level plateau Nicholas stopped so he could admire the panorama.

'Wonderful,' he whispered.

'Beautiful,' was Alice's contribution as she immersed herself in the splendour of the view.

They sat transfixed, without speaking, for ten minutes.

The plateau on which they had stopped sloped down steadily to a loch. The encroaching hills enclosed the water like a rare jewel nestling against the earth and rock and heather. Delicate gradations of colour were reflected off the loch. Trees swayed before a gentle breeze, the murmuring of their leaves the only sound to accompany the perfect scene.

'If ever I feel the need, I will recall this scene,' sighed Alice.

'The overall picture or the convent specifically?' queried Nicholas.

'The convent?' asked a puzzled Alice.

'Over the other side of the loch, barely noticeable but just peeping through the trees.'

'Oh! Ah, there, I see it now.'

'It must have been looking you over before revealing itself.'

'I hope it liked what it saw.'

'More important, do you like what you see?'

'Yes, but there are deeper things here and in me that have to come together.'

'True,' agreed Nicholas. 'But, Alice, don't be swayed by what you are seeing now. There's enchantment in the air today, but it may not always be there. Remember that another magical moment got you into this mess in the first place. Come on, we had better find out what awaits us.'

He started the engine, released the brake and let the car move slowly forward, hoping that his sister would find what she sought here – happiness.

33

The front door opened before them and a nun stepped out and signalled them to park to the right of it.

The blouse-like top of her black dress, buttoned at the neck, fitted close to her waist from where its folds fell evenly to her ankles. A small black knitted skullcap failed to hide every strand of her hair. She had delicate ivory skin and wore a warm smile of welcome, Nicholas was glad to see. He judged her to be in her early thirties and was struck by the sense of peace and contentment that radiated from her.

'Good day to you, and welcome to Saint Mary's Convent,' she greeted them. 'We don't get many visitors here. I am Sister Martha.' She gave a little chuckle. 'The name fits me perfectly – so many workaday things to see to. I am responsible for household matters at the convent, the practical necessities of life here. I saw you arriving from my office window, please come in.'

As she started to lead the way Nicholas said, 'I

am Nicholas Ware and this is my sister Alice.'

'I am pleased to meet you.'

As they entered her office the brother and sister noticed that everything on the desk was precisely placed, and that the shelves covering the wall behind were neatly stacked with files, ledgers and books.

'Please sit down.' Sister Martha indicated two armchairs as she went to her own chair at the other side of the desk. As soon as she saw Alice and Nicholas were comfortably seated she sat down, folding her hands together and placing them before her.

'Now tell me what brings you here? Is this what the outside world would call a social call? Have you come upon us by chance? Or maybe you were directed by the Good Lord?'

Nicholas glanced at his sister and saw by her expression that she wanted him to make the introduction. 'I will not skirt round that question,' he began. 'It is only fair to you, to your community and to Alice that you have all the facts.'

As he stopped momentarily, Sister Martha added, 'And to you, no doubt? I say that because you must be involved, for whatever reason, if you felt obliged to bring your sister here. Whatever you disclose will remain confidential, you can rest assured.'

'Thank you for making that clear, Sister,' said Alice firmly. Not wanting at this point to give away too much information, she said, 'I heard of your convent from a friend, but know very little about the establishment.'

'We are very remote here, so I don't imagine

294

you have arrived out of curiosity. I think maybe you have a particular reason for coming.'

'Yes. A personal reason that only my brother knows about but which has led me to believe I may like to join your order.'

The nun held up her hand. 'I do not wish to know what that reason might be. That will be the concern of our abbess, to whom I will take you shortly. For now, all that I am concerned about is sorting out accommodation for you and that requires me to know the possible length of your stay. In your case, Alice, you may not know. In Nicholas's, we have what is termed a guesthouse for travellers and short-stay visitors including relatives. So let us start by fixing you both up with rooms.'

They followed her along two corridors and on to a covered way that linked with two further buildings.

'This is our guest wing for females. Across this small cloister is one for male visitors, with no direct connection between the two. Your meals are shared with the community – convent rules and times are posted on your door. As visitors you are not members of the community so are not obliged to follow the times listed there, but you would get more out of your visit if you did so.' She took them to see the room Alice would occupy.

She could not hide her surprise. She had expected to be met by Spartan conditions whereas she found a room that was well appointed, with bed, wardrobe, armchair and a dressing table, all hand-made with loving care.

Sister Martha noted her reaction and with a

smile explained, 'One of our community, Sister Anne, is an expert carpenter who learned the trade from her father. As you see, she has put her skill to good use for the community.'

So the little tour went on, with Nicholas finding his room the equal of his sister's. He felt more comfortable now about leaving her behind in this out-of-the way place.

'If you will excuse me for a few moments, I will check if Mother Abbess is available to see you.' Sister Martha slipped quietly away, to return shortly afterwards and say, 'She will see you now.' While leading the way back into the main building, Sister Martha told them a little about the organisation of the convent.

'A community such as ours is run by the nuns themselves according to the talents at their disposal. So I am in charge of hospitality and the everyday running of the convent, except for the catering which is in the hands of Sister Letitia. We grow what we can in our garden, but in consultation with her I put out orders for further provisions to local farmers. So, you see, it is very much a help-one-another community, using our talents to the best of our abilities.'

Within a few minutes they were meeting the abbess in her office, the hub of the community in which the individual lives of its inhabitants and their welfare, the daily and long-term upkeep of the property, and above all their religious worship, were supervised.

'Abbess Loyola, I bring you the two visitors I mentioned earlier, Miss Alice Ware and her brother Nicholas.' With the newcomers' attention fixed on the abbess, Sister Martha passed a finger across her forehead. A sign that she considered it might prove useful to the abbess for Martha to stay present at her superior's interview with the newcomers.

The elderly nun rose from her seat behind the desk and came to greet them with her hand outstretched. They both felt friendship in her gentle grip and in the simple blessing she made over them with her hand.

'I am pleased to meet you. Please do sit down.' The elderly abbess indicated the two seats that had been placed facing the desk. 'Don't go, Sister Martha,' she added. 'You should hear a little more about why these two people are here. If they are seeking help in some way, it would be as well for you to hear of it.'

Alice's apprehension disappeared as the abbess's soothing voice washed over her, instilling in her the confidence to speak. She looked from her hands, which she had clasped together on her lap, and met the encouragement in the nun's friendly eyes.

Sister Martha drew up a chair unobtrusively.

'I would say that you have experienced convent life before?' said the abbess. Alice's show of surprise at this observation was not lost on the nun. 'You are wondering how I judged that. Well, I have interviewed many girls, mostly before I came here, who were wondering if they had a vocation born in their schooldays at a convent. Nearly all of them looked round my office, comparing it to the one they had experienced in their schooldays. You did the same.'

Alice blushed, but found the abbess's observation kindly put and felt an encouraging warmth in the nun's interest in her.

'Am I right, Alice?' she prompted.

She gave a little smile in return. 'Yes, Mother.'

When she offered no further information, Abbess Loyola said, 'You do not want to tell me where that convent was?'

'Not at the moment,' replied Alice.

'You think I might trace your parents through that information?'

'You could do.'

'And you have a good reason for not wanting them to know where you are?'

'Yes, Mother.'

'Very well. That is your right unless it becomes obvious that I must intervene for the sake of your welfare. We'll set that aside for now. So, are you here because you want to take up the religious life?'

'I am not sure, Mother. I think so. Recently certain problems have come into my life and I need to try to see whether I have a true vocation or where else my future might lie.'

'Where else might that be?'

'I don't know.'

'Have you sought advice from your mother and father?'

'No.'

'Your parish priest?'

'No.'

'The chaplain to the convent where you were at school?'

'No.'

'So none of them knows you are here?'

'No one knows except for my brother Nicholas.'

The abbess nodded thoughtfully, paused and then said, 'When any girl comes here with the thought of joining the convent, we do like to know who should be contacted if required.'

'In my case, it should be Nicholas.'

'Is there a good reason why your parents should not be told?'

'Only because, as yet, I don't want them to know where I am. I don't wish them to influence my decision. Only Nicholas need know for the present.'

The abbess looked directly at him. 'Does that sit easily with you, Nicholas?'

He had been listening to the questions and answers carefully. 'Yes. I believe I can read behind your questions and know what your next one is likely to be. I can say here and now that my sister is not with child. Her reasons for being here are complicated but they have led her to find solace in her faith. She sought my advice and proposed that she should come here to try and find her way forward. I attempted to persuade her to inform Mother and Father, but she does not wish to do that yet.'

'Yet?' The abbess inclined her head and gave a puzzled frown. 'So you think she intends to tell them eventually?'

'Yes, I do, once she has made her own mind up about what she wants to do.'

Both of them turned to Alice. 'Is that right, my dear?' asked the abbess.

She nodded in agreement, adding, 'I hope that will not be too long, but I cannot judge when it will be or the course I wish to take. I thought I might be able to do everything more easily if I escaped from the world.'

'So you came here to do just that?'

'As I said, Mother, I have lived in a convent previously and I need to reflect on the calling I might or might not have.'

The abbess leaned back in her chair, studying both Alice and Nicholas thoughtfully. The silence that had come over the room was almost palpable. Alice shot a quick glance at Nicholas and caught a very light movement of his head, warning her. She said nothing more.

The abbess steepled her fingers before her. It would be easier if she knew more about what had marked this young life but she knew she would not get any further details from Alice or her brother, who obviously had a strong regard for her and would help in any way he could without betraying her wishes.

After a few moments she glanced at Sister Martha, who had remained motionless throughout the exchange. Having her sit in on the new arrivals' interviews gave the abbess someone with whom to discuss her impressions of them, which often proved invaluable.

'Alice, it is no good beating about the bush. From the little I have gleaned, I believe you are suffering from what I call a problem of conscience. The fact that you have kept the details from people who are dear to you tells me you are facing a dilemma that, if not solved properly, could leave

300

its mark on you and others for the rest of your lives. Yes, you may want to become a nun but you need time to sort out your old life first. Here you will be given the peace and tranquillity in which you can do that. And if you have the religious calling, you will eventually be able to profess it to the Order.'

She awaited Alice's reaction. The moments stretched. Nicholas thought he should say something but saw the abbess raise a finger, warning him not to. They waited. Then Alice started as if she had thrown off something that was holding her back.

'Thank you, Mother Abbess,' she said quietly. 'You have been very understanding. You have pointed out a path for me to take and generously offered me the sanctuary of the convent. I do not know if will eventually take my vows but I believe this is the right place to make a decision that will shape the rest of my life.'

34

Tears began to fall as Alice watched the car swing round the loch and climb the hill above. Envy swelled within her for a moment – Nicholas was heading home!

It faded with the reminder that he would have to face their mother and father and fend off all the questions they would fire at him about what had happened in South Africa to stop the wedding and where Alice was now.

She dabbed her eyes with her handkerchief and straightened her shoulders, determined to follow the road she had chosen which, at the moment, was one of uncertainty. Her gaze swept over the water. How easy it would be to banish for good the problems she had caused herself during a few minutes of reckless unrestraint. Here and now she could put that right. She made a slight movement of her feet towards the water.

'Ah, Alice, there you are.'

The voice startled her. Her thoughts whirled in confusion. She swung round. 'Oh, Sister Martha!'

The nun made no reference to what she had supposed Alice was about to do. Instead she said soothingly, 'Should we take a walk? It is never good to be alone after seeing a loved one depart, no matter where or what the circumstances are.' She came alongside Alice, who fell into step beside her. 'Have you ever been in Scotland before?' Sister Martha deliberately made the query casual.

'No.'

'It is a lovely country and we are privileged to be able to live amongst such beauty.'

'Have you always been here since you became a nun?'

'No. I joined a convent straight from school. It was near Glasgow where I lived. That was a mistake; it nearly led to my leaving religious orders completely. I was too near home. I need not go into all the details of my life since I moved on except to say that eventually I heard of this place, and after one visit I decided I would try again.'

'It obviously worked for you; you are still here.

But did you find it hard at the start?'

'Yes, I did. It was very different living here from what I had been used to. Remember, I had been a city girl. But after a month here I knew this was where I needed to be. I set about involving myself and adapting my life to the world I had chosen. You'll only be taking simple vows so if you find convent life is not what you want, you can always leave. You may think you have already seen something of that life but you'll get a shock when you move from the comparative comfort of the guest room to the austerity of a novice's.'

After the lunchtime meal of soup, bread and rice pudding, Alice was taken to meet the elderly nun in charge of the novitiate.

'I am Sister Winifred,' she introduced herself and then, turning to a young nun standing beside her, said, 'This is Sister Celia. She has been with us two weeks so is in a similar position to you, Alice – here on simple vows. Sister Celia, Sister Alice has joined us today. You are the only applicants we have at the moment so you form our postulancy. You will remain so for six months after which you will become novices and will be in our novitiate for two years. Then comes three years in the juniorate, after which you make your final vows. I hope you will embrace our life and eventually take solemn vows. Sit down and I will tell you what we expect from you here.'

She related how their days would be divided up. 'You will spend your time at religious services and in private devotion, but when you are not attending to these you will also have various tasks to accomplish as well as domestic work.'

When Sister Winifred had finished with them, Alice was allowed time to settle in.

'My room's next to yours. I will see you again soon,' whispered Sister Celia as she parted from Alice at the door that would introduce her to her new life.

When she stepped inside Alice felt overcome by deep loneliness. She sank back against the door and wept. Through her tears she glanced around the room. This really was Spartan compared to the guest room she had occupied yesterday. There was not even a mirror on the wall. Then she had been a guest, now she was on the bottom rung of convent life and that was not easy to take after the world she had grown up in.

'Oh, Nicholas, I miss you!' she cried aloud.

She pushed herself away from the door, sank down on the bed and gave way to her misery.

Nicholas took two days to reach Yorkshire, allowing himself time to consider what he should tell his parents.

His heart was beating a little faster as his taxi cab drew to a halt in front of Wooton Hall. He sat still for a moment, stealing himself. Then he drew a deep breath and swung out of the vehicle. He strode in at the front door just as a maid was bringing a tray of tea from the kitchen. Startled to see him, she almost dropped it. He steadied it for her, smiled and said quietly, 'I'm no ghost. Are my parents in the drawing room?'

'Yes, sir.'

'I'll take the tray in and surprise them.'

'Very good, sir,' she said. 'I'll bring the extra

cup for you.'

He took the tray and she scurried past him to open the lounge door. He mouthed a silent 'Thank you'.

His father was deep into his newspaper and his mother was dozing in her usual armchair.

'Your tea is served,' Nicholas announced as he slid the tray on to the small table placed conveniently between his parents.

They both started, and stared at their son in disbelief.

'What? You! What are you doing here?' spluttered his father.

'Nicholas! Why aren't you in Africa?' his mother asked, still hazy with sleep.

'It's a long story.'

His parents waited impatiently, all interest in the tea gone. Nicholas took a sip from his own cup and it seemed to settle him. 'There is much to tell you and much that I cannot. Some things can only be told when Alice decides to make them known.'

'Make what known?' his mother demanded in a no-nonsense tone of voice.

'I will tell you now, the wedding has not taken place. She returned to England with me.' Nicholas remembered what Alice wanted her parents to believe. 'She did not like Africa nor what she saw of the life of an Army wife.'

'Why?' asked his mother as she exchanged a glance of disbelief with Sir Raymond.

'And why isn't Alice here?' he snapped. 'Or is she in trouble?' There was no mistaking what he was enquiring about.

'It is nothing like that!' Nicholas's retort came sharp and clear. 'Believe me, I would tell you more if I could, but I have sworn to my sister that I would reveal nothing more of what she experienced in Africa. That is up to her.'

'We should know,' said his father, quietly but forcefully. 'We are her parents.'

'I agree, but I am sworn to secrecy. Believe me, the circumstances are such that the whole story will be better coming from her, when she wants to tell it.'

'Does Steven's mother know?' Lady Ware demanded angrily.

'I don't know. I doubt it, if she has not already contacted you.'

'Then I shall go and see her at once. I want to learn what has happened.'

'I wouldn't do that, Mother. I think, like yourself and Alice, the Cheeveys won't want to talk about it. They will not wish to lose face. Please be aware that Alice wants what she has to tell you to remain a secret for now.'

Lady Cecilia shook her head in disbelief and anger. A long pause followed and then she stated, 'Very well, but do at least tell us where she is.'

Nicholas held up his hands as if to prevent further questioning. 'Please don't persist in this. I will tell you more about Africa but only enough to allay any fears you may have. I will *not* betray my sister's wishes. Believe me, it is for her own good and for her peace of mind. She will certainly tell you everything herself when she feels the time is right. But I beg of you not to keep pestering me to reveal more. I won't do it. Let me say again, Alice is perfectly safe, in very good health, but wants peace and quiet on her own in order to make certain decisions that she has promised to share with us when she feels the time is right.'

His mother and father, knowing the strength of their son's brotherly love, knew they should bow to Alice's wishes for the time being. They did not want Nicholas to leave them as well as, it seemed, their daughter had.

Alice started. The morning handbell was sounding outside her door. She dragged her mind free from sleep, trying to remember what they had been told about all the bells. Ah, yes, this one was for a first call to church. She tumbled quickly off the bed, with a quick straightening of the bed-clothes and then her habit. She stepped out of the door. It was only 5 a.m.

'I was just coming to see if you had heard the bell,' said Sister Celia. 'We'd better be quick. We don't want to miss the service. Someone would notice.'

'That's a hard bed,' whispered Alice in disgust. 'But you were right when you told me I wouldn't be bothered at the end of an exhausting day.' However, she couldn't escape the reminders of it prompted by her aches and pains: prayers, kitchen, prayers, kitchen, scrubbing, peeling, lifting heavy pans, prayers, kitchen, washing, chapel, more work, on and on. Tomorrow it would be the same, and the day after that, and again and again. Why had she come here? What had she done to deserve this? The word Africa mocked her then.

307

Would the memories ever be exorcised?

Every night Alice wept herself to sleep until the first two weeks of silence were over. When the nuns had lined the cloister after morning service, the abbess informed the community that Sister Alice had joined Sister Celia in serving their simple vows as members of the community. The nuns clapped and, as they broke lines, congratulations and welcomes flowed, almost overpowering Alice with sound after her enforced silence. When she reached her room she flopped on to her bed. There were no tears, but sighs of relief that the silence was over and the atmosphere had lightened. But the chores had not.

'Look at my hands,' Alice muttered to Celia one morning. 'Red raw after all that soda.' And later, 'How many more potatoes am I going to peel?'

Celia smiled. Turning Alice's hands over, she said, 'You haven't peeled potatoes before. Look how many times you've nicked your fingers with the knife.'

'I'd be pleased by a change of job,' sighed Alice.

'Don't be too keen for that. I reckon it's coming and you might not like it.'

'What have you heard?'

'Nothing. I'm only surmising.'

'Come on, tell me.'

'You'll have noticed that patch of waste ground to the right of the kitchen door?'

'Yes.'

'Haven't you noticed two nuns doing some measuring there?'

'I didn't think about what they were doing.'

'Mark my words, in a day or two's time, you

and I will be delegated a patch each to cultivate, growing vegetables and potatoes for the community and possibly flowers for the altar.'

'It will be a change from the kitchen and wonderful to be outside. Fresh air and sunshine!' Alice stretched at the thought of it.

Sister Celia chuckled. 'We'll see what you think after a week of it.'

Seven days later, after a day spent in their gardens with breaks only to attend religious services and meals, Alice remembered Celia's warning. 'I see what you meant,' she said as they left their patches. 'My back is aching, my legs are protesting, and just look at my hands. The fingers of the gloves they gave us were soon worn through and now my hands are filthy. Oh, there's dirt down my fingernails. I'll never get it out with that miserable brush I was given. And my nails used to be so beautiful.' She shook her head sadly as a vision of her previous life swam across her mind.' She paused a moment then added, 'I wish...'

Celia interrupted her with a sharp note in her voice. 'Don't start wishing for things you can't have or get unless you are thinking of leaving. If you are, get it over with or you'll be upsetting my plans.'

'And what are those?' asked Alice, piqued by the criticism.

'I was going to tell you later. I will definitely take each step towards finally making my solemn vows.'

Alice stared at her. 'You know that already?'

'Yes.'

'I can't contemplate it yet.'

'I'm sure it will come, Alice. You are a good person.'

Those words returned to her as she got into bed that night. A good person? What would Celia think of her if she knew the whole story?

35

Alice sat nervously facing the abbess across the superior's desk.

Sensing that she was ill at ease, Mother Abbess Loyola leaned forward and said gently, 'You requested this interview. Is something troubling you?'

Alice hesitated then the words tumbled out. 'After six months I realise that I would like to join the community on a permanent basis.'

'I had hoped this would happen,' said the abbess, with satisfaction in her voice. 'I am pleased you have taken some time to reach this decision. It shows you have considered it carefully. Better that than rush into a decision you might regret later. Of course this novitiate remains the early stage of your commitment. You will be clothed in your habit, make simple vows, live with the community and follow the monastic timetable. You and Sister Celia have reached the same decision. I know that the rest of the nuns will be as pleased as I am. I have never had any doubts that you would make a good member of the community but I did not voice that to you because I did not want to exert any pressure. So if you are absolutely sure you want to make the first step, I'll set everything in motion.

'Sister Winifred will have explained the various steps so I'll not go into them again. We are only concerned now with your simple commitment, but we like to make it special so let us find a suitable date.' She flicked at a calendar and studied it. 'Ah, this should fit in nicely for both you and Sister Celia ... a month today.' She looked up quickly to catch Alice's reaction but gained no enlightenment from her serious expression.

Back in her room Alice wrote to her brother,

Dear Nicholas,

I have just come from seeing the abbess, requesting her approval of my decision to join the community. She has agreed. So I will be here for two years as a novice during which time I can still renounce my simple vows. However, I don't think that will happen, as I experienced such joy when the abbess accepted me.

The date when Sister Celia and I will be clothed is set for a month today.

I hope you will be able to come. It would mean so much to me to have you here.

I think now is the time to tell Mother and Father where I am, without mentioning the facts about my having to leave South Africa. Would you please do that for me, and tell them I will write to them in the hope that they too will attend my clothing?

Your loving and grateful sister,
Alice.

Nicholas had been visiting a bank in York on estate business. Before heading home, he picked up Alice's latest letter from the prearranged address he and his sister had agreed on.

He opened the envelope immediately, relief spreading over him with every word he read. While he would have to continue keeping some aspects of her life in South Africa a secret, he could now at least reveal where his sister was living. He lost no time in reaching Wooton Hall where he rode straight to the stables to leave his horse. A wall-clock told him that his mother and father would be in the dining room about to start lunch.

'I didn't expect to see you until later today,' remarked his mother.

'All was well at the bank, I hope?' queried Sir Raymond.

'Yes,' replied Nicholas, as he rang the bell for the maid. 'But I have some news that I thought you would wish to hear immediately so I came straight home.' The maid appeared and Nicholas asked for another place to be set. When she had done so and closed the door, he added, 'I've had a letter from Alice.'

His parents had put down their cutlery and were watching him intently, hungry for news of their daughter. With Nicholas's announcement the atmosphere in the room became charged with expectation.

'It will be easier if I tell you where Alice is, what she has been doing and her hopes for her life ahead,' Nicholas began. His parents listened attentively. 'When Alice left South Africa, she was confused by what was happening in her life. She

312

realised that it was best she return to England, and of course I was able to accompany her and see her safely home.'

'But she didn't come home,' his father pointed out.

'That's right. Why?' asked his mother.

'As I explained at the time, she was embarrassed to be returning so soon, and unmarried too.'

'What has happened has happened. Now we must do our best to support her,' said Sir Raymond stoically. He looked at Nicholas. 'Well, where is she? Why is she not here with us? Surely she must have known that we would help her all we could?'

'I think she did know that, Father, but she was ashamed of her own failure and the knowledge that she had let you down. She wanted to make amends to you, to me, and above all to herself.'

Sir Raymond nodded thoughtfully as he said quietly, 'Good girl. With that sort of spirit she will be all right. Well, Nicholas, where is she?'

There was a short silence. Then: 'She is in St Mary's Convent, about twenty miles from Fort William in Scotland.'

Raymond and Cecilia gasped at this unexpected news. They looked at their son in disbelief. This was the last thing they had expected to hear.

'But...' Sir Raymond let his question trail away, lost in the mystery of it all.

Lady Cecilia sat dumbstruck, trying to come to terms with what this news could mean: the loss of her daughter for ever behind the closed doors of a convent. She just had to put the question. 'Is this an enclosed Order, Nicholas?'

'No, Mother, it isn't. There are strict rules, but it is not enclosed.'

His mother breathed a sigh of relief. 'At least that's something. You've seen her, Nicholas?'

'Yes, on two or three occasions, and we have kept in touch by letter. I can assure you, Alice is well and happy. She seems to be taking to life in the convent very well. After all, she spent her school days in one. St Mary's is only a small convent, established from a larger one for nuns seeking isolation permanently or just from time to time. That was one reason why Alice chose this Order, because it had the facility of remoteness. That was what she wanted in order to give herself a chance to recover from her African experience.'

'And has she done that?' asked Sir Raymond.

'I believe she has, but you and Mother can judge for yourselves. Alice is entering the novitiate and taking simple vows in just under a month's time. She asked me to inform you of that and expresses her hope that you will attend that ceremony?' Nicholas did not wait for an answer but went on quickly when he saw his mother grappling with what this might mean, 'It does not necessarily mean she is, at this point, committing herself to the life of a nun for ever. This step means that she will be a member of the convent but will remain under simple vows for six months, after which she will take the next step towards eventually committing herself fully to the religious life.'

'So there is still a chance she may change her mind and leave?' asked his mother anxiously and with some hope in her voice.

'Yes.'

'Good. Then I will write to her at once.'

'Mother, write to her by all means ... she will love hearing from you ... but please be careful what you say. Don't put any pressure on her. I can tell Alice is on the verge of making a decision that could make or break her. Hopefully whatever she decides will be right for her.'

'Are we going to break this news to Emma?'

'I would wait until after you have seen Alice,' said Nicholas. And, trying to make light of the matter, added, 'If Alice decides at some point after she has seen you that she will forsake convent life, there will be no need to tell Mrs Cheevey she ever contemplated joining an Order of nuns.'

His mother and father took his point and agreed that nothing should be made public until events in Scotland had unfolded.

Lady Cecilia wrote to her daughter:

Dear Alice,

Nicholas has just told us where you are. Your father and I are deeply relieved by this news but must say that we wish you had come home immediately on your return from South Africa. Nicholas has explained the reasoning behind this but I do feel it is not the whole story. Maybe one day we will know.

However, we are now trying to come to terms with your desire to become a nun. Nicholas has given us your reasons for this and has told us of your forthcoming simple vows. Alice, your father and I will be delighted to attend that service and look forward immensely to seeing you again and also the convent in which you will be living. It is in beautiful countryside,

315

Nicholas tells us. Well, we look forward to seeing it for ourselves. I have no doubt your brother is already planning our journey and stay.

Alice, you have no idea how wonderful it is to be in touch with you once more and we sincerely hope that contact is never broken again.

Take care, my dear.

Lady Cecilia signed the letter and called for her husband to sign it too. He did so with a flourish that expressed his joy at the coming reunion with his daughter.

Alice was overjoyed to receive that letter. In the privacy of her bleak room she hugged herself with delight. There had been no disagreement or reproaches. Now in the time remaining until her simple profession, she could look forward to that day being made extra special by their attendance.

36

Nicholas's mother had assumed correctly that her son would already be making arrangements for their journey north. He wanted everything to be in place in plenty of time so that there would be no last minute hitches.

'There are several letters for you, Nicholas,' said Lady Cecilia when he arrived in the dining room for lunch a week after his parents had received the letter from Alice.

He opened them, laying aside five and then looking up at her. 'There you are, all our accommodation is settled so you need have no worries except to pack the clothes you will require.'

'That's a relief,' said his mother, contentment in her voice as she sank back against her chair. 'And now, with everything arranged, we can relax and anticipate meeting our daughter again.'

'Very true,' agreed Nicholas. But he had not anticipated yet another twist in the tortuous course of Alice's life.

It came two days later in the form of a letter from Steven.

Dear Nicholas,

I am now in England, which I know will come as a surprise. The reason I am writing to you is to ask if we could meet. The letter you sent me a while ago made me realise there are still things I need to ask you, things that trouble me about the way I parted from Alice and my severity towards her. Thank you, by the way, for your discretion with our parents in the matter of the wedding and Alice's return from Africa.

Please say you will meet me? I'll come anywhere you like. No one else knows I am writing to you, and it will stay that way.

I remember saying to you once that I thought you and I could get on well. We are not brothers, but something tells me we may rely on each other's good faith.

Yours in hope,
Steven

Nicholas's first impulse was to tear this letter up

and let the pieces flutter away with the breeze.

Normally he would have received his mail when his parents were present. Had fate stepped in today by bringing the letter to him while he was alone? His parents need never know that he had received it – he could just forget it. But he read it through again, more slowly, seeking something that would exonerate him from revealing its existence. He stared at it – then realised that behind Steven's cautious words there was a cry for help. Could Nicholas ignore this? He thought about their last meeting and the way Steven had deliberately evoked it in the letter. There was no mistaking the fact that Steven was relying on him to do the right thing.

Nicholas replied to him at an address in London. Two days later he rode into York, handed his horse over to the stable boys at the hotel and walked briskly inside.

'Good day, sir,' a clerk greeted him pleasantly.

'Mr Nicholas Ware. Have you a message for me?'

'Yes, sir. Mr Cheevey awaits you in the small lounge, sir.'

A bell-boy, hovering close by, sprang forward. 'Follow me, sir.'

As soon as Nicholas entered the room, Steven was on to his feet and giving him a friendly smile.

'It is good to see you, Nicholas, and I am so grateful that you agreed to meet me.' They shook hands. 'Shall we sit here?' Steven invited.

As they were making themselves comfortable a waiter appeared, carrying a tray with two glasses of whisky and a small jug of water.

'I took the liberty of ordering,' said Steven, 'recalling that you liked a single malt.'

Nicholas acknowledged this and added, 'It shall be no other.' They each took a sip of whisky.

'Do your parents keep well?' asked Steven.

'Remarkably so,' replied Nicholas. 'Time is a healer, particularly when allowed it to be.' Then he added quickly, before Steven could utter another word, 'I have no idea why you requested this meeting but I don't think it was merely a social call or that it is an attempt to retrieve a broken friendship. So why are we meeting?'

'You are correct, and right to come straight to the point too,' said Steven. 'It is no use our pretending there is not a shadow hanging over us. As I said in my letter, there are things I must lay to rest with Alice. I need to know where she is.'

Nicholas was thankful that, at that moment, the waiter came up to check everything was satisfactory. He diverted Steven with a question of his own.

'The clerk referred to you just now as Mr Cheevey,' Nicholas commented.

Steven nodded his head.

'I realised that because of the shame I felt, and for other reasons, I had to leave the Army, so, here I am back in Britain for good. I am staying with friends in London for the time being. Nicholas, I must make my peace with Alice before facing my parents. So here I am, seeking your help.'

Nicholas did not reply at first, taken aback by Steven's abandoning the military life and his changed manner. He seemed almost humble now.

'Steven,' Nicholas began, 'before we continue

discussing your attempt to find Alice, may I ask you something?'

'Whatever you wish.'

'Do you miss Army life?'

Steven was surprised by the question, which seemed to him to have no bearing on his search for Alice. He hesitated then replied thoughtfully.

'When I made the decision to leave, I thought I would. After all, I really know no other life. I enjoyed being in a man's world. Once I had made the break, however, strange as it may seem, I didn't miss it as much as I thought I would. Now I feel sure it was the right decision to leave. I suppose in a way I am lucky, I will always have Heatherfold.' He gave a little smile. 'Strange how life plays tricks on you, isn't it? I was the Army man, talked about as the one who would have a glittering military career, while Matthew had no interest in it; hated it, in fact. Then something happens in my private life and everything is turned upside down. I am now aiming to make Heatherfold my life, while Matthew's resignation was not accepted and he is making a name for himself in clandestine operations, at the moment still in South Africa, keeping an eye on the Boers, but willing to serve in that capacity anywhere in the world. But why did you want to know that? It has no bearing on my need to see Alice.'

'You never know how things will turn out. You and Matthew have had a change of roles. Other people too have changed the course of their life,' Nicholas said carefully.

Steven looked thoughtful and then said, 'So what can you tell me about your sister?'

Nicholas looked at him squarely. 'I do know where she is.' He saw the light of expectancy and hope coming to Steven's eyes. 'But I am bound by certain promises I made to her about keeping her whereabouts secret.'

'But surely you...'

Nicholas cut in sharply, 'No, I cannot disclose them to you. Don't try to persuade me or you will only meet a complete and lasting silence.'

Steven knew that to be true. He knew the loyalty that existed between this brother and sister. He eyed Nicholas, wondering how to get the information he required. Nicholas facing him with a non-committal expression on his face, wondering how far he could, or should, betray his sister's trust. His main concern was her happiness, but did he know where that lay and had he the right to play God with other people's lives? Besides, wasn't it already too late?

37

'I do appreciate what you have told me, Steven, and will give your request due consideration. Certain promises were made to Alice, but I will reach a decision within the next ten days.' Nicholas saw disappointment cloud Steven's face and added, 'I will keep my promise. Please be patient. I only hope I come to the right decision for everyone.'

'I understand,' Steven conceded. 'You can reach me at my London address.'

He added, 'I would be grateful if you did not pass it on to anyone, not even my mother. I wish to make contact with Alice before I communicate with Deepdale, if you would please bear that in mind.'

'Your whereabouts shall remain secret,' Nicholas promised.

They talked for a few more minutes before they rose from their chairs, shook hands and left the hotel; a hopeful Steven for London, a thoughtful Nicholas for Wooton Hall.

Nicholas tried to make the journey north as pleasant as possible for his parents. He sensed that they were apprehensive about the forthcoming meeting with their daughter. After all, the last time they had seen her was before she left for South Africa with marriage strongly in mind; yet now they were to see her as a nun, accepted to serve simple vows in a convent in Scotland. It was a huge change for them to encompass.

'It is good to see you, sir,' the proprietor of the hotel in Fort William said as he and his wife shook hands with Nicholas. He felt awkward before his parents at this demonstration of his regular visits to see Alice. But they uttered no word of reproach.

He left them in their room to recover from their journey.

As the door closed on him, Raymond stepped over to his wife and took her in his arms. He looking lovingly into her eyes.

'This is a new path in our lives, Cecilia. Let us make it a happy one, especially for Alice. Whatever her reason for deserting Steven and Africa, we will not probe. We brought her and Nicholas up to make their own judgements, so long as they were not destructive. We have stood by them so far. We should continue to do so.'

Cecilia gave a little nod of agreement as she looked into his eyes. 'You are a wise man, Raymond. I am lucky to have you.'

'It is a partnership we have created together,' he replied.

She reached up and kissed him. With his arms still round her, she leaned back and met his loving gaze that said everything necessary without a word being spoken.

Even though they had been determined to face the next day with open minds, they awoke to it with fear of the unknown weighing heavily on their minds. When Nicholas joined his parents in the dining room for breakfast he guessed their thoughts. Will Alice have changed? Has the convent taken her from us? Will she no longer be our daughter?

He attempted to raise their spirits, talking about the beauty of Alice's chosen retreat and how it should not take too long to reach it.

Their questions loomed again when he turned the car off the better road heading north from Fort William.

They had travelled only half a mile when his mother cast doubt on the location. 'Where on earth are we going? This is a godforsaken road.'

'But look at the beautiful mountain scenery, Mother,' countered Nicholas.

She heaved a sigh that projected her doubts

about Alice's choice of such an out-of-the-way place. 'We'll never see our daughter again!' she said, giving way to her doubts.

'Cecilia, never is an awful long time,' responded her husband, trying to ease her mind and make her recall the promises they had made each other the previous night.

Cecilia fell into silence, seeming to hug herself as if to ward off the threat of the mountains closing in. Nicholas sensed his mother's increasing withdrawal but gave up on trying to ease her mind; he knew what lay ahead and hoped the unexpected would make enough of an impact to impress his mother and change her mind about Alice's new home.

The track began to climb the gentle incline that Nicholas remembered well from the time he'd first brought his sister to the convent. As the countryside unfolded he was pleased to see the sun breaking through the thinning clouds. The road grew steeper then flattened. Nicholas began to slow down. Then, as the magnificent panorama unfolded in its full glory, he stopped. His mother and father were both silent and he sensed they had been mesmerised by its beauty.

The water of the loch, bejewelled by the sunlight, seemed to be creating a dance of welcome for them. After their first gasps of wonder they could do nothing but absorb the beauty that lay around them.

'Wonderful,' said Raymond quietly, as if he had no right to break the peace.

'It's magnificent,' whispered Cecilia.

Nicholas, thankful for the fine weather, remained silent, pleased that his parents were impressed.

'Where is the convent?' asked his father.

'The other side of the loch, slightly to our right. Its roof is just visible among the trees. It will become clearer as I drive round the waterside.'

Nicholas started the car. As he drove they fell silent, absorbing the atmosphere and imprinting on their minds a picture of the place where their daughter was living.

As he was slowing to halt near the front door, a nun appeared and stood waiting until the car had halted.

'Mr Nicholas, it is good to see you again on this great day.' She turned to his parents. 'You must be Alice's mother and father.' She smiled warmly as she shook hands and introduced herself. 'I am Sister Martha. Part of my duties is to look after any guests we have. So may I say welcome to St Mary's Convent on this great day when we will welcome Alice into our community.' She spread her hands and indicated the scene around them. 'God has been good in allowing us beautiful weather. Now, I am sure you would welcome a drink. Will it be tea or coffee?'

They all opted for coffee and, as they passed through the front door, Sister Martha gave their order to a young maid who was standing in the hall. After their outdoor clothes had been taken care of the nun led them into a room arranged to accommodate meetings between the sisters and visiting friends and relatives.

'When will we be able to see Alice?' Cecilia asked.

She had noticed Sister Martha giving a discreet signal to a young nun standing nearby.

'I have sent someone to tell the abbess you are here. She will come to meet you and take coffee with you. Then we will go to the chapel for the clothing ceremony. It is simple and short because it is the first in a series of such ceremonies over five or six years before final vows are taken. After the initial clothing you will have lunch with the community. Then, because it is a special day and we regard it as a holiday, all the nuns have free time to enjoy themselves within the boundaries of our land until our evening meal at seven. So you will have plenty of time to spend with Alice.'

'And beyond that?' Lady Cecilia queried.

'For the first year in the novitiate Alice is allowed four visiting times, one for each season of the year.' Sister Martha saw disappointment cloud Lady Cecilia's face. 'I am sorry, but those are the rules of our Order. It is a testing time for our new arrivals, to enable them and us to judge if they are suited to the life. I hope you will be able to see it as we do.'

'Right and proper,' approved Sir Raymond with a glance at his wife, who nodded her agreement.

Before any more could be said the door opened and the abbess came in. She introduced herself immediately and greeted the newcomers with warmth as if they had been friends all their lives. 'Lady Cecilia, Sir Raymond, it is indeed a pleasure to meet Alice's parents, and of course to see Nicholas again.' She took in both Lady Cecilia and Sir Raymond with her gaze as she added, 'You have a caring son. You should be proud of his concern for his sister.'

The compliment struck home. Both parents felt a rush of pride in him and also sensed their confidence strengthen, both in the convent and what it might mean to Alice. They were further reassured when, in answer to a question from Sir Raymond, the abbess informed them, 'You must understand that neither I nor any of my nuns used persuasion to get your daughter to leave home and join us. She sought us out. Her brother had full knowledge of what she was doing and, like my nuns, sensibly did not try to impose any judgement of his own on her. Nor should any of us try to influence the decision Alice will have to make as to whether she continues in the life of a nun or returns to the outside world. At various times here she will have the opportunity to change her mind, but once she makes her solemn vows she is bound to the Order.'

So the conversation continued, drawing from the Wares a greater respect and confidence in this abbess and the small community of nuns Alice had chosen to join. The door opened and a sister came in. 'Excuse me, Mother Abbess, Celia's parent's, Mr and Mrs Warriner, have arrived.'

'Thank you. Please show them in,' the abbess replied.

A smiling sister, erring a little on the shy side, ushered in Celia's parents to meet the abbess who deftly introduced the two families and soon had them on friendly terms. Celia's mother and father were accompanied by their son of seventeen and his thirteen-year-old sister.

Then the abbess looked at her watch. 'I will

have to go now and get ready for the clothing. I will leave you all in the capable hands of Sister Martha.' As she stood up, she added, 'I will see you after the ceremony, then it is lunch. You will be dining with me at the top table and we will be following custom so the newly clothed will be seated there too.'

Lady Cecilia spoke up as the abbess turned to leave. 'I am sure Mr and Mrs Warriner won't mind my speaking for us all, but may I offer you our sincere thanks for all you are doing for our daughters?'

Mr and Mrs Warriner smiled and nodded in agreement. 'Thank you,' said the abbess.

Sister Martha came to collect them. 'I will be your guide from now until after lunch.' She chatted with them until she glanced at the clock on the wall. 'Let us make our way to the chapel now.'

She escorted them into the main hall, constructed entirely of wood with six tall windows either side, which allowed light to flood the space with a sense of joy. They passed through a door into a passage with three closed doors in it. When they reached the end Sister Martha opened one of the doors and stood to one side to allow them to enter the chapel. It was a place that inspired respect, with a special air of tranquillity that touched them all. The pews were arranged so as to leave a central aisle leading to the east wall with its lancet windows. Sister Martha stood for a few minutes, allowing the peace to seep into her guests.

Cecilia remarked on the atmosphere and the sister gave a small smile as she softly replied, 'All our visitors mention that and it pleases us. I am sure both Alice and Celia will have felt it and perhaps found here their reason for joining us.' She glanced at her watch. 'Let me get you seated and I'll give you a brief summary of the order of service.'

When she had done that she said, 'I'll join my fellow nuns in the procession and meet up with you again later. Any questions before I leave you?'

No one had any. The two families were left alone. They exchanged smiles but respected the silence, which now had been charged with expectancy. They heard the door from the hall open, accompanied by the gentle footfalls of the nuns.

The Wares stood to silent attention but, their desire to see Alice being too strong to resist, they half turned to watch the nuns escort their two new sisters down the aisle. Three nuns walked on either side of Alice and Celia.

Lady Cecilia swallowed hard to hold back the tears when she saw her daughter. Alice was dressed in the plain grey habit she was now to exchange for the black garment and headdress worn by the community. She walked in step with her escort, her hands joined in prayer in front of her, head bowed. Her family's eyes were on her. She glanced up and met their gazes. A smile crossed her lips and she winked at them.

Raymond's heart soared. His little girl was still there! Cecilia found joy in her gesture and winked back. Nicholas knew he had not lost a sister.

The clothing and its following service had been kept simple, the prayers appropriate to the occasion and the hymns ably harmonised by such a small community. Alice had now taken the name of Sister Catherine and Celia that of Sister Felicity.

When they had left the chapel Sister Martha rejoined them and asked them to wait with her in the hall for a few minutes. The reason for that became obvious when the abbess appeared with two new novices smiling beside her.

'I am so glad you are all here today,' she greeted them quickly. 'I won't take up your time now, you'll want to be with your daughters. I'll see you all shortly at lunch.'

She had barely moved away when Cecilia took her daughter in her arms. Silent tears of joy flowed from them both. Alice was the first to speak. 'Mother, I want to say how sorry I was not to come to you when I returned from South Africa, but there was much I wanted to sort out without any distraction.'

'I was sorry too,' said her mother. She eased Alice out of the hug but still held her. She glanced at her husband, standing beside them, and then said to Alice, 'That is all in the past now ... memories to be shed. Better to realise it was not the life for you than attempt to make it so. I know you can still walk away from this convent but, if you are happy here, all well and good. Whatever you choose to do, you will have our blessing.' She turned to her husband, her glance telling him to reassure their daughter.

'You look happy, Alice. Whatever put you off Africa – we don't want to know. It is in the past, gone and forgotten. Your mother and I and Nicholas will always love you.'

The matter that might have come between them was settled. A new life lay before them. Sister Martha soon came in to escort them to the refectory.

The rest of the day passed off pleasantly. Alice introduced her fellow nuns who took the opportunity to mingle with the Wares without occupying too much of their time. Inevitably the moment came to say goodbye and heartstrings were tugged, but this was Alice's day and their parting had to be kept under control.

It was only when she passed from their sight, as they drove away, that her mother let the tears flow and her father cried softly too.

After a few minutes Nicholas eased the situation. 'I'm sure Alice will be happy here, if this is the life she finally settles to. I hope you can accept whatever she chooses?'

'Alice's happiness is our only concern. She has to look ahead and make any decision herself. I don't think your mother or I had appreciated before today what you must have done for Alice. It hurt us at the time that you would not tell us where she was but now I am sure we both accept your reason for doing so. She needed time to herself after Africa. We both owe a big debt to you.'

'What are brothers for if they can't help their sisters?' Nicholas said casually, but his mind was already drifting to the further dilemma that faced him.

He still felt an obligation to look after his sister. Her happiness was paramount to him. Should he reveal his meeting with Steven? Would it upset Alice to hear of it? Might leaving things unsaid be the best solution in this case? Nicholas wondered if Steven would attempt to find her, and if he did, would Alice feel her brother had betrayed her trust? Where did her happiness truly lie, within the convent or without?

So many answers rested with him, but which was the path that would ensure Alice's lasting happiness?

38

Despondency was beginning to take hold of Steven Cheevey as he walked into his hotel after he had spent the morning wandering round London's minor bookshops. Normally his hope of finding a rare book devoted to the Polar Regions to add to his collection would have been incentive enough, but today the passion was not there.

Time was running short on the promise made to him by Nicholas Ware.

Steven wondered if he had misinterpreted Nicholas's friendliness. Perhaps deep down he was wary of revisiting their troubled encounters in Africa. Steven knew how devoted Nicholas was to his sister and that he would want to protect Alice from anything that might harm her. So maybe he would forget his promise and let sleeping dogs lie. Perhaps the matter was over and done with and Steven would have to rethink his future.

There was no spring in his step and no smile for the clerk at his post behind the reception desk.

'My key, please.'

The man took the key from its hook, and as he turned back plucked something from the wall rack. 'A letter for you, sir.'

'Thank you.' A tremor touched Steven's lips; his heart began to beat faster. Was this it? Was this the message he had been waiting for? He couldn't wait until he returned to his room so he crossed the lobby to an isolated seat and tore the envelope open, withdrawing two sheets of paper. One sheet read: *Alice is at St Mary's Convent twenty miles north of Fort William. She took her simple vows yesterday.* It took moments for the meaning to sink in. Simple vows! Yesterday! The words thundered in his mind. He was too late then ... or was he? Simple implied another higher level of vows, one that Alice had not as yet taken. He turned eagerly to the next sheet of paper and read: *I am trusting you with this address because I think you have a right to make your peace with Alice. If that causes her any hurt, you will have me to answer to. Nicholas.*

Joy and excitement surged through Steven. Finally he knew where Alice was. He must go to Scotland immediately and leave any contact with his mother until his return. He crossed the lobby with a quick step. 'Can you find out when the next train to Edinburgh is, please?'

Steven re-read Nicholas's letter several times on his journey north. After a restless night at the Railway Hotel in Edinburgh he made his way to the desk and asked, 'Have you the name of a reliable firm that hires out motor vehicles, please?'

Within half an hour he was packed, his hotel bill

paid and he was waiting impatiently for the vehicle, which he had been told would be brought to the hotel at ten o'clock. When it arrived he noted that the maps he had requested were on the passenger seat. He was on his way.

The sound of the handbell in the corridor woke Alice. The desire to sleep longer was strong in her. She chastised herself for contemplating this and rose from her bed. She shivered at the cold, which worsened when she washed with icy water from the ewer she had filled the previous night before retiring to bed. She dressed quickly, paused in the corridor, and hearing no movement in Sister Felicity's room knocked on the door, fulfilling the promise they had made to each other. She heard a groan and then an acknowledgement. She hurried to the chapel where the small community was beginning to assemble, each in her allotted seat in order of seniority.

As she knelt in silent prayer awaiting the start of the service Alice kept an eye on the door, hoping her friend would not be late. At any moment the abbess would be starting the service. The door opened. Alice relaxed in relief when Sister Felicity, breathing hard, came in. The service began, starting the new day. The same routine stretched endlessly before the new sisters for the next five years. Three days a week, after lunch and communal prayers had been said, they had two hours of free time to spend in pursuit of their vocation.

'Sister Catherine.' Alice, realising the call was for her, responded and saw Sister Martha coming towards her as the nuns left the chapel for their free time. 'Would you like to walk with me? The morning rain has stopped.'

'I would like that, Sister. Sister Felicity wishes to do some reading that Sister Winifred has recommended.'

The two women put on their overcoats and left the convent.

'I've grown to enjoy walking in our grounds,' said Sister Martha as they set off.

'Even though you were born a city girl?'

Sister Martha gave a little laugh. 'Oh, yes! Perhaps that's why, and because one of the older nuns, who died shortly after I joined, showed me the beauty of the convent grounds in a way that I had not previously considered as being an integral part of this place and the life it offered. I think of her often and thank her for what she showed me.'

'What did she tell you?'

'You would like to hear that?'

'It might help me, as it did you.'

'If it does my mentor will be pleased.'

'You think she will know?'

'Of course.'

Their chat had assumed a course that Alice was beginning to find interesting. Their walk had brought them to the front of the convent, where they stopped to admire the view across the loch.

A car appeared over the brow of the hill and immediately swung to a stop. The driver's door opened, a young man stepped quickly out of the driver's seat and ran towards four nuns whose conversation he interrupted.

Alice's heart missed a beat but she rebuked

herself for the thought that had come to her. Why had she...? She cut her question short only to replace it with another. Why had the man's stature and movement struck her? Unless... One of the nuns pointed to the convent and then indicated the visitors' door. He moved back to his car. Alice tensed; her mind raced. She jumped to her feet, startling Sister Martha, and called, 'I need to go, Sister. Sorry.'

'Are you all right?' queried Sister Martha.

'Yes...'

With that Alice was hurrying into the convent by the front door and making her way hastily to her room. She sat down on the edge of her bed, her mind in a whirl. Steven here? So near to her! Only Nicholas could have disclosed her whereabouts. Why had he betrayed her trust? What had gone on since Steven's arrival?

She waited for the inevitable. It came – a knock on the door. She knew it was be no good pretending she wasn't there.

'The abbess wishes to see you immediately,' she was informed by a nun.

Alice could only murmur 'Thank you' and go straight to the office.

The abbess, sitting behind her desk, was looking thoughtful when Alice walked in. 'There is a gentleman requesting to see you, Mr Steven Cheevey. It is unusual for me to grant such a request without prior notice. The gentleman seemed troubled and entreated me to allow this meeting. He is a retired Army officer whose roots are in Scotland. His request and disturbed state of mind seem genuine, though he has made no attempt to disclose the causes of his distress. You may know more about him. I think it only right for you to decide whether you wish to meet him or not.' She looked questioningly at Alice.

Confusion raged within her as Alice battled with her decision. After a long pause she said, 'I know this man, Mother. He has come a long way to see me. I could say he has come all the way from Africa. I think perhaps I should see him.'

'Very well, I have left him with Sister Winifred in the guest wing.'

'Thank you, Mother.'

The abbess nodded. 'I will see him again before he leaves and then you will come to me and we will talk.'

'Yes, Mother.' Alice tried to prevent her voice from shaking but knew she hadn't been successful in that. Her heart began to race as she walked to the guest wing.

She paused, drew a deep breath, and, unable to control her trembling hand, swung the door open. As she stepped inside the room Sister Winifred asked Alice if she should stay, but at the shake of her head the nun slipped quietly out, leaving a silence sparking with tension between Alice and the man who faced her. 'Steven, what are you doing here?' she asked.

'I needed to see you, Alice.'

'Why?'

'I treated you too harshly in South Africa.'

'I deserved it.'

'If I had taken time to think everything through, I would have done things differently. My love for you had been badly bruised ... I could not think straight. I thought I wanted you out of my life. I acted too quickly. I realised that when I stood on the dock in Cape Town and watched the ship taking you from me, but I could do nothing then. It was too late. I too have done things I'm not proud of; not like yours they are in the past. Can we forget? Nicholas informed me that neither your parents nor mine knew anything of what had happened to you next so I tried through all kinds of other ways to reach you, but was never successful. Eventually I decided to leave the Army, saying I had an estate to run. That is what I intend doing and I want you beside me to...'

'Stop, Steven! Look at my habit. It is that of a nun.'

'But you are Alice ... the woman I still love.'

'Please, Steven, no more. What's done is done.'

He saw her eyes dampening, her face filled with emotion. 'Alice, forgive me, I will not pressure you any longer but I would ask you to reconsider your recent decision. Do you really see yourself spending the rest of your life as a nun, bound and tied by a final profession? You have so much more to give. Please, please, reconsider. Please accept a new life with me as mistress of Heatherfold.'

'I take it this is a proposal?'

'I could not be more earnest. I've got to say this now because once I leave here I may not be allowed to see you face to face again.' Alice could not deny the sincerity of his plea.

Tears flowed down her cheeks. 'When I first considered becoming a nun, I was seeking an escape from the wounds you had inflicted on me, wounds that I richly deserved, but the more I thought

338

about it, the more I saw it as a way of life that I could embrace, and in it find peace. Then I came here to St Mary's and I was sure I was right.'

'But now I have made you have second thoughts.' Steven held out his hands to her. 'Maybe finding you was fortuitous. Maybe it was right for Nicholas to give me the address. Maybe you and I are still meant to be together.'

Alice bit her lip. Her mind was racing. She looked hard at Steven and saw the man she had loved, not the man who had cast her so cruelly out of his life. 'Steven, will you please go?'

He shook his head.

'You must. You have been with me long enough.'

'From now to eternity will not be long enough for me.'

The moment of charged silence that filled the room was broken when Alice said, 'I will think this over after I have talked to my abbess. You may think she will try and persuade me to do what she wants, become another nun fully pledged to her community for evermore. But she is not like that. She was once a woman of the world and certainly wants what is best for her convent. Her advice will be impartially given. I promise you, I will let you know my decision as soon as I make it. I can't say any more now.' She looked into his eyes and saw the depth of his feeling for her.

Steven held her gaze, gently took hold of her hands and said tenderly 'So now I must wait in hope, my love.'

Epilogue

The butler threaded his way through the fifty guests assembling in the main hall.

'A letter for you, Mrs Cheevey,' he said, raising his voice a little to overcome the buzz of excited conversation.

Emma took the envelope from him. 'Thank you.' Her tone held an element of surprise. The mail had been delivered as usual at mid-morning and it had already been dealt with. She glanced at the envelope and saw that it had an unusual date stamp. The postman must have found it after his round and made a second call. Emma did not recognise the handwriting. With so much more to occupy her, she pushed the letter into the pocket of her dress.

At that moment cheering and clapping swept through the hall. She started to move towards her son then stopped and looked back. 'Come along, John, you should be with me.'

He gave a little shake of his head. 'This is a special occasion for the Cheeveys. Go to your husband and son. I'll be waiting for you.'

Emma gave him a warm appreciative smile. 'I am lucky to have you.' She went to join Steven, who was receiving the congratulations conveyed by telegram from the officers with whom he had served in South Africa as well as from his brother. Emma approached Robert, who was singing the

340

praises of his son's choice of bride. She gave him a smile of encouragement as he adjusted his hold on his stick.

His words were lost in the surge of excitement that caused everyone to turn their attention to the stairs down which a smiling Alice descended, taking each step in a stately manner. Her simply cut dress was high-waisted, with a high-necked lace cape covering her shoulders. The short train touched only a few inches of the floor allowing the bride to move freely among her guests, who admired her diadem of fresh orange blossom. There was a lump in Sir Raymond's throat as he watched his daughter advancing and he was grateful for Cecilia's support as she slipped her hand in his and gave it a squeeze.

Nicholas, who had been in conversation with Mrs Cheevey, had been about to move on when she stopped him with a touch on the arm. 'A late delivery was given to me. I'm sure it must be meant for the new Mrs Cheevey. As best man, I think you had better have it.' She fished the letter from her pocket and handed it to him. It took him a few minutes before he could get a word with his sister and hand over the envelope. Curious, Alice seized a moment to herself and opened the envelope. She drew out a sheet of paper and unfolded it. Her eyes skimmed the writing and then began to fill with tears.

Nicholas saw them and looked at her with concern. 'What's wrong?'

She gave a little smile. 'Nothing,' she said. 'But please call for order.'

He did as he was bid and moved two steps up

the stairs. 'Quiet, please!' He called it three times before the request was fully adhered to, during which time a concerned Steven had come to join Alice. Silence fell, filled with curiosity and interest as Alice indicated to Steven that she was all right.

'Ladies and gentlemen, I have just received a letter that I would like to read to you because it has just crowned my wonderful day with more happiness.' She paused to brush away a tear.

Dear Alice and Steven,

May my community and I wish you both all the happiness you deserve. It is never easy to make the decisions you have done. We pray that they will fortify you in your lives together.

We think of you fondly and may God's blessing be upon you now and always.

Yours sincerely,

Mother Loyola

Abbess of St Mary's Convent

Steven took his wife's arm and turned her to face him. As their lips met they both knew that the mistakes of the past had been forgiven.

Acknowledgements

Twenty-five years ago Lynn Curtis set me on the path to Piatkus Publishers. Since then she has been my copy editor for every Jessica Blair book. To her go my heartfelt thanks. They also go to Judy Piatkus, who took my first novel and began an association that continued when Piatkus became an imprint of the Little, Brown Book Group which it remains to this day. Throughout that time I have always had great help and support from the staff working in whatever capacity for Piatkus. To them all, past and present, I send a very warm and sincere thank you. You have made my association with Piatkus a joy, and still do.

I could not have become an author without the unstinting support and encouragement of my late wife, Joan, and our children who have always taken a keen interest in my writing. Judith vets my work as I produce it. Her twin Geraldine checks the finished novel. Anne and Duncan are ever ready with their support, and research whenever it is required. To say merely thank you to them does not seem enough, but they know how sincerely I mean it.

Of course all this would be of no avail if I had no readers. I am grateful to all of you.

The publishers hope that this book has given you enjoyable reading. Large Print Books are especially designed to be as easy to see and hold as possible. If you wish a complete list of our books please ask at your local library or write directly to:

Magna Large Print Books
Magna House, Long Preston,
Skipton, North Yorkshire.
BD23 4ND

This Large Print Book for the partially sighted, who cannot read normal print, is published under the auspices of

THE ULVERSCROFT FOUNDATION